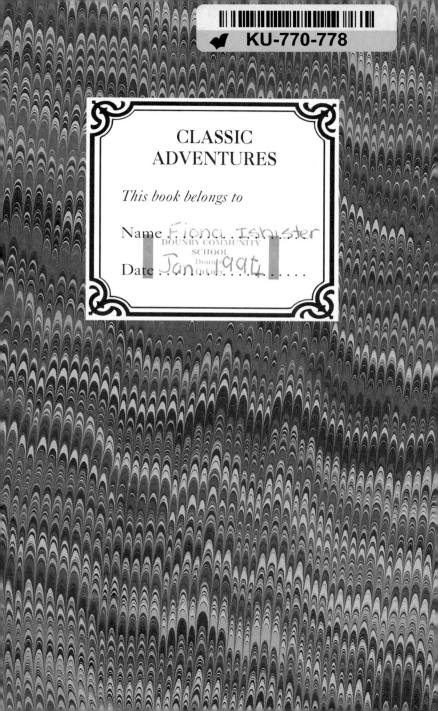

KU-770-778

CLASSIC ADVENTURES

This book belongs to

Name Fiona Isbister

Date Jan 1994

Twenty Thousand Leagues Under the Sea

First published in this (abridged) edition in 1955
by Wm. Collins Sons and Co. Ltd.
This facsimile edition
© Fabbri Publishing Ltd 1991
Printed and bound in Spain by Printer
Industria Gráfica, Barcelona

ISBN 1-85587-309-5

Twenty Thousand Leagues Under the Sea

By
Jules Verne

The Classic Adventures Series

CONTENTS

6 CONTENTS

CHAPTER ONE

A FLOATING REEF

IN THE year 1866 the whole maritime population of Europe and America was excited by a mysterious and inexplicable phenomenon. This excitement was not confined to merchants, sailors, sea-captains, shippers and naval officers of all countries, but the governments of many states on the two continents were deeply interested.

The excitement was caused by an enormous "something" that ships were often meeting. It was a long, spindle-shaped, and sometimes phosphorescent object, much larger and more rapid than a whale.

The different accounts that were written of this object in various log-books agreed generally as to its structure, wonderful speed, and the peculiar life with which it appeared endowed.

By taking the average of observations made at different times—rejecting the timid estimates that assigned to this object a length of 200 feet, as well as the exaggerated opinions which made it out to be a mile in width and three in length —we may fairly affirm that it surpassed all the dimensions allowed by the ichthyologists of the day, if it existed at all. It did exist, that was undeniable, and with that leaning towards the marvellous that characterises humanity, we cannot wonder at the excitement it produced in the entire world.

On the 20th of July, 1866, the steamer *Governor Higgenson*, of the Calcutta and Burnach Steam Navigation Company, met this moving mass five miles off the east coast of Australia. Captain Baker thought at first that he was in presence of an unknown reef; he was preparing to take its exact position, when two columns of water, projected by the inexplicable object, went hissing up a hundred and fifty feet into the air. Unless there was an intermittent geyser on the reef, the *Governor Higgenson* had to do with some aquatic mammal, unknown till then, which threw out columns of water mixed with air and vapour from its blowholes.

A similar occurrence happened on the 23rd of July in the same year to the *Columbus*, of the West India and Pacific Steam Navigation Company, in the Pacific Ocean. It was, therefore, evident that this extraordinary cetaceous creature could transport itself from one place to another with surprising velocity, seeing there was but an interval of three days between the two observations, separated by a distance of more than 700 nautical leagues.

Fifteen days later, two thousand leagues from the last place it was seen at, the *Helvetia*, of the Compagnie Nationale, and the *Shannon*, of the Royal Mail Steamship Company, sailing to windward in that part of the Atlantic between the United States and Europe, each signalled the monster to the other in 42° 15' N. lat. and 60° 35' W. long. As the *Shannon* and the *Helvetia* were of smaller dimensions than the object, though they measured 300 feet over all, the minimum length of the mammal was estimated at more than 350 feet. Now the largest whales are never more than sixty yards long, if so long.

In all the great centres the monster became the fashion; it was sung about in the cafés, scoffed at in the newspapers, and represented at all the theatres. It gave opportunity for hoaxes of every description. In all newspapers short of copy imaginary beings reappeared, from the white whale, the terrible "Moby Dick" of the Northern regions, to the inordinate "kraken," whose tentacles could fold round a vessel of 500 tons burden and drag it down to the depths of the ocean. The accounts of ancient times were reproduced: the opinions of Aristotle and Pliny, who admitted the existence of these monsters, and the Norwegian tales about Bishop Pontoppidan, those of Paul Heggede, and lastly the report of Mr. Harrington, whose good faith could not be put in question when he affirmed that, being on board the *Castillian*, in 1857, he saw this enormous serpent, which until then had only frequented the seas of the old *Constitutionnel* newspaper.

During the first months of the year 1867 the question seemed to be buried out of sight and mind, when fresh facts brought it again before the public. It had then changed from a scientific problem to be solved to a real and serious danger to be avoided. The question took another phase. The monster again became an island or rock. On the 5th of March, 1867, the *Moravian*, of the Montreal Ocean Company, struck her starboard quarter on a rock which no chart gave in that point. She was then going at the rate of thirteen knots under the combined efforts of the wind and her 400 horse-power. Had it not been for the more than ordinary strength of the hull in the *Moravian* she would have been broken by the shock, and have gone down with 237 passengers.

The accident happened about daybreak. The officers on watch hurried aft, and looked at the sea with the most scrupulous attention. They saw nothing except what looked like a strong eddy, three cables' length off, as if the waves had been violently agitated. The bearings of the place were taken exactly, and the *Moravian* went on her way without apparent damage. Had she struck on a submarine rock or some enormous fragment of wreck? They could not find out, but during the examination made of the ship's bottom when under repair, it was found that part of her keel was broken.

This fact, extremely grave in itself, would perhaps have been forgotten, like so many others, if three weeks afterwards it had not happened again under identical circumstances, only, thanks to the nationality of the ship that was this time victim of the shock, and the reputation of the company to which the vessel belonged, the circumstance was immensely commented upon.

On the 13th of April, 1867, with a smooth sea and favourable breeze, the Cunard steamer *Scotia* was going at the rate of thirteen knots an hour under the pressure of her 1000 horse-power.

At 4.17 p.m., as the passengers were assembled at dinner in the great saloon, a slight shock was felt on the hull of the *Scotia*, on her quarter a little aft of the paddle.

The *Scotia* had not struck anything, but had been struck by some sharp and penetrating rather than blunt surface. The shock was so slight that not one on board would have been uneasy at it had it not been for the carpenter's watch, who rushed upon deck, calling out—"She is sinking! She is sinking!"

Captain Anderson went down immediately into the hold and found that a leak had sprung in the fifth compartment, and the sea was rushing in rapidly. Happily there were no boilers in this compartment, or the fires would have been at once put out. Captain Anderson ordered the engines to be immediately stopped, and one of the sailors dived to ascertain the extent of the damage. Some minutes after it was ascertained that there was a large hole about two yards in diameter in the ship's bottom. Such a leak could not be stopped, and the *Scotia*, with her paddles half submerged, was obliged to continue her voyage. She was then 300 miles from Cape Clear, and after three days' delay, which caused great anxiety in Liverpool, she entered the company's docks.

The engineers then proceeded to examine her in the dry dock, which she had been placed. They could scarcely believe their eyes; at two yards and a half below water-mark was a regular rent in the shape of an isosceles triangle. The place where the piece had been taken out of the iron plates was so sharply defined that it could not have been done more neatly by a punch. The perforating instrument that had done the work was of no common stamp, or after having been driven with prodigious force, and piercing an iron plate one and three-eighths of an inch thick, it had been withdrawn by some wonderful retrograde movement.

Such was the last fact, and it again awakened public opinion on the subject. After that all maritime disasters not satisfactorily accounted for were put down to the account of the monster. All the responsibility of the numerous wrecks annually recorded at Lloyd's was laid to the charge of this fantastic animal, and thanks to the "monster," communication between the two continents became more and more difficult; the public loudly demanding that the seas should be rid of the formidable cetacean at any price.

CHAPTER TWO

FOR AND AGAINST

AT THE period when these events were happening I was returning from a scientific expedition into the region of Nebraska. In my quality of Assistant Professor in the Paris Museum of Natural History, the French Government had attached me to that expedition. I arrived at New York, loaded with precious collections made during my six months in Nebraska, at the end of March. My departure from France was fixed for the beginning of May. Whilst I waited and was occupying myself with classifying my mineralogical, botanical and zoological riches, the incident happened to the *Scotia*.

When I arrived at New York the subject was hot. The hypothesis of a floating island or reef, which was supported by incompetent opinion, was quite abandoned, for unless the shoal had a machine in its stomach, how could it change its position with such marvellous rapidity? For the same reason the idea of a floating hull or gigantic wreck was given up.

There remained, therefore, two possible solutions of the enigma which created two distinct parties; one was that the object was a colossal monster, the other that it was a submarine vessel of enormous motive power. This last hypothesis, which, after all, was admissible, could not stand against inquiries made in the two hemispheres. It was hardly probable that a private individual should possess such a machine. Where and when had he caused it to be built, and how could he have kept its construction secret? Certainly a government might possess such a destructive engine, and it was possible in these disastrous times, when the power of weapons of war has been multiplied, that, without the knowledge of others, a state might possess so formidable a weapon.

But the hypothesis of a war machine fell before the declaration of different governments, and as the public interest suffered from the difficulty of transatlantic communication, their veracity could not be doubted. Besides, secrecy would be even more difficult to a government than to a private individual. After inquiries made in England, France, Russia, Prussia, Spain, Italy, America, and even Turkey, the hypothesis of a submarine monitor was definitely rejected.

On my arrival at New York, several persons did me the honour of consulting me about the phenomenon in question. The Honourable Pierre Aronnax, Professor in the Paris Museum, was asked by the *New York Herald* to give his opinion on the matter. I subjoin an extract from the article which I published on the 30th of April:

"After having examined the different hypotheses one by one, and all other suppositions being rejected, the existence of a marine animal of excessive strength must be admitted.

"The greatest depths of the ocean are totally unknown to us. What happens there? What beings can live twelve or fifteen miles below the surface of the sea? We can scarcely conjecture what the organisation of these animals is. However the solution of the problem submitted to me may affect the form of the dilemma, we either know all the varieties of beings that people our planet or we do not. If we do not know them all—if there are still secrets of ichthyology for us—nothing is more reasonable than to admit the existence of fishes or cetaceans of an organisation suitable to the strata inaccessible to soundings, which for some reason or other come up to the surface at intervals.

"If, on the contrary, we do know all living species, we must, of course, look for the animal in question amongst the already classified marine animals, and in that case I should be disposed to admit the existence of a gigantic narwhal.

"The common narwhal, or sea-unicorn, is often sixty feet long. This size increased five or tenfold, and a strength in proportion to its size being given to the cetacean, and its offensive arms being increased in the same proportion, you obtain the animal required. It will have the proportions given by the officers of the *Shannon*, the instrument that perforated the *Scotia*, and the strength necessary to pierce the hull of the steamer.

"In fact, the narwhal is armed with a kind of ivory sword or halberd, as some naturalists call it. It is the principal tusk, and is as hard as steel. Some of these tusks have been found imbedded in the bodies of whales, which the narwhal always attacks with success. Others have been with difficulty taken out of ships' bottoms, which they pierced through and through like a gimlet in a barrel. The Museum of the Paris Faculty of Medicine contains one of these weapons, two and a quarter yards in length and fifteen inches in diameter at the base.

"Now, suppose this weapon to be ten times stronger, and its possessor ten times more powerful, hurl it at the rate of twenty miles an hour, and you obtain a shock that might produce the catastrophe required. Therefore, until I get fuller information, I shall suppose it to be a sea-unicorn of colossal dimensions, armed, not with a halberd, but with a spur like ironclads or battering rams, the massiveness and motive power of which it would possess at the same time. This inexplicable phenomenon may be thus explained, unless something exists over and above anything ever conjectured, seen, or experienced, which is just possible."

My article was well received, and provoked much discussion amongst the public. It rallied a certain number of partisans. The solution which it proposed left freedom to the imagination. The human mind likes these grand conceptions of supernatural beings.

But if some people saw in this nothing but a purely scientific problem to solve, others more positive, especially in America and England, were of opinion to purge the ocean of this formidable monster, in order to reassure transmarine communications.

Public opinion having declared its verdict, the United States were first in the field, and preparations for an expedition to pursue the narwhal were at once begun in New York. A very fast frigate, the *Abraham Lincoln*, was put in commission, and the arsenals were opened to Captain Farragut, who actively hastened the arming of his frigate.

But, as generally happens, from the moment it was decided to pursue the monster, the monster was not heard of for two months. It seemed as if this unicorn knew about the plots that were being weaved for it. It had been so much talked of, even through the Atlantic Cable! Would-be wits pretended that the cunning fellow had stopped some telegram in its passage, and was now using the knowledge for his own benefit.

So when the frigate had been prepared for a long campaign, and furnished with formidable fishing apparatus they did not know where to send her to. Impatience was increasing with the delay, when on July 2 it was reported that a steamer of the San Francisco Line, from California to Shanghai, had met with the animal three weeks before in the North Pacific Ocean.

The emotion caused by the news was extreme, and twenty-four hours, only were granted to Captain Farragut before he sailed. The ship was already victualled and well stocked with coal. The crew were there to a man, and there was nothing to do but to light the fires.

Three hours before the *Abraham Lincoln* left Brooklyn Pier I received the following letter:

"SIR,—If you would like to join the expedition of the *Abraham Lincoln*, the United States Government will have great pleasure in seeing France represented by you in the enterprise. Captain Farragut has a cabin at your disposition.

"Faithfully yours,

"J. B. HOBSON, Secretary of Marine."

CHAPTER THREE

AS MONSIEUR PLEASES

THREE seconds before the arrival of J. B. Hobson's letter I had no more idea of pursuing the unicorn than of attempting the North-West Passage. Three seconds after having read the secretary's letter I had made up my mind that ridding the world of this monster was my veritable vocation and the single aim of my life.

"Conseil!" I called in an impatient tone. "Conseil!"

Conseil was my servant, a faithful fellow who accompanied me on all my journeys, a brave Dutchman I had great confidence in; he was phlegmatic by nature, regular from principle, zealous from habit, showing little astonishment at the varied surprises of life, very skilful with his hands, apt at any service, and, in spite of his name, never giving any counsel, even when asked for it.

Conseil had followed me during the last ten years wherever science had directed my steps. He never complained of the length or fatigue of a journey, or of having to pack his trunks for any country, however remote, whether China or Congo. He went there or elsewhere without questioning the wherefore. His health defied all illness, and he had solid muscles, but no nerves—not the least appearance of nerves—of course, I mean in his mental faculties. He was thirty years old, and his age to that of his master was as fifteen is to twenty. May I be excused for saying that I was forty?

But Conseil had one fault. He was intensely formal, and would never speak to me except in the third person, which was sometimes irritating.

"Conseil!" I repeated, beginning my preparations for departure with a feverish hand.

Conseil appeared.

"Did monsieur call me?" said he on entering.

"Yes, my boy. Get yourself and me ready to start in two hours."

"As it pleases monsieur," answered Conseil calmly.

"You know about the monster, Conseil—the famous narwhal. We are going to rid the seas of it. A glorious mission, but—dangerous too. We don't know where we are going to. Those animals may be very capricious! But we will go, whether or no! We have a captain who will keep his eyes open."

"As monsieur does, I will do," answered Conseil.

"But think, for I will hide nothing from you. It is one of those voyages from which people do not always come back."

"As monsieur pleases."

A quarter of an hour afterwards our trunks were ready. Conseil had packed them by sleight of hand, and I was sure nothing would be missing, for the fellow classified shirts and clothes as well as he did birds or mammals.

The hotel lift deposited us in the large vestibule of the first floor. I went down the few stairs that led to the ground floor I paid my bill at the vast counter, always besieged by a considerable crowd. I gave the order to send my cases of stuffed animals and dried plants to Paris, and, Conseil following me, I sprang into a vehicle.

Our luggage was at once sent on board, and we soon followed it. I asked for Captain Farragut. One of the sailors conducted me to the poop, where I found myself in the presence of a pleasant-looking officer, who held out his hand to me.

"Monsieur Pierre Aronnax?" he said.

"Himself," replied I. "Do I see Captain Farragut?"

"In person. You are welcome, Professor. Your cabin is ready for you."

I bowed, and leaving the commander to his duties, went down to the cabin prepared for me.

The *Abraham Lincoln* had been well chosen and equipped for her new destination. She was a frigate of great speed, furnished with overheating apparatus that allowed the tension of the steam to reach seven atmospheres. Under that pressure the *Abraham Lincoln* reached an average speed of eighteen miles and three-tenths an hour good speed, but not enough to wrestle with the gigantic cetacean.

The interior arrangements of the frigate were in keeping with her nautical qualities. I was well satisfied with my cabin, which was situated aft, and opened on the wardroom.

The Abraham Lincoln was soon moving majestically amongst a hundred ferry-boats and tenders loaded with spectators, passed the Brooklyn quay, on which, as well as on all that part of New York bordering on the East River, crowds of spectators were assembled. Thousands of hand-kerchiefs were waved above the compact mass, and saluted the *Abraham Lincoln* until she reached the Hudson at the point of that elongated peninsula which forms the town of New York.

Her escorts of boats and tenders followed her till she reached the lightboat, the two lights of which mark the entrance to the New York Channel.

Three o'clock was then striking. The pilot went down into his boat and rejoined the little schooner which was waiting under lee, the fires were made up, the screw beat the waves more rapidly, and the frigate coasted the low yellow shore of Long Island, and at 8 p.m., after having lost sight in the north-west of the lights on Fire Island, she ran at full steam on to the dark waters of the Atlantic.

CHAPTER FOUR

NED LAND

CAPTAIN FARRAGUT was a good seaman, worthy of the frigate he was commanding. His ship and he were one. He was the soul of it. No doubt arose in his mind on the question of the cetacean, and he did not allow the existence of the animal to be disputed on board. He believed in it like simple souls believe in the Leviathan—by faith, not by sight. The monster existed, and he had sworn to deliver the seas from it. Either Captain Farragut would kill the narwhal or the narwhal would kill Captain Farragut—there was no middle course.

As to the crew, all they wanted was to meet the unicorn, harpoon it, haul it on board, and cut it up. Captain Farragut had offered a reward of 2,000 dollars to the first cabin-boy, sailor, or officer who should signal the animal. I have already said that Captain Farragut had carefully provided all the tackle necessary for taking the gigantic cetacean. A whaler would not have been better furnished. We had every known engine, from the hand harpoon to the barbed arrow of the blunderbuss and the explosive bullets of the deck-gun. On the forecastle lay a perfect breech-loader, very thick at the breech and narrow in the bore, the model of which had been in the Paris Exhibition of 1867. This weapon, of American make, could throw with ease a conical projectile, weighing nine pounds, to a mean distance of ten miles. Thus the *Abraham Lincoln* not only possessed every means of destruction, but, better still, she had on board Ned Land, the king of harpooners.

Ned Land was a Canadian of uncommon skill, who had no equal in his perilous employment. He possessed ability, *sang-froid*, audacity, and subtleness to a remarkable degree, and it would have taken a sharp whale or a singularly wily

18

cachalot to escape his harpoon. He was about forty years of age, tall (more than six feet high), strongly built, grave, and taciturn, sometimes violent, and very passionate when put out. His person, and especially the power of his glance, which gave a singular expression to his face, attracted attention.

I believe that Captain Farragut had done wisely in engaging this man. He was worth all the rest of the ship's company as far as his eye and arm went. I could not compare him to anything better than a powerful telescope which would be a cannon always ready to fire as well.

I now depict this brave companion as I knew him afterwards, for we are old friends, united in that unchangeable friendship which is born and cemented in mutual danger. Ah, brave Ned, I only hope I may live a hundred years more to remember you longer.

CHAPTER FIVE

AT RANDOM

THE voyage of the *Abraham Lincoln* for some time was marked by no incident. At last a circumstance happened which showed off the wonderful skill of Ned Land and the confidence that might be placed in him.

On the 30th of June, the frigate, being then off the Falkland Islands, spoke to some American whalers, who told us they had not met with the narwhal. But one of them, the captain of the *Munroe*, knowing that Ned Land was on board the *Abraham Lincoln*, asked for his help in capturing a whale they had in sight. Captain Farragut, desirous of seeing Ned Land at work, allowed him to go on board the *Munroe*, and fortune favoured our Canadian so well, that instead of one whale he harpooned two with a double blow, striking one right in the heart, and capturing the other after a pursuit of some minutes.

Certainly if the monster ever had Ned Land to deal with I would not bet in its favour.

On the 6th of July, about 3 p.m., we doubled, fifteen miles to the south, the solitary island to which some Dutch sailors gave the name of their native town, Cape Horn. The next day the frigate was in the Pacific.

"Keep a sharp look-out!" cried all the sailors.

Both eyes and telescopes, a little dazzled certainly by the thought of 2,000 dollars, never had a minute's rest. Day and night they observed the surface of the ocean; and even nyctalops, whose faculty of seeing in the darkness increased their chances fifty per cent, would have had to keep a sharp look-out to win the prize.

But vain excitement! The *Abraham Lincoln* would modify her speed, run down the animal signalled, which always turned out to be a simple whale or common cachalot, and disappeared amidst a storm of execration.

We were at last on the scene of the last frolics of the monster; and the truth was, no one lived really on board. The entire crew were under the influence of such nervous excitement as I could not give the idea of. They neither ate nor slept. Twenty times a day some error of estimation, or the optical delusion of a sailor perched on the yards, caused intolerable frights; and these emotions, twenty times repeated, kept us in a state too violent not to cause an early reaction.

And, in fact, the reaction was not slow in coming. For three months—three months, each day of which lasted a century—the *Abraham Lincoln* ploughed all the waters of the North Pacific, running down all the whales signalled, making sharp deviations from her route, veering suddenly from one tack to another, and not leaving one point of the Chinese or Japanese coast unexplored. And yet nothing was seen but the immense waste of waters—nothing that resembled a gigantic narwhal, nor a submarine islet, nor a wreck, nor a floating reef, nor anything at all supernatural.

The reaction, therefore, began. Discouragement at first took possession of all minds, and opened a breach for incredulity. A new sentiment was experienced on board, composed of three-tenths of shame and seven-tenths of rage. They called themselves fools for being faken in by a chimera, and were still more furious at it. The mountains of arguments piled up for a year fell down all at once, and all everyone thought of was to make up the hours of meals and sleep which they had so foolishly sacrificed.

With the mobility natural to the human mind, they threw themselves from one excess into another. The warmest partisans of the enterprise became final'y its most ardent detractors. The reaction ascended from the depths of the vessel, from the coal-hole, to the officers' ward-room, and certainly, had it not been for very strong determination on the part of Captain Farragut, the head of the frigate would have been definitely turned southward.

However, this useless search could be no further prolonged. No crew of the American Navy had ever shown more patience or zeal; its want of success could not be imputed to it. There was nothing left to do but to return. A representation in this sense was made to the commander. The commander kept his ground. The sailors did not hide their dissatisfaction, and the service suffered from it. I do not mean that there was revolt on board, but after a reasonable period of obstinacy the commander, like Columbus before him, asked for three days' patience. If in three days the monster had not reappeared, the man at the helm should give three turns of the wheel, and the *Abraham Lincoln* should make for the European seas.

Two days passed. The frigate kept up steam at half-pressure. Large quantities of bacon were trailed in the wake of the ship, to the great satisfaction of the sharks. The frigate lay to, and her boats were sent in all directions, but the night of the 4th of November passed without unveiling the submarine mystery.

Japan lay less than 200 miles to leeward Eight bells had just struck as I was leaning over the starboard side. Conseil, standing near me, was looking straight in front of him The crew, perched in the ratlins, were keeping a sharp look-out in the approaching darkness. Officers with their night-glasses swept the horizon.

Looking at Conseil, I saw that the brave fellow was feeling slightly the general influence—at least it seemed to me so. Perhaps for the first time, his nerves were vibrating under the action of a sentiment of curiosity.

"Well, Conseil," said I, "this is your last chance of pocketing 2,000 dollars."

"Will monsieur allow me to tell him that I never counted upon the reward, and if the Union had promised 100,000 dollars it would never be any the poorer."

"You are right, Conseil. It has been a stupid affair, after all. We have lost time and patience, and might just as well have been in France six months ago."

"Yes, in monsieur's little apartments, classifying monsieur's fossils, and monsieur's babiroussa would be in its cage in the Jardin des Plantes, attracting all the curious people in Paris."

"Yes, Conseil, and besides that we shall get well laughed at."

"Certainly," said Conseil tranquilly. "I think they will laugh at monsieur And I must say——"

"What, Conseil?"

"That it will serve monsieur right! When one has the honour to be a *savant* like monsieur, one does not expose——"

Conseil did not finish his compliment. In the midst of general silence Ned Land's voice was heard calling out:

"Look out, there! The thing we are looking for is on our weather beam!"

CHAPTER SIX

WITH ALL STEAM ON

AT THIS cry the entire crew rushed towards the harpooner. Captain, officers, masters, sailors and cabin-boys, even the engineers left their engines, and the stokers their fires. The order to stop her had been given, and the frigate was only moving by her own momentum. The darkness was then profound, and although I knew the Canadian's eyes were very good, I asked myself what he could have seen, and how he could have seen it. My heart beat violently.

At two cables' length from the *Abraham Lincoln* on her starboard quarter, the sea seemed to be illuminated below the surface. The monster lay some fathoms below the sea, and threw out the very intense but inexplicable light mentioned in the reports of several captains. This light described an immense and much-elongated oval, in the centre of which was condensed a focus the over-powering brilliancy of which died out by successive gradations.

A general cry rose from the frigate.

"Silence!" called out the captain. "Up with the helm! Reverse the engines!"

The frigate thus tried to escape but the supernatural animal approached her with a speed double her own.

Stupefaction, more than fear, kept us mute and motionless. The animal gained upon us. It made the round of the frigate, which was then going at the rate of fourteen knots, and enveloped her with its electric ring like luminous dust. Then it went two or three miles off, leaving a phosphoric trail like the steam of an express locomotive. All at once, from the dark limits of the horizon, where it went to gain its momentum, the monster rushed towards the frigate with frightful rapidity, stopped suddenly at a distance of twenty feet, and then went out, not diving, for its brilliancy did

23

not die out by degrees, but all at once, as if turned off. Then it reappeared on the other side of the ship, either going round her or gliding under her hull. A collison might have occurred at any moment, which might have been fata. to us.

I was astonished at the way the ship was worked. She was being attacked instead of attacking; and I asked Captain Farragut the reason. On the captain's generally impassive face was an expression of profound astonishment.

"M. Aronnax," he said, "I do not know with how formidable a being I have to deal, and I will not imprudently risk my frigate in the darkness. We must wait for daylight, and then we shall change parts."

All the crew remained up that night. No one thought of going to sleep. The *Abraham Lincoln* not being able to compete in speed, was kept under half-steam. On its side the narwhal imitated the frigate, let the waves rock it at will, and seemed determined not to leave the scene of combat.

Towards midnight, however, it disappeared, dying out like a large glowworm. At seven minutes to one in the morning a deafening whistle was heard, like that produced by a column of water driven out with extreme violence.

About 2 a.m. the luminous focus reappeared, no less intense, about five miles to the windward of the frigate. Notwithstanding the distance and the noise of the wind and and sea, the loud strokes of the animal's tail were distinctly heard, and even its panting breathing. When the enormous narwhal came up to the surface to breathe, it seemed as if the air rushed into its lungs like steam in the vast cylinders of a 2000 horse-power engine.

"Hum!" thought I, "a whale with the strength of a cavalry regiment would be a pretty whale!"

Until daylight we were all on the *qui-vive*, and then the fishing tackle was prepared. The first mate loaded the blunderbusses, which throw harpoons the distance of a mile, and long duck-guns with explosive bullets, which inflict mortal wounds even upon the most powerful animals.

Ned Land contented himself with sharpening his harpoon—a terrible weapon in his hands.

Day began to break, and with the first glimmer of dawn the electric light of the narwhal disappeared. At 7 a.m. a very thick sea-fog obscured the atmosphere, and the best glasses could not pierce it.

I climbed the mizenmast and found some officers already perched on the mastheads.

At 8 a.m. the mist began to clear away. Suddenly, like the night before, Ned Land's voice was heard calling:

"The thing in question on the port quarter!"

All eyes were turned towards the point indicated. There, a mile and a half from the frigate, a large black body emerged more than a yard above the waves. Its tail, violently agitated, produced a considerable eddy. Never did caudal appendage beat the sea with such force. An immense track, dazzlingly white, marked the passage of the animal, and described a long curve.

The frigate approached the cetacean, and I could see it well. The accounts of it given by the *Shannon* and *Helvetia* had rather exaggerated its dimensions, and I estimated its length at 150 feet only. As to its other dimensions, I could only conceive them to be in proportion.

The crew were waiting impatiently for their captain's orders. Farragut, after attentively examining the animal, had the chief engineer called.

"Is your steam up?" asked the captain.

"Yes, Captain," answered the engineer.

"Then make up your fires and put on all steam."

The *Abraham Lincoln*, propelled by her powerful screw, went straight at the animal, who let her approach to within half a cable's length, and then, as if disdaining to dive, made a little attempt at flight, and contented itself with keeping its distance.

This pursuit lasted about three-quarters of an hour, without the frigate gaining four yards on the cetacean. It was quite evident she would never reach it at that rate.

The captain twisted his beard impatiently.

"Ned Land!" called the captain, "do you think I had better have the boats lowered?"

"No, sir," answered Ned Land, "for that animal won't be caught unless it chooses."

"What must be done, then?"

"Force steam if you can, Captain, and I, with your permission, will post myself under the bowsprit, and if we get within a harpoon length I shall hurl one."

"Very well," said the captain. "Engineer, put on more pressure."

Ned Land went to his post, the fires were increased, the screw revolved forty-three times a minute, and the steam poured out of the valves. The log was heaved, and it was found that the frigate was going eighteen miles and five-tenths an hour. But the animal went eighteen and five-tenths an hour too.

During another hour the frigate kept up that speed without gaining a yard. It was humiliating for one of the quickest vessels in the American Navy. The crew began to get very angry. The sailors swore at the animal, who did not deign to answer them. The captain not only twisted his beard, he began to gnaw it too. The engineer was called once more.

"Have you reached your maximum of pressure?" asked the captain.

"Yes sir."

The captain ordered him to do all he could without absolutely blowing up the vessel, and coal was at once piled up on the fires. The speed of the frigate increased. Her masts shook again. The log was again heaved, and this time she was making nineteen miles and three-tenths.

"All steam on!" called out the captain.

The engineer obeyed. The manometer marked ten degrees. But the cetacean did the nineteen miles and three-tenths as easily as the eighteen and five-tenths.

What a chase! I cannot describe the emotion that made my whole being vibrate again. Ned Land kept at his post, harpoon in hand. The animal allowed itself to be approached several times. Sometimes it was so near that the Canadian raised his hand to hurl the harpoon, when the animal rushed away at a speed of at least thirty miles an hour, and even during our maximum of speed it bullied the frigate, going round and round it.

A cry of fury burst from all lips. We were not further advanced at twelve o'clock than we had been at eight. Captain Farragut then made up his mind to employ more direct means.

The forecastle gun was immediately loaded and pointed. It was fired, but the ball passed some feet above the cetacean, which kept about half a mile off.

"Let someone else try!" called out the captain. "Five hundred dollars to whomsoever will hit the beast!"

An old gunner with a grey beard—I think I see now his calm face as he approached the gun—put it into position and took a long aim. A loud report followed and mingled with the cheers of the crew.

The bullet reached its destination; it struck the animal, but, gliding off the rounded surface, fell into the sea two miles off.

"Malediction!" cried the captain; "that animal must be clad in six-inch iron plates. But I'll catch it, if I have to blow up my frigate!"

It was to be hoped that the animal would be exhausted, and that it would not be indifferent to fatigue like a steam-engine. But the hours went on, and it showed no signs of exhaustion.

It must be said, in praise of the *Abraham Lincoln*, that she struggled on indefatigably. I cannot reckon the distance we made during this unfortunate day at less than 300 miles. But night came on and closed round the heaving ocean.

At that minute, I believed our expedition to be at an end, and that we should see the fantastic animal no more.

I was mistaken, for at 10.50 p.m. the electric light reappeared, three miles windward to the frigate, clear and intense as on the night before.

The narwhal seemed motionless. Perhaps fatigued with its day's work, it was sleeping in its billowy cradle. That was a chance by which the captain resolved to profit.

He gave his orders. The *Abraham Lincoln* was kept up at half-steam, and advanced cautiously so as not to awaken her adversary. It is not rare to meet in open sea with whales fast asleep, and Ned Land had harpooned many a one in that condition. The Canadian went back to his post under the bowsprit.

The frigate noiselessly approached, and stopped at two cables' length from the animal. No one breathed. A profound silence reigned on deck. We were not 1,000 feet from the burning focus, the light of which increased and dazzled our eyes.

At that minute, leaning on the forecastle bulwark, I saw Ned Land below me, holding the martingale with one hand and with the other brandishing his terrible harpoon, scarcely twenty feet from the motionless animal.

All at once he threw the harpoon, and I heard the sonorous stroke of the weapon, which seemed to have struck a hard body.

The electric light suddenly went out, and two enormous water-spouts fell on the deck of the frigate, running like a torrent from fore to aft, upsetting men, and breaking the lashing of the spars.

A frightful shock followed. I was thrown over the rail before I had time to stop myself, and fell into the sea.

CHAPTER SEVEN

A WHALE OF AN UNKNOWN SPECIES

ALTHOUGH I was surprised by my unexpected fall, I still kept a very distinct impression of my sensations. I was at first dragged down to a depth of about twenty feet. I was a good swimmer, and this plunge did not make me lose my presence of mind. Two vigorous kicks brought me back to the surface.

My first care was to look for the frigate. Had the crew seen me disappear? Had the *Abraham Lincoln* veered round? Would the captain have a boat lowered? Might I hope to be saved?

The darkness was profound. I perceived a black mass disappearing in the east, the beacon lights of which were dying out in the distance. It was the frigate. I gave myself up.

"Help! help!" cried I, swimming towards the frigate with desperate strokes.

My clothes embarrassed me. The water glued them to my body. They paralysed my movements. I was sinking.

"Help!" rang out again in the darkness.

This was the last cry I uttered. My mouth filled with water. I struggled not to be sucked into the abyss.

Suddenly my clothes were seized by a vigorous hand, and I felt myself brought back violently to the surface of the water, and I heard—yes, I heard these words uttered in my ear:

"If monsieur will have the goodness to lean on my shoulder, monsieur will swim much better."

I seized the arm of my faithful Conseil.

"You!" I cried—"you!"

"Myself," answered Conseil, "at monsieur's service."

"Did the shock throw you into the sea too?"

29

"No; but being in the service of monsieur, I followed him."

The worthy fellow thought that quite natural.

"What about the frigate?" I asked.

"The frigate!" answered Conseil, turning on his back; "I think monsieur will do well not to count upon the frigate."

"Why?"

"Because, as I jumped into the sea, I heard the man at the helm call out, 'The screw and the rudder are broken.'"

"Broken?"

"Yes, by the monster's tusk. It is the only damage she has sustained, I think, but without a helm she can't do anything for us."

"Then we are lost!"

"Perhaps," answered Conseil tranquilly. "In the meantime we have still several hours before us, and in several hours many things may happen."

The *sang-froid* of Conseil did me good. I swam more vigorously, but encumbered by my garments, which dragged me down like a leaden weight, I found it extremely difficult to keep up. Conseil perceived it.

"Will monsieur allow me to make a slit?" said he. And, slipping an open knife under my clothes, he slit them rapidly from top to bottom. Then he quickly helped me off with them whilst I swam for both. I rendered him the same service, and we went on swimming near each other.

The collision had happened about 11 p.m. About 1 a.m. I was taken with extreme fatigue, and all my limbs became stiff with cramp. Conseil was obliged to keep me up, and the care of our preservation depended upon him alone. I heard the poor fellow breathing hard, and knew he could not keep up much longer.

Just then the moon appeared through the fringe of a large cloud that the wind was driving eastward. The surface of the sea shone under her rays. I lifted my head and saw the frigate. She was five miles from us, and only looked like a dark mass, scarcely distinguishable. I saw no boats.

I tried to call out, but it was useless at that distance. My swollen lips would not utter a sound. Conseil could still speak, and I heard him call out "Help!" several times.

We suspended our movements for an instant and listened. It might be only a singing in our ears, but it seemed to me that a cry answered Conseil's.

"Did you hear?" I murmured.

"Yes, yes!"

And Conseil threw another despairing cry into space. This time there could be no mistake. A human voice answered ours. Was it the voice of some other victim of the shock, or a boat hailing us in the darkness? Conseil made a supreme effort, and, leaning on my shoulder whilst I made a last struggle for us both, he raised himself half out of the water, and I heard him shout. Then my strength was exhausted, my fingers slipped, my mouth filled with salt water, I went cold all over, raised my head for the last time, and began to sink.

At that moment I hit against something hard, and I clung to it in desperation. Then I felt myself lifted up out of the water, and I fainted. I soon came to, thanks to the vigorous friction that was being applied to my body, and I half opened my eyes.

"Ned!" I cried.

"The same, sir, looking after his prize," replied the Canadian.

"Were you thrown into the sea when the frigate was struck?"

"Yes, sir, but, luckier than you, I soon got upon a floating island."

"An island?"

"Yes, or if you like better, on our giant narwhal."

"What do you mean, Ned?"

"I mean that I understand now why my harpoon did not stick into the skin, but was blunted."

"Why, Ned, why?"

"Because the beast is made of sheet-iron plates."

I wriggled myself quickly to the top of the half-submerged

being or object on which we had found refuge. I struck my foot against it. It was evidently a hard and impenetrable body, and not the soft substance which forms the mass of great marine mammalia. But this hard body could not be a bony carapace like that of antediluvian animals. I could not even class it amongst amphibious reptiles, such as tortoises and alligators, for the blackish back that supported me was not scaly but smooth and polished.

The blow produced a metallic sound, and, strange as it may appear, seemed caused by being struck on riveted plates. Doubt was no longer possible. The animal, monster, natural phenomenon that had puzzled the entire scientific world, and misled the imagination of sailors in the two hemispheres, was, it must be acknowledged, a still more astonishing phenomenon, a phenomenon of man's making. The discovery of the existence of the most fabulous and mythological being would not have astonished me in the same degree. It seems quite simple that anything prodigious should come from the hand of the Creator, but to find the impossible realised by the hand of man was enough to confound the imagination.

We were lying upon the top of a sort of submarine boat, which looked to me like an immense steel fish. Ned Land's mind was made up on that point, and Conseil and I could only agree with him.

"But then," said I, "this apparatus must have a locomotive machine, and a crew inside of it to work it."

"Evidently," replied the harpooner, "and yet for the three hours that I have inhabited this floating island, it has not given sign of life."

"The vessel has not moved?"

"No, M. Aronnax. It is cradled in the waves, but it does not move."

"We know, without the slightest doubt, however, that it is endowed with great speed, and as a machine is necessary to produce the speed, and a mechanician to guide it, I conclude from that that we are saved."

"Hum," said Ned Land in a reserved tone of voice.

At that moment, and as if to support my arguments, a boiling was heard at the back of the strange apparatus, the propeller of which was evidently a screw, and it began to move. We only had time to hold up to its upper part, which emerged about a yard out of the water. Happily its speed was not excessive.

"As long as it moves horizontally," murmured Ned Land, "I have nothing to say. But if it takes it into its head to plunge, I would not give two dollars for my skin!"

The Canadian might have said less still. It therefore became urgent to communicate with whatever beings were shut up in the machine. I looked on its surface for an opening a panel, a "manhole," to use the technical expression; but the lines of bolts, solidly fastened down on the joints of the plates, were clear and uniform.

Besides, the moon then disappeared and left us in profound obscurity. We were obliged to wait till daybreak to decide upon the means of penetrating to the interior of this submarine boat.

Thus, then, our safety depended solely upon the caprice of the mysterious steersmen who directed this apparatus, and if they plunged we were lost! Unless that happened I did not doubt the possibility of entering into communication with them. And it was certain that unless they made their own air they must necessarily return from time to time to the surface of the ocean to renew their provision of breathable molecules. Therefore there must be an opening which put the interior of the boat into communication with the atmosphere.

At last this long night slipped away. My incomplete memory does not allow me to retrace all the impressions of it. A single detail returns to my mind. During certain lullings of the sea and wind, I thought several times I heard vague sounds, a sort of fugitive harmony produced by far-off chords. What, then, was the mystery of this submarine navigation, of which the entire world vainly sought the explanation? What beings lived in this strange boat? What mechanical agent allowed it to move with such prodigious speed?

When daylight appeared the morning mists enveloped us, but they soon rose, and I proceeded to make an attentive examination of the sort of horizontal platform we were on, when I felt myself gradually sinking.

"Mille diables!" cried Land, kicking against the sonorous metal, "open, inhospitable creatures!"

But it was difficult to make oneself heard amidst the deafening noise made by the screw. Happily the sinking ceased.

Suddenly a noise like iron bolts being violently withdrawn was heard from the interior of the boat. One of the iron plates was raised, a man appeared, uttered a strange cry, and disappeared immediately.

Some moments after, eight strong fellows, with veiled faces, silently appeared, and dragged us down into their formidable machine.

CHAPTER EIGHT

MOBILIS IN MOBILE

THE narrow panel had scarcely closed upon me when I was enveloped by profound darkness. My eyes, dazzled by the light outside, could distinguish nothing. I felt my naked feet touch the steps of an iron ladder. Ned Land and Conseil, firmly held, followed me. At the bottom of the ladder a door opened and closed again immediately with a sonorous bang.

We were alone. Where? I neither knew nor could I imagine. All was darkness, and such absolute darkness, that after some minutes I had not been able to make out even those faint glimmers of light which float in the darkest nights.

I groped my way about. When I had gone about five

steps I came to an iron wall made of riveted plates. Then turning, I knocked against a wooden table, near which were several stools. The flooring of this prison was hidden under thick matting, which deadened the noise of our footsteps. The walls revealed no traces of either door or window. Conseil, going round the reverse way, met me, and we returned to the centre of the room, which measured about twenty feet by ten. As to its height, Ned Land, notwithstanding his tall stature, could not measure it.

Half an hour passed away without bringing any change in our position, when from the extreme of obscurity our eyes passed suddenly to the most violent light. Our prison was lighted up all at once—that is to say, it was filled with a luminous matter so intense that at first I could not bear its brilliancy. I saw from its whiteness and intensity that was the same electric light that shone around the submarine boat like a magnificent phosphoric phenomenon. After having involuntarily closed my eyes I opened them again, and saw that the luminous agent was escaping from a polished half-globe, which was shining in the top part of the room.

The sudden lighting of the cabin had allowed me to examine its least details. It only contained the table and five stools. The invisible door seemed hermetically closed. No noise reached our ears. All seemed dead in the interior of this machine. Was it moving, or was it motionless on the surface of the ocean, or deep in its depths? I could not guess.

However, the luminous globe was not lighted without a reason. I hoped that the men of the crew would soon show themselves, and my hope was well founded. A noise of bolts and bars being withdrawn was heard, the door opened, and two men appeared. One was short in stature, vigorously muscular, with broad shoulders, robust limbs, large head, abundant black hair, thick moustache, and all his person imprinted with that southern vivacity which characterises the Provençal inhabitants of France.

The second deserves a more detailed description. I read

at once his dominant qualities on his open face—self-confidence, because his head was firmly set on his shoulders, and his black eyes looked round with cold assurance—calmness, for his pale complexion announced the tranquillity of his blood—energy, demonstrated by the rapid contraction of his eyebrows; and, lastly, courage, for his deep breathing denoted vast vital expansion. I felt involuntarily reassured in his presence, and augured good from it. He might be of any age from thirty-five to fifty. His tall stature, wide forehead, straight nose, clear-cut mouth, magnificent teeth, taper hands, indicated a highly nervous temperament. This man formed certainly the most admirable type I had ever met with. One strange detail was that his eyes, rather far from each other, could take in nearly a quarter of the horizon at once. This faculty—I verified it later on—was added to a power of vision superior even to that of Ned Land. When the unknown fixed an object he frowned, and his large eyelids closed round so as to contract the range of his vision, and the result was a look that penetrated your very soul. With it he pierced the liquid waves that looked so opaque to us as if he read to the very depths of the sea.

The two strangers had on caps made from the fur of the sea-otter, sealskin boots and clothes of a peculiar texture, which allowed them great liberty of movement.

The taller of the two—evidently the chief on board—examined us with extreme attention without speaking a word. Then he turned towards his companion, and spoke to him in a language I could not understand. It was a sonorous, harmonious and flexible idiom, of which the vowels seemed very variously accented.

The other answered by shaking his head and pronouncing two or three perfectly incomprehensible words. Then, from his looks, he seemed to be questioning me directly.

I answered in good French that I did not understand his language; but he did not seem to know French, and the situation became very embarrassing.

"If monsieur would relate his story," said Conseil, "these gentlemen may understand some words of it."

I began the recital of my adventures, articulating clearly all my syllables, without leaving out a single detail. I gave our names and qualities. The man with the soft, calm eyes listened to me calmly, and even politely, with remarkable attention. But nothing in his face indicated that he understood me. When I had done he did not speak a single word.

There still remained one resource, that of speaking English. Perhaps they would understand that almost universal language. I knew it, and German too, sufficiently to read it correctly, but not to speak it fluently.

"It is your turn now, Land," I said to the harpooner. "Make use of your best English, and try to be more fortunate than I."

Ned did not need urging, and began the same tale in English, and ended by saying what was perfectly true, that we were half dead with hunger. To his great disgust the harpooner did not seem more intelligible than I. Our visitors did not move a feature. It was evident that they neither knew the language of Arago nor Faraday. I was wondering what to do next, when Conseil said to me:

"If monsieur will allow me, I will tell them in German."

"What! do you know German?" I cried.

"Like a Dutchman, sir."

"Well do your best, old fellow."

And Conseil, in his tranquil voice, told our story for the third time, but without success.

I then assembled all the Latin I had learnt at school, and told my adventures in that dead language. Cicero would have stopped his ears and sent me to the kitchen, but I did the best I could with the same negative result.

After this last attempt the strangers exchanged a few words in their incomprehensible language, and went away without a gesture that could reassure us. The door closed upon them.

"It is infamous!" cried Ned Land, who broke out again

for the twentieth time. "What! French, English, German and Latin are spoken to those rascals, and not one of them has the politeness to answer."

"My friends," said I, "we must not despair. We have been in worse situations before now. Do me the pleasure of waiting before you form an opinion of the commander and crew of this vessel."

"My opinion is already formed," answered Ned Land. "They are rascals——"

"Well, and of what country?"

"Of Rascaldom!"

"My worthy Ned, that country is not yet sufficiently indicated on the map of the world, and I acknowledge that the nationality of those two men is difficult to determine. Neither English, French, nor German, that is all we can affirm. However, I should be tempted to admit that the commander and his second were born under low latitudes. There is something meridional in them. But are they Spaniards, Turks, Arabians, or Indians? Their physical type does not allow me to decide; as to their language, it is absolutely incomprehensible."

"That is the disadvantage of not knowing every language," answered Conseil, "or the disadvantage of not having a single language."

"That would be of no use," answered Ned Land. "Do you not see that those fellows have a language of their own— a language invented to make honest men who want their dinners despair? But in every country in the world, to open your mouth, move your jaws, snap your teeth and lips, is understood. Does it not mean in Quebec as well as the Society Islands, in Paris as well as the Antipodes, 'I am hungry—give me something to eat!'"

"Oh," said Conseil, "there are people so unintelligent——"

As he was saying these words the door opened, and a steward entered. He brought us clothes similar to those worn by the two strangers, which we hastened to don.

Meanwhile, the servant—dumb and deaf too in all appearance—had laid the cloth for three.

"This is something like," said Conseil, "and promises well."

"I'll bet anything there's nothing here fit to eat," said the harpooner. "Tortoise liver, fillets of shark, or beefsteak from a sea-dog, perhaps!"

"We shall soon see," said Conseil

The dishes with their silver covers were symmetrically placed on the table. We had certainly civilised people to deal with, and had it not been for the electric light which inundated us, I might have imagined myself in the Adelphi Hotel in Liverpool, or the Grand Hotel in Paris. There was neither bread nor wine, nothing but pure fresh water, which was not at all to Ned Land's taste. Amongst the dishes that were placed before us I recognised several kinds of fish delicately cooked; but there were some that I knew nothing about, though they were delicious. I could not tell to what kingdom their contents belonged. The dinner service was elegant and in perfect taste; each piece was engraved with a letter and motto of which the following is a facsimile:

Mobilis in Mobile
N

Mobile in a mobile element! The letter N was doubtless the initial of the enigmatical person who commanded at the bottom of the sea.

Ned and Conseil did not observe so much. They devoured all before them, and I ended by imitating them.

But at last even our appetite was satisfied, and we felt overcome with sleep. A natural reaction after the fatigue of the interminable night during which we had struggled with death.

My two companions lay down on the carpet, and were soon fast asleep. I did not go so soon, for too many thoughts filled my brain; too many insoluble questions asked me for a solution; too many images kept my eyes open. Where were we? What strange power was bearing us along? I felt, or rather I thought I felt, the strange machine sinking down to the lowest depths of the sea. Dreadful nightmares took possession of me. I saw a world of unknown animals in these mysterious asylums, amongst which the submarine boat seemed as living, moving and formidable as they. Then my brain grew calmer, my imagination melted into dreaminess, and I fell into a deep sleep.

CHAPTER NINE

NED LAND'S ANGER

I DO not know how long our sleep lasted, but it must have been a long time, for it rested us completely from our fatigues. I awoke first. My companions had not yet moved.

I had scarcely risen from my rather hard couch when I felt all my faculties clear, and looked about me.

Nothing was changed in the room. The prison was still a prison, and the prisoners prisoners. The steward, profiting by our sleep, had cleared the supper things away. Nothing indicated an approaching change in our position, and I asked myself seriously if we were destined to live indefinitely in that cage.

This prospect seemed to me the more painful, because, though my head was clear, my chest was oppressed. The heavy air weighed upon my lungs. We had evidently consumed the larger part of the oxygen the cell contained, although it was large. One man consumes in one hour the oxygen contained in 176 pints of air, and this air, then loaded with an almost equal quantity of carbonic acid, becomes unbearable.

It was, therefore, urgent to renew the atmosphere of our prison, and most likely that of the submarine boat also. Thereupon a question came into my head: "How did the commander of this floating dwelling manage? Did he obtain air by chemical means, by evolving the heat of oxygen contained in chlorate of potassium, and by absorbing the carbonic acid with caustic potassium? In that case he must have kept up some relations with land in order to procure the materials necessary to this operation. Did he confine himself simply to storing up air under great pressure in reservoirs and then let it out according to the needs of his crew? Perhaps. Or did he use the more convenient, economical, and consequently more probably means of contenting himself with returning to breathe on the surface of the water like a cetacean, and of renewing for twenty-four hours his provision of atmosphere? Whatever his method might be, it seemed to me prudent to employ it without delay.

I was reduced to multiplying my respirations to extract from our cell the small quantity of oxygen it contained, when, suddenly I was refreshed by a current of fresh air, loaded with saline odours. It was a sea breeze, life-giving, and charged with iodine. I opened my mouth wide, and my lungs became saturated with fresh particles. At the same time I felt the boat roll, and the iron-plated monster had evidently just ascended to the surface of the ocean to breathe like the whales. When I had breathed fully, I looked for the ventilator which had brought us the beneficent breeze, and, before long, found it.

I was making these observations when my two companions awoke nearly at the same time, doubtless through the influence of the reviving air. They rubbed their eyes, stretched themselves, and were on foot instantly.

"Did monsieur sleep well?" Conseil asked me, with his usual politeness.

"Very well. And you, Land?"

"Soundly, Mr. Professor. But if I am not mistaken, I am breathing a sea breeze."

A seaman could not be mistaken in that, and I told the Canadian what had happened while he was asleep.

"That accounts for the roarings we heard when the supposed narwhal was in sight of the *Abraham Lincoln*."

"Yes, Mr. Land, that is its breathing."

"I have not the least idea what time it can be, M. Aronnax, unless it be dinner-time."

"Dinner-time, Ned? Say, breakfast-time at least, for we have certainly slept something like twenty-four hours."

"I will not contradict you," answered Ned Land, "but dinner or breakfast, the steward would be welcome. I wish he would bring one or the other."

"The one and the other," said Conseil.

"Certainly," answered the Canadian, "we have right to two meals and, for my own part, I shall do honour to both."

"Well, Ned, we must wait," I answered. "It is evident that those two men had no intention of leaving us to die of hunger, for in that case there would have been no reason to give us dinner yesterday."

"Unless it is to fatten us!" answered Ned.

"I protest," I answered. "We have not fallen into the hands of cannibals."

"One swallow does not make a summer," answered the Canadian seriously. "Who knows if those fellows have not been long deprived of fresh meat, and in that case these healthy and well-constituted individuals like the Professor, his servant and me——"

"Drive away such ideas, Land," I answered, "and above all do not act upon them to get into a rage with our hosts, for that would only make the situation worse."

"Anyway," said the harpooner, "I am devilishly hungry and, dinner or breakfast, the meal does not arrive!"

Then the conversation was suspended, and each of us began to reflect on his own account.

Ned Land, tormented by the twinges of his robust stomach, became more and more enraged, and I really feared an explosion when he would again be in the presence of the men on board. He rose, moved about like a wild beast in a cage, and struck the wall with his fist and foot.

Two more hours rolled on, and Ned's anger increased; he cried and called at the top of his voice, but in vain. The iron walls were deaf. The boat seemed quite still. The silence became quite oppressive.

I dare no longer think how long our abandonment and isolation in this cell might last. The hopes that I had conceived after our interview with the commander of the vessel vanished one by one. The gentle look of this man, the generous expression of his face, the nobility of his carriage, all disappeared from my memory. I again saw this enigmatical personage such as he must necessarily be, pitiless and cruel. I felt him to be outside the pale of humanity, inaccessible to all sentiment of pity, the implacable enemy of his fellow men, to whom he had vowed imperishable hatred.

But was this man going, then, to let us perish from inanition, shut up in this narrow prison, giving up to the horrible temptations to which ferocious famine leads? This frightful thought took a terrible intensity in my mind, and imagination helping, I felt myself invaded by unreasoning fear. Conseil remained calm. Ned was roaring. At that moment a noise was heard outside. Steps clanged on the metal slabs. The bolts were withdrawn, the door opened, the steward appeared.

Before I could make a movement to prevent him, the Canadian had rushed upon the unfortunate fellow, knocked him down and fastened on his throat. The steward was choking under his powerful hand.

Conseil was trying to rescue his half-suffocated victim from the hands of the harpooner, and I was going to join my efforts to his, when, suddenly, I was riveted to my place by these words, spoken in French:

"Calm yourself, Mr. Land, and you, Professor, please to listen to me."

CHAPTER TEN

NEMO

THE MAN who spoke thus was the commander of the vessel. When Ned Land heard these words he rose suddenly.

The almost strangled steward went tottering out on a sign from his master; but such was the power of the commander on his vessel that not a gesture betrayed the resentment the man must have felt towards the Canadian. Conseil, interested in spite of himself, and I stupefied, awaited the result of this scene in silence.

The commander, leaning against the angle of the table, with his arms folded, looked at us with profound attention. After some minutes of a silence which none of us thought of interrupting, he said in a calm and penetrating voice:

"Gentlemen, I speak French, English, German and Latin equally well. I might, therefore, have answered you at our last interview, but I wished to know you first, and afterwards to ponder on what you said. The stories told by each of you agreed in the main, and assured me of your identity. I know now that accident has brought me into the presence of M. Pierre Aronnax, Professor of Natural History in the Paris Museum, charged with a foreign scientific mission, his servant Conseil, and Ned Land, of Canadian origin, harpooner on board the frigate *Abraham Lincoln*, of the United States Navy."

I bent my head in sign of assent. There was no answer necessary. This man expressed himself with perfect ease and without the least foreign accent. And yet I felt that he was not one of my countrymen. He continued the conversation in these terms:

"I dare say you thought me a long time in coming to pay you this second visit. It was because, after once knowing your identity, I wished to ponder upon what to do with you. I hesitated long. The most unfortunate conjecture of circumstances has brought you into the presence of a man who has broken all ties that bound him to humanity. You came here to trouble my existence——"

"Unintentionally," said I.

"Unintentionally," he repeated, raising his voice a little. "Is it unintentionally that the *Abraham Lincoln* pursues me in every sea? Was it unintentionally that you took passage on board her? Was it unintentionally that your bullets struck my vessel? Did Mr. Land throw his harpoon unintentionally?"

"You are doubtless unaware," I answered, "of the commotion you have caused in Europe and America. When the *Abraham Lincoln* pursued you on the high seas, everyone on board believed they were pursuing a marine monster."

A slight smile curled round the commander's lips, then he went on in a calmer tone:

"Dare you affirm, M. Aronnax, that your frigate would not have pursued a submarine vessel as well as a marine monster?"

This question embarrassed me, for it was certain that Captain Farragut would not have hesitated. He would have thought it as much his duty to destroy such a machine as the gigantic narwhal he took it to be.

"You see, sir," continued the commander, "I have the right to treat you as enemies."

I answered nothing, and for a very good reason; the unknown had force on his side, and it can destroy the best arguments.

"I have long hesitated," continued the commander. "Nothing obliges me to give you hospitality. I could place you upon the platform of this vessel, upon which you took refuge; I might sink it beneath the waters and forget that you ever existed. I should only be using my right."

"The right of a savage, perhaps," I answered, "but not that of a civilised man."

"Professor," quickly answered the commander, "I am not what is called a civilised man. I have done with society entirely for reasons that seem to me good; therefore I do not obey its laws, and I desire you never to allude to them before me again."

This was uttered clearly. A flash of anger and contempt had kindled in the man's eyes, and I had a glimpse of a terrible past in his life. He had not only put himself out of the pale of human laws, but he had made himself independent of them, free, in the most rigorous sense of the word, entirely out of their reach. Who, then, would dare to pursue him in the depths of the sea, when on its surface he baffled all efforts attempted against him? What armour, however thick, could support the blows of his spur? No man could ask him for an account of his works. God, if he believed in Him, his conscience, if he had one, were the only judges he could depend upon.

After a rather long silence the commander went on speaking.

"I have hesitated, therefore," he said, "but I thought that my interest might be reconciled with that natural pity to which every human being has a right. You may remain on my vessel, since fate has brought you to it. You will be free, and in exchange for this liberty which, after all, will be relative. I shall only impose one condition upon you. Your word of honour to submit to it will be sufficient."

"Speak, sir," I answered. "I suppose this condition is one that an honest man can accept?"

"Yes; it is this: It is possible that certain unforeseen events may force me to consign you to your cabin for some hours, or even days. As I do not wish to use violence, I expect from you, in such a case, more than from all others, passive obedience. By acting thus I take all the responsibility; I acquit you entirely, by making it impossible for you to see what ought not to be seen. Do you accept the condition?"

So things took place on board which were, at least, singular and not to be seen by people who were not placed beyond the pale of social laws.

"We accept," I replied. "Only I ask your permission to

address to you one question—only one. What degree of liberty do you intend giving us?"

"The liberty to move about freely and observe even all that passes here—except under rare circumstances—in short, the liberty that my companions and I enjoy ourselves."

It was evident that we did not understand each other.

"Pardon me, sir," I continued, "but this liberty is only that of every prisoner to pace his prison. It is not enough for us."

"You must make it enough."

"Do you mean to say we must for ever renounce the idea of seeing country, friends and relations again?"

"Yes, sir. But to renounce the unendurable worldly yoke that men call liberty is not perhaps so painful as you think."

"I declare," said Ned Land, "I'll never give my word of honour not to try to escape."

"I did not ask for your word of honour, Mr. Land," answered the commander coldly.

"Sir," I replied, carried away in spite of myself, "you take advantage of your position towards us. It is cruel!"

"No, sir, it is kind. You are my prisoners of war. I keep you when I could, by a word, plunge you into the depths of the ocean. You attacked me. You came and surprised a secret that I mean no man inhabiting the world to penetrate—the secret of my whole existence. And you think that I am going to send you back to that world? Never! In retaining you, it is not you I guard, it is myself!"

These words indicated that the commander's mind was made up, and that argument was useless.

"Then, sir," I answered, "you give us the simple choice between life and death?"

"As you say."

"My friends," said I, "to a question thus put there is nothing to answer. But no word of honour binds us to the master of this vessel."

"None, sir," answered the unknown.

Then, in a gentler voice, he went on:

"Now, allow me to finish what I have to say to you. I know you, M. Arronax. You, if not your companions, will not have so much to complain of in the chance that has bound you to my lot. You have carried your investigations as far as terrestrial science allowed you. But on board my vessel you will have an opportunity of seeing what no man has seen before. Thanks to me, our planet will give up her last secrets."

I cannot deny that these words had a great effect upon me. My weak point was touched, and I forgot for a moment that the contemplation of these divine things was not worth the loss of liberty. Besides, I counted upon the future to decide that grave question, and so contented myself with saying:

"What name am I to call you by, sir?"

"Captain Nemo," answered the commander. "That is all I am to you, and you and your companions are nothing to me but the passengers of the *Nautilus.*"

The captain called and a steward appeared. The captain gave him his orders in that foreign tongue which I could not understand. Then turning to the Canadian and Conseil:

"Your meal is prepared in your cabin," he said to them. "Be so good as to follow that man."

My two companions in misfortune left the cell where they had been confined for more than thirty hours.

"And now, M. Aronnax, our breakfast is ready. Allow me to lead the way."

I followed Captain Nemo into a sort of corridor lighted by electricity, similar to the waist of a ship. After going about a dozen yards, a second door opened before me into a kind of dining-room, decorated and furnished with severe taste. High oaken sideboards, inlaid with ebony ornaments, stood at either end of the room, and on their shelves glittered china, porcelain and glass of inestimable value. The plate that was on them sparkled in the light which shone from the ceiling, tempered and softened by fine painting. In the centre of the room was a table richly spread. Captain Nemo pointed to my seat.

"Sit down," said he, "and eat like a man who must be dying of hunger."

The breakfast consisted of a number of dishes, the contents of which were all furnished by the sea; of some I neither knew the nature nor mode of preparation. They were good, but had a peculiar flavour which I soon became accustomed to. They appeared to be rich in phosphorus.

Captain Nemo looked at me. I asked him no questions, but he guessed my thoughts, and said:

"Most of these dishes are unknown to you, but you can eat of them without fear. They are wholesome and nourishing. I have long renounced the food of the earth, and I am none the worse for it. My crew, who are healthy, have the same food."

"Then all these dishes are the produce of the sea?" said I.

"Yes, Professor, the sea supplies all my needs. Sometimes I cast my nets in tow, and they are drawn in ready to break. Sometimes I go and hunt in the midst of this element, which seems inaccessible to man, and run down the game of submarine forests. My flocks, like those of Neptune's old shepherd, graze fearlessly the immense ocean meadows. I have a vast estate there, which I cultivate myself, and which is always stocked by the Creator of all things."

I looked at Captain Nemo with some astonishment, and answered:

"I can quite understand that your nets should furnish excellent fish for your table, and that you should pursue aquatic game in your submarine forests; but I do not understand how a particle of meat can find its way into your bill of fare."

"What you believe to be meat, Professor, is nothing but fillet of turtle. Here also are dolphins' livers, which you might take for ragout of pork. My cook is a clever fellow, who excels in preparing these various products of the sea. Taste all these dishes. Here is a conserve of holothuria, which a Malay would declare to be unrivalled in the world; here is a cream furnished by the cetacea, and the sugar by the great fucus of the North Sea; and, lastly, allow me to offer you some anemone preserve, which equals that made from the most delicious fruits."

Whilst I was tasting, more from curiosity than as a gourmet, Captain Nemo enchanted me with extraordinary stories.

"Not only does the sea feed me," he continued, "but it clothes me too. These materials that clothe you are wrought from the byssus of certain shells; they are dyed with the purple of the ancients, and the violet shades which I extract from the aplysis of the Mediterranean. The perfumes you will find on the toilet of your cabin are produced from the distillation of marine plants. Your bed is made with the softest wrack-grass of the ocean. Your pen will be a whale's fin, your ink the liquor secreted by the calamary. Everything now comes to me from the sea, and everything will one day return to it!"

"You love the sea, Captain?"

"Yes, I love it. The sea is everything. Its breath is pure and healthy. It is an immense desert where man is never alone, for he feels life quivering around him on every side. The sea does not belong to despots. On its surface iniquitous rights can still be exercised, men can fight there, devour each other there, and transport all terrestrial horrors there. But at thirty feet below its level their power ceases, their influence dies out, their might disappears. Ah, sir, live in the bosom of the waters! There alone is independence! There I recognise no masters! There I am free!"

Captain Nemo stopped suddenly in the midst of this burst of enthusiasm. Had he let himself be carried out of his habitual reserve? Had he said too much? During some moments he walked about much agitated. Then his nerves became calmer, his face regained its usual calm expression, and turning towards me:

"Now, Professor," said he, "if you wish to visit the *Nautilus*, I am at your service."

CHAPTER ELEVEN

THE "NAUTILUS"

CAPTAIN NEMO rose, and I followed him. A folding door, contrived at the back of the room, opened, and I entered a room about the same size as the one I had just left.

It was a library. High bookcases of black rosewood supported on their shelves a great number of books in uniform binding. They went round the room, terminating at their lower part in large divans, covered with brown leather, curved so as to afford the greatest comfort. Light, movable desks, made to slide in and out at will, were there to rest one's book while reading. In the centre was a vast table, covered with pamphlets, amongst which appeared some newspapers, already old. The electric light flooded this harmonious whole, and was shed from four polished globes half sunk in the volutes of the ceiling. This room, so ingeniously fitted up, excited my admiration, and I could scarcely believe my eyes.

Books of science, ethics, and literature—written in every language—were there in quantities; but I did not see a single work on political economy amongst them; they seemed to be severely prohibited on board. A curious detail was that all these books were classified indistinctly, in whatever language they were written, and this confusion showed that the captain of the *Nautilus* could read with the utmost facility any volume he might take up by chance.

"This room is not only a library," said Captain Nemo; "it is a smoking-room too."

"A smoking-room?" cried I. "Do you smoke here, then?"

"Certainly."

"Then, sir, I am forced to believe that you have kept up relations with Havana?"

"No, I have not," answered the captain. "Accept this cigar, M. Arronax; although it does not come from Havana, you will be pleased with it if you are a connoisseur."

I took the cigar that was offered me; its shape was something like that of a *Londres*, but it seemed to be made of leaves of gold. I lighted it at a little brazier which was supported on an elegant bronze pedestal, and drew the first whiffs with the delight of an amateur who has not smoked for two days.

"It is excellent," said I, "but it is not tobacco."

"No," answered the captain. "This tobacco comes neither from Havana nor the East. It is a sort of seaweed, rich in nicotine, with which the sea supplies me, but somewhat sparingly. If you do not regret the *Londres*, M. Aronnax, smoke these as much as you like."

As Captain Nemo spoke he opened the opposite door to the one by which we had entered the library, and I passed into an immense and brilliantly-lighted saloon. It was a vast four-sided room, with panelled walls, measuring thirty feet by eighteen, and about fifteen feet high. A luminous ceiling, decorated with light arabesques, distributed a soft, clear light over all the marvels collected in the museum. For it was, in fact, a museum in which an intelligent and prodigal hand had gathered together all the treasures of nature and art with the artistic confusion of a painter's studio.

About thirty pictures by the first artists, uniformly framed and separated by brilliant drapery, were hung on tapestry of severe design. I saw there works of great value, most of which I had admired in the special collections of Europe, and in exhibitions of paintings. The amazement which the captain of the *Nautilus* had predicted had already begun to take possession of me.

"Professor," then said this strange man, "you must excuse the unceremonious way in which I receive you, and the disorder of this room."

"Sir," I answered, "without seeking to know who you are, may I be allowed to recognise in you an artist?"

"Only an amateur, sir. Formerly I liked to collect these works of art. I was a greedy collector and an indefatigable antiquary, and have been able to get together some objects of great value. These are my last gatherings from that world which is now dead to me. In my eyes your modern artists are already old; they have two or three thousand years of existence, and all masters are of the same age in my mind."

"And these musicians?" said I, pointing to the works of Weber, Rossini, Mozart, and many others, scattered over a large piano-organ fixed in one of the panels of the room.

"These musicians," answered Captain Nemo, "are contemporaries of Orpheus, for all chronological differences are effaced in the memory of the dead; and I am dead, as much dead as those of your friends who are resting six feet under the earth!"

Captain Nemo ceased talking, and seemed lost in a profound reverie. I looked at him with great interest, analysing in silence the strange expressions of his face.

I respected his meditation, and went on passing in review the curiosities that enriched the saloon. They consisted principally of marine plants, shells, and other productions of the ocean, which must have been found by Captain Nemo himself. In the centre of the saloon rose a jet of water lighted up by electricity, and falling into a basin formed of a single tridacne shell, measuring about seven yards in circumference; it, therefore, surpassed in size the beautiful tridacnes given to Francis I of France by the Venetian Republic, and that now form two basins for holy water in the church of Saint Sulpice in Paris.

Apart and in special apartments were chaplets of pearls of the greatest beauty, which the electric light pricked with points of fire; pink pearls, torn from the pinnamarina of the Red Sea; green pearls from the haliotyde iris; yellow, blue, and black pearls, the curious productions of different molluscs from every ocean, and certain mussels from the water-courses of the North; lastly, several specimens of priceless value, gathered from the rarest pintadines. Some of these pearls were bigger than a pigeon's egg, and were worth more than the one Tavernier sold to the Shah of Persia for 3,000,000 francs, and surpassed the one in the possession of the Imaum of Muscat, which I had believed unrivalled.

It was impossible to estimate the worth of this collection. Captain Nemo must have spent millions in acquiring these various specimens, and I was asking myself from whence he had drawn the money to gratify his fancy for collecting, when I was interrupted by these words: "You are examining my shells, Professor. They certainly must be interesting to a naturalist, but for me they have a greater charm, for I have collected them all myself, and there is not a sea on the face of the globe that has escaped my search."

"I understand, Captain—I understand the delight of moving amongst such riches. You are one of those people who lay up treasures for themselves. There is not a museum in Europe that possess such a collection of marine products. But if I exhaust all my admiration upon it, I shall have none left for the vessel that carries it. I do not wish to penetrate into your secrets, but I must confess that this *Nautilus*, with the motive power she contains, the contrivances by which she is worked, the powerful agent which propels her, all excite my utmost curiosity. I see hung on the walls of this room instruments the use of which I ignore."

"When I told you that you were free on board my vessel, I meant that every portion of the *Nautilus* was open to your inspection. The instruments you will see in my room, Professor, where I shall have much pleasure in explaining their use to you. But come and look at your own cabin."

I followed Captain Nemo, who, by one of the doors opening from each panel of the drawing-room, regained the waist of the vessel. He conducted me aft, and there I found, not a cabin, but an elegant room with a bed, toilet-table, and several other articles of furniture. I could only thank my host.

"Your room is next to mine," said he, opening a door; "and mine opens into the saloon we have just left."

I entered the captain's room; it had a severe, almost monkish, aspect. A small iron bedstead, an office desk, some articles of toilet—all lighted by a strong light. There were no comforts, only the strictest necessaries.

Captain Nemo pointed to a seat.

"Pray sit down," he said.

I obeyed, and he began thus:

CHAPTER TWELVE

EVERYTHING BY ELECTRICITY

"Sir," said Captain Nemo, showing me the instruments hung on the walls of the room, "here are the instruments necessary for the navigation of the *Nautilus*. Here, as in the saloon, I have them always before me, and they indicate my position and exact direction in the midst of the ocean. You are acquainted with some of them."

"Yes," I answered; "I understand the usual nautical instruments. But I see others that doubtless answer the peculiar requirements of your vessel. That dial with a movable needle is a manometer, is it not?"

"Yes, by communication with the water it indicates the exterior pressure and gives our depth at the same time."

"And these other instruments, the use of which I cannot guess?"

"Here I ought to give you some explanation, Professor. There is a powerful, obedient, rapid, and easy agent which lends itself to all uses, and reigns supreme here. We do everything by its means. It is the light, warmth and soul of my mechanical apparatus. This agent is electricity."

"Yes, Captain, you possess an extreme rapidity of movement which does not well agree with the power of electricity. Until now its dynamic force has been very restricted, and has only produced little power."

"Professor," answered Captain Nemo, "my electricity is

not everybody's, and you will permit me to withhold any further information."

"I will not insist, sir; I will content myself with being astonished at such wonderful results. A single question, however, I will ask, which you need not answer if it is an indiscreet one. The elements which you employ to produce this marvellous agent must necessarily be soon consumed. The zinc, for instance, that you use—how do you obtain a fresh supply? You now have no communication with the land?"

"I will answer your question," replied Captain Nemo. "In the first place I must inform you that there exist, at the bottom of the sea, mines of zinc, iron, silver and gold, the working of which would most certainly be practicable; but I am not indebted to any of these terrestrial metals. I was determined to seek from the sea alone the means of producing my electricity."

"From the sea?"

"You know the composition of sea-water? Chloride of sodium forms a notable proportion of it. Now it is this sodium that I extract from sea-water, and of which I compose my ingredients. Mixed with mercury it takes the place of zinc for the voltaic pile. The mercury is never exhausted; only the sodium is consumed, and the sea itself gives me that. Besides, the electric power of the sodium piles is double that of zinc ones."

"I clearly understand, Captain, the convenience of sodium in the circumstances in which you are placed. The sea contains it. Good. But you still have to make it, to extract it, in a word. And how do you do that? Your pile would evidently serve the purpose of extracting it; but the consumption of sodium necessitated by the electrical apparatus would exceed the quantity extracted. You would consume more than you would produce."

"I do not extract it by the pile, Professor I employ nothing but the heat of coal."

"Coal!" I urged.

"We will call it sea-coal if you like," replied Captain Nemo.

"And are you able to work submarine coal-mines?"

"You shall see me so employed, M. Aronnax. I only ask you for a little patience; you have time to be patient here. I get everything from the ocean. It produces electricity, and electricity supplies the *Nautilus* with light—in a word, with life."

"But not with the air you breathe."

"I could produce the air necessary for my consumption, but I do not, because I go up to the surface of the water when I please. But though electricity does not furnish me with the air to breathe, it works the powerful pumps which store it up in special reservoirs, and which enable me to prolong at need, and as long as I like, my stay in the depths of the sea."

"Captain," I replied, "I can do nothing but admire. You have evidently discovered what mankind at large will, no doubt, one day discover, the veritable dynamic power of electricity."

"Whether they will discover it I do not know," replied Captain Nemo coldly. "However that may be, you now know the first application that I have made of this precious agent. It is electricity that furnishes us with a light that surpasses in uniformity and continuity that of the sun itself. Look now at this clock! It is an electric one, and goes with a regularity that defies the best of chronometers. I have divided it into twenty-four hours, like the Italian clocks, because there exists for me neither night nor day, sun nor moon, only this factitious light that I take with me to the bottom of the sea. Look! just now it is 10 a.m."

"Exactly so."

"This dial hanging in front of us indicates the speed of the *Nautilus*. An electric wire puts it into communication with the screw. Look! just now we are going along at the moderate speed of fifteen miles an hour. But we have not finished yet, M. Aronnax," continued Captain Nemo, rising, "if you will follow me we will visit the stern of the *Nautilus*."

I followed Captain Nemo across the waist, and in the centre of the boat came to a sort of well that opened between two watertight partitions. An iron ladder, fastened by an iron hook to the partition, led to the upper end. I asked the captain what it was for.

"It leads to the boat," answered he.

"What! have you a boat?" I exclaimed in astonishment.

"Certainly, an excellent one, light and unsinkable, that serves either for fishing or pleasure trips."

"Then when you wish to embark you are obliged to go up to the surface of the water."

"Not at all. The boat is fixed on the top of the *Nautilus* in a cavity made for it. It has a deck, is quite watertight, and fastened by solid bolts. This ladder leads to a man-hole in the hull of the *Nautilus*, corresponding to a similar hole in the boat. It is by this double opening that I get to the boat. The one is shut by my men in the vessel, I shut the one in the boat by means of screw pressure, I undo the bolts, and the little boat darts up to the surface of the sea with prodigious rapidity. I then open the panel of the deck, carefully closed before, I mast it, hoist my sail, take my oars, and am off."

"But how do you return?"

"I do not return to it; it comes to me."

"At your order?"

"At my order. An electric wire connects us. I telegraph my orders."

"Really," I said, intoxicated by such marvels, "nothing can be more simple!"

After having passed the companion ladder that led to the platform, I saw a cabin about twelve feet long, in which Conseil and Ned Land were devouring their meal. Then a door opened upon a kitchen nine feet long, situated between the vast store-rooms of the vessel. There electricity, better than gas itself, did all the cooking. The wires under the stoves communicated with platinum sponges, and gave out a heat which was regularly kept up and distributed. They also heated a distilling apparatus which, by evaporation, furnished excellent drinking water. A bathroom, comfortably furnished with hot and cold water taps, opened out of this kitchen.

Next to the kitchen was the berth-room of the vessel, eighteen feet long. But the door was closed, and I could not see how it was furnished which might have given me an idea of the number of men employed on board the *Nautilus*. At the far end was a fourth partition, which separated this room from the engine-room. A door opened, and I entered the compartment where Captain Nemo— certainly a first-rate engineer—had arranged his locomotive machinery. It was well lighted, and did not measure less than sixty-five feet. It was naturally divided into two parts; the first contained the materials for producing electricity, and the second the machinery that moved the screw. I was at first surprised at a smell *sui generis* which filled the compartment. The captain saw that I perceived it.

"It is only a slight escape of gas produced by the use of the sodium, and not much inconvenience, as every morning we purify the vessel by ventilating it in the open air."

In the meantime I was examining the machinery with great interest.

"You see," said the captain, "I use Bunsen's elements, not Ruhmkorff's—they would not have been powerful enough. Bunsen's are fewer in number, but strong and large, which experience proves to be the best. The electricity produced passes to the back, where it works by electro-magnets of great size on a peculiar system of levers and cog-wheels that transmit the movement to the axle of the screw. This one, with a diameter of nineteen feet and a thread twenty-three feet, performs about a hundred and twenty revolutions in a second."

"What speed do you obtain from it?"

"About fifty miles an hour."

"Captain Nemo," I replied, "I recognise the results, and do not seek to explain them. I saw the *Nautilus* worked in the presence of the *Abraham Lincoln*, and I know what to think of its speed. But it is not enough to be able to walk; you must see where you are going; you must be able to direct yourself to the right or left, above or below. How do you reach the great depths, where you find an increasing resistance, which is rated by hundreds of atmospheres? How do you return to the surface of the ocean, or maintain yourself at the proper depth? Am I indiscreet in asking you this question?"

"Not at all, Professor," answered the captain, after a slight hesitation. "As you are never to leave this submarine boat, come into the saloon—it is our true study—and there you shall learn all you want to know about the *Nautilus*."

CHAPTER THIRTEEN

FIGURES

A MOMENT afterwards we were seated on a divan in the saloon, with our cigars. The captain spread out a diagram that gave the plan of the *Nautilus*. Then he began his description in these terms:

"Here, M. Aronnax are the different dimensions of the vessel you are in. It is a very elongated cylinder, with conical ends much like a cigar in shape. The length of this cylinder is exactly 232 feet, and its maximum breadth is 26 feet. Its lines are sufficiently long, and its slope lengthened out to allow the displaced water to escape easily, and opposes no obstacle to its speed. It surface is 1,011 metres and 45 centimetres; its volume, 1,500 cubic metres and two-tenths, which is the same as saying that it is entirely immersed. It displaces 50,000 feet of water, and weighs 1,500 tons

"When I made the plans for this vessel—destined for submarine navigation—I wished that when it was in equilibrium nine-tenths of it should be under water, and one-tenth only should emerge. Consequently, under these conditions, it only ought to displace nine-tenths of its volume, or 1,356 cubic metres and 48 centimetres—that is to say, it only ought to weigh the same number of tons. I therefore did not exceed this weight in constructing it according to the above-named dimensions.

"The *Nautilus* is composed of two hulls, one inside the other, and joined by T-shaped irons, which made it very strong. Owing to this cellular arrangement it resists as if it were solid. Its sides cannot yield; they adhere spontaneously, and not by the closeness of their rivets; and the homogeneity of their construction, due to the perfect union of the materials, enables my vessel to defy the roughest seas.

"Then when the *Nautilus* is afloat, one-tenth is out of the water. I have placed reservoirs of a size equal to this tenth capable of holding 150.72 tons, and when I fill them with water the vessel becomes completely immersed. These reservoirs exist in the lowest parts of the *Nautilus*. I turn on taps, they fill, and the vessel sinks just below the surface of the water."

"Well, Captain, I can understand your being able to keep just level with the surface of the ocean. But lower down, when you plunge below that surface, does not your submarine apparatus meet with a pressure from below, which must be equal to one atmosphere for every thirty feet of water?"

"True, sir."

"Then unless you fill the *Nautilus* entirely, I do not see how you can draw it down into the bosom of the liquid mass."

"Professor," answered Captain Nemo, "you must not confound statics with dynamics, or you will expose yourself to grave errors. There is very little work necessary to reach the lowest depths of the ocean, for bodies have a tendency ' to sink.' Follow my reasoning."

"I am listening to you, Captain."

"When I wished to determine the increase of weight that

must be given to the *Nautilus* to sink it, I had only to occupy myself with the reduction in volume which sea-water experiences as it becomes deeper and deeper."

"That is evident " said I.

"Now if water is not absolutely incompressible, it is, at least, very slightly compressible—in fact, according to the most recent calculations ·0000436 in an atmosphere or in each thirty feet of depth. If I wish to go to the depth of 1000 metres, I take into account the reduction of volume under a pressure of 100 atmospheres. I ought, therefore, to increase the weight so as to weight 1,513·79 tons instead of 1,507·2 tons. The augmentation will only be 6·77 tons. Now I have supplementary reservoirs capable of embarking 100 tons. When I wish to remount to the surface, I have only to let out this water, and empty all the reservoirs, if I desire that the *Nautilus* should emerge one-tenth of its total capacity "

To this reasoning, founded upon figures, I had nothing to object.

"I admit your calculations, Captain," I replied, "and I should be foolish to dispute them, as experience proves them every day, but I foresee a real difficulty."

"What is that, sir?"

"When you are at the depth of 1,000 yards the sides of the *Nautilus* support a pressure of 100 atmospheres. If, therefore, at this moment, you wish to empty the supplementary reservoirs to lighten your vessel and ascend to the surface, the pumps must conquer this pressure of 100 atmospheres, which is that of 100 kilogrammes for every square centimetre. Hence a power——"

"Which electricity alone can give me," hastened to say Captain Nemo. "The dynamic power of my machines is nearly infinite. The pumps of the *Nautilus* have prodigious force, which you must have seen when their columns of water were precipitated like a torrent over the *Abraham Lincoln*. Besides, I only use supplementary reservoirs to obtain middle depths of 1,500 to 2,000 metres, and that in order to save my apparatus. When the fancy takes me to visit the depths of the ocean at two or three leagues below its surface, I use longer means, but no less infallible."

"What are they, Captain?" I asked.

"That involves my telling you how the *Nautilus* is worked."

"I am all impatience to hear it."

"In order to steer my vessel horizontally I use an ordinary rudder, worked by a wheel and tackle. But I can also move the *Nautilus* by a vertical movement, by means of two inclined planes fastened to the sides and at the centre of flotation, planes that can move in every direction, and are worked from the interior by means of powerful levers. When these planes are kept parallel with the boat it moves horizontally; when slanted, the *Nautilus*, according to their inclination, and under the influence of the screw, either sinks according to an elongated diagonal, or rises diagonally as it suits me. And even when I wish to rise more quickly to the surface I engage the screw, and the pressure of the water causes the *Nautilus* to rise vertically like a balloon into the air."

"Bravo! Captain," I cried. "But how can the helmsman follow the route you give him in the midst of the waters?"

"The helmsman is placed in a glass cage jutting from the top of the *Nautilus* and furnished with lenses."

"Capable of resisting such pressure?"

"Perfectly. Glass, which a blow can break, offers, nevertheless, considerable resistance. During some fishing experiments we made in 1864, by electric light, in the Northern Seas, we saw plates less than a third of an inch thick resist a pressure of sixteen atmospheres. Now the glass that I use is not less than thirty times thicker "

"I see now. But, after all, it is dark under water; how do you see where you are going?"

"There is a powerful electric reflector placed behind the helmsman's cage, the rays from which light up the sea for half a mile in front."

"Ah, now I can account for the phosphorescence in the supposed narwhal that puzzled me so. May I now ask you if the damage you did to the *Scotia* was due to an accident?"

"Yes, it was quite accidental. I was sailing only one fathom below the surface when the shock came. Had it any bad result?"

"None, sir. But how about the shock you gave the *Abraham Lincoln*?"

"Professor, it was a great pity for one of the best ships in the American Navy; but they attacked me and I had to defend myself! Besides, I contented myself with putting it out of the power of the frigate to harm me; there will be no difficulty in getting her repaired at the nearest port."

"Ah, Commander!" I cried, with conviction, "your *Nautilus* is certainly a marvellous boat. But how could you construct this admirable craft in secret?"

"I had each separate portion made in different parts of the globe, and it reached me through a disguised address. The keel was forged at Creuzot the shaft of the screw at Penn and Co.'s, of London; the iron plates of the hull at Laird's of Liverpool; the screw itself at Scott's of Glasgow. Its reservoirs were made by Cail and Co., of Paris; the engine by the Prussian Krupp; the prow in Motala's workshop in Sweden; the mathematical instruments by Hart Brothers, of New York, etc.; all of these people had my orders under different names."

"But how did you get all the parts put together?"

"I set up a workshop upon a desert island in the ocean. There, my workmen—that is to say, my brave companions whom I instructed—and I put together our *Nautilus*. When the work was ended, fire destroyed all trace of our proceedings on the island, which I should have blown up if I could."

"It must have cost you a great deal."

"An iron vessel costs £45 a ton. The *Nautilus* weighs 1,500 tons. It came, therefore, to £67,500 and £80,000 more for fitting up; altogether, with the works of art and collections it contains, it cost about £200,000."

"You must be rich?"

"Immensely rich, sir; I could, without missing it, pay the English national debt."

I stared at the singular person who spoke. Was he taking advantage of my credulity?

CHAPTER FOURTEEN

THE BLACK RIVER

"Now, Professor," said Captain Nemo, "we will, if you please, take our bearings and fix the starting-point of this voyage. It wants a quarter to twelve. I am going up to the surface of the water."

The captain pressed an electric bell three times. The pumps began to drive the water out of the reservoirs; the needle of the manometer marked by the different pressures the ascensional movement of the *Nautilus*, then it stopped.

"We have arrived," said the captain.

We went to the central staircase which led up to the platform, climbed the iron steps, and found ourselves on the top of the *Nautilus*.

The platform was only three feet out of the water. The front and back of the *Nautilus* were of that spindle shape which caused it justly to be compared to a cigar. I noticed that its iron plates slightly overlaid each other, like the scales on the body of our large terrestrial reptiles. I well understood how, in spite of the best glasses, this boat should have been taken for a marine animal.

Towards the middle of the platform, the boat, half sunk in the vessel, formed a slight excrescence. Fore and aft rose two cages of medium height, with inclined sides, and partly enclosed by thick lenticular glasses. In the one was the helmsman who directed the *Nautilus*; and in the other a powerful electric lantern that lighted up his course.

The sea was beautiful, the sky pure. The long vessel could hardly feel the broad undulations of the ocean. A slight breeze from the east rippled the surface of the water. The horizon was quite clear, making observation easy. There was nothing in sight—not a rock nor an island, no *Abraham Lincoln*, nothing but a waste of waters.

Captain Nemo took the altitude of the sun with his sextant to get his latitude. He waited some minutes till the planes came on a level with the edge of the horizon. Whilst he was observing, not one of his muscles moved, and the instrument would not have been more motionless in a hand of marble.

"It is noon. Professor, when you are ready——"

I cast a last look at the sea, slightly yellowed by the Japanese coast, and went down again to the saloon.

There the captain made his point, and calculated his longitude chronometrically, which he controlled by preceding observations of horary angles. Then he said to me:

"Thirty-seven degrees and fifteen minutes longitude west of the Paris meridian, and thirty degrees and seven minutes north latitude—that is to say, about three hundred miles from the coasts of Japan. To-day, the 8th of November, at noon, our voyage of exploration under the waters begins."

"God preserve us!" I answered.

"And now, Professor," added the captain, "I leave you to your studies. I have given ENE. as our route at a depth of fifty yards. Here are maps on which you can follow it. The saloon is at your disposition, and I ask your permission to withdraw."

Captain Nemo bowed to me. I remained alone, absorbed in my thoughts. All of them referred to the commander of the *Nautilus*. Should I ever know to what nation belonged the strange man who boasted of belonging to none? This hatred which he had vowed to humanity—this hatred which perhaps sought terrible means of revenge—what had provoked it? I, whom hazard had just cast upon his vessel —I, whose life he held in his hands, he had received me coldly, but with hospitality. Only he had never taken the hand I had held out to him. He had never held out his to me."

For a whole hour I remained buried in these reflections,

seeking to pierce the mystery that interested me so greatly. Then my eyes fell upon the vast planisphere on the table, and I placed my finger on the very spot where the given latitude and longitude crossed.

The sea has its large rivers like continents. They are special currents, known by their temperature and colour. The most remarkable is known under the name of the Gulf Stream. Science has found out the direction of five principal currents—one in the North Atlantic, a second in the South Atlantic, a third in the North Pacific, a fourth in the South Pacific, and a fifth in the South Indian Ocean It is probable that a sixth current formerly existed in the North Indian Ocean, when the Caspian and Aral Seas, united to the great Asiatic lakes, only formed one vast sheet of water.

At the point on the planisphere where my finger lay, one of these currents was rolling—the Black River of the Japanese, which, leaving the Gulf of Bengal, where the perpendicular rays of a tropical sun warm it, crosses the Straits of Malacca, runs along the coast of Asia, turns into the North Pacific as far as the Aleutian Islands, carrying with it the trunks of camphor-trees and other indigenous productions, contrasting by the pure indigo of its warm waters with the waves of the ocean. It was this current that the *Nautilus* was going to follow. I saw that it lost itself in the immensity of the Pacific, and felt myself carried along by it. Just then Ned Land and Conseil appeared at the door of the saloon.

"I have seen nothing, heard nothing," said the Canadian. "I have not even perceived the ship's crew. Is it by chance, or can it be electric too?"

"Electric!"

"Faith, anyone would think so. But you, M. Aronnax," said Ned Land, who stuck to his idea, "can you tell me how many men there are on board? Are there twenty, fifty, a hundred?"

"I know no more than you, Land; abandon at present all idea of either taking the *Nautilus* or escaping from it. This vessel is a masterpiece of modern industry, and I should regret not to have seen it. Many people would accept our position only to move amidst such marvels. The only thing to do is to keep quiet and watch what passes."

"Watch!" exclaimed the harpooner, "but there's nothing to watch; we can't see anything in this iron prison. We are moving along blindfolded."

Ned Land had scarcely uttered these words when it became suddenly dark. The light in the ceiling went out, and so rapidly that my eyes ached with the change, in the same way as they do after passage from profound darkness to the most brilliant light.

We remained mute and did not stir, not knowing what surprise, agreeable or disagreeable, awaited us. But a sliding noise was heard. It was like as if panels were being drawn back in the sides of the *Nautilus*.

"It is the end of all things!" said Ned Land.

Suddenly light appeared on either side of the saloon, through two oblong openings. The liquid mass appeared vividly lighted up by the electric effluence.

Two crystal panes separated us from the sea. At first I shuddered at the thought that this feeble partition might break, but strong copper bands bound it, giving an almost infinite power of resistance.

The sea was distinctly visible for a mile round the *Nautilus*. What a spectacle! What pen could describe it? Who could paint the effect of the light through those transparent sheets of water, and the softness of its successive gradations from the lower to the upper beds of the ocean?

The transparency of the sea is well known, and its limpidity is far greater than that of fresh water. The mineral and organic substances which it holds in suspension increase its transparency. In certain parts of the ocean at the Antilles, under seventy-five fathoms of water, the sandy bottom can be seen with clearness, and the penetrating strength of the sun's rays only appears to stop at 150 fathoms. But in this fluid medium through which the *Nautilus* was travelling, the electric light was produced in the very bosom of the waves. It was not luminous water, but liquid light.

The *Nautilus* did not seem to be moving. It was because there were no landmarks. Sometimes, however, the lines of water, furrowed by her prow, flowed before our eyes with excessive speed.

Lost in wonder, we stood before these windows, and none of us had broken this silence of astonishment when Conseil said:

"Well, friend Ned, you wanted to look; well, now you see!"

"It is curious!" exclaimed the Canadian, who, forgetting his anger and projects of flight, was under the influence of irresistible attraction. "Who wouldn't come for the sake of such a sight?"

"Now I understand the man's life," I exclaimed. "He has made a world of marvels for himself."

"But I don't see any fish," said the Canadian.

"What does it matter to you, friend Ned," answered Conseil, "since you know nothing about them?"

"I! A fisherman!" cried Ned Land.

And thereupon a dispute arose between the two, for each had some knowledge of fish, though in a very different way.

"Well, friend Conseil," said the harpooner, finally leaning against the glass of the panel, "there are some varieties passing now."

"Yes!—some fish," cried Conseil. "It is like being at an aquarium."

"No," I answered, "for an aquarium is only a cage, and those fish are as free as birds in the air."

"Well, now, Conseil, tell me their names!—tell me their names!" said Ned Land.

"I?" answered Conseil; "I could not do it; that is my master's business."

And, in fact, the worthy fellow, though an enthusiastic classifier, was not a naturalist, and I do not know if he could have distinguished a tunny-fish from a bonito. The Canadian, on the contrary, named them all without hesitation.

"A balister," said I.

"And a Chinese balister too!" answered Ned Land.

The Canadian was not mistaken. A shoal of balisters with fat bodies, grained skins, armed with a spur on their dorsal fin, were playing round the *Nautilus* and agitating the four rows of quills bristling on either side of their tails. Nothing could be more admirable than their grey backs, white stomachs, and gold spots that shone amidst the waves. Amongst them undulated skates like a sheet abandoned to the winds, and with them I perceived, to my great joy, the Chinese skate, yellow above, pale pink underneath, with three darts behind the eye—a rare species.

For two hours a whole aquatic army escorted the *Nautilus*. Amidst their games and gambols, whilst they rivalled each other in brilliancy and speed, I recognised the green wrasse, the surmullet, marked with a double black stripe; the goby, with its round tail, white with violet eyes; the Japanese mackerel, with blue body and silver head; gilt heads with a black band down their tails; aulostones with flute-like noses, real sea-woodcocks, of which some specimens attain a yard in length; Japanese salamanders; sea-eels, serpents six feet long with bright little eyes and a huge mouth bristling with teeth.

Suddenly light again appeared in the saloon. The iron panels were again closed. The enchanting vision disappeared. But long after that I was dreaming still, until my eyes happened to fall on the instruments hung on the partition. The compass still indicated the direction of NNE., the manometer indicated a pressure of five atmospheres, corresponding to a depth of 1000 fathoms, and the electric log gave a speed of fifteen miles an hour.

I expected Captain Nemo, but he did not appear. The clock was on the stroke of five. Ned Land and Conseil returned to the cabin, and I regained my room.

I passed the evening reading, writing and thinking. Then sleep overpowered me, and I stretched myself on my zostera couch and slept profoundly, whilst the *Nautilus* glided rapidly along the current of the Black River.

CHAPTER FIFTEEN

A WRITTEN INVITATION

THE NEXT day, the 9th of November, I awoke after a long sleep that had lasted twelve hours. Conseil came, as was his custom, to ask " how monsieur had passed the night," and to offer his services. He had left his friend the Canadian sleeping like a man who had never done anything else in his life.

I was soon clothed in my byssus garments. Their nature provoked many reflections from Conseil. I told him they were manufactured with the lustrous and silky filaments which fasten a sort of shell, very abundant on the shores of the Mediterranean, to the rocks. Formerly beautiful materials—stockings and gloves—were made from it, and they were both very soft and very warm. The crew of the *Nautilus* could, therefore, be clothed at a cheap rate, without help of either cotton-trees, sheep or silkworms of the earth.

When I was dressed I went into the saloon. It was deserted. The whole day passed without my being honoured with a visit from Captain Nemo. The panels of the saloon were not opened. Perhaps they did not wish us to get tired of such beautiful things.

The direction of the *Nautilus* kept NNE., its speed at twelve miles, its depth between twenty-five and thirty fathoms.

The next day the same desertion, the same solitude. I did not see one of the ship's crew. Ned and Conseil passed the greater part of the day with me. They were astonished at the absence of the captain. Was the singular man ill? Did he mean to alter his plans about us?"

After all, as Conseil said, we enjoyed complete liberty; we were delicately and abundantly fed. Our host kept to the terms of his treaty. We could not complain, and, besides, the singularity of our destiny reserved us such great compensations that we had no right to accuse it.

That day I began the account of these adventures, which allowed me to relate them with the most scrupulous exactness, and, curious detail, I wrote it on paper made with marine zostera.

Five days passed thus and altered nothing in our position. Captain Nemo did not appear.

I had made up my mind that I was not going to see him again, when on the 16th of November, on entering my room with Ned Land and Conseil, I found a note directed to me upon the table.

I opened it. It was written in a bold, clear hand, of Gothic character, something like the German types.

The note contained the following:

"To Professor ARONNAX, on board the *Nautilus*.

"Captain Nemo invites Professor Aronnax to a hunt to-morrow morning in the forest of the island of Crespo. He hopes nothing will prevent the professor joining it, and he will have much pleasure in seeing his companions also."

"A hunt!" cried Ned.

"And in the forests of Crespo Island," added Conseil.

I consulted the planisphere as to the whereabouts of the island of Crespo, and in 32° 40′ north lat. and 167° 50′ west long. I found a small island, reconnoitred in 1801 by Captain Crespo, and marked in old Spanish maps as Rocca de la Plata, or "Silver Rock." We were then about 1800 miles from our starting-point, and the course of the *Nautilus*, a little changed, was bringing it back towards the southeast.

The next day, when I awoke, I felt that the *Nautilus* was perfectly still, I dressed quickly and went to the saloon.

Captain Nemo was there waiting for me. He rose, bowed, and asked me if it was convenient for me to accompany him.

"May I ask you, Captain," I said, "how it is that, having

broken all ties with earth, you possess forests in Crespo Island?"

"Professor," answered the captain, "my forests are not terrestrial forests but submarine forests."

"Submarine!" I exclaimed.

"Yes, Professor."

"And you offer to take me to them?"

"Yes, and dry-footed too."

"But how shall we hunt?—with a gun?"

"Yes, with a gun."

I thought the captain was gone mad, and the idea was expressed on my face, but he only invited me to follow him like a man resigned to anything. We entered the dining-room, where breakfast was laid.

"M. Aronnax," said the captain, "will you share my breakfast without ceremony? We will talk as we eat. You will not find a restaurant in our walk, though you will a forest. Breakfast like a man who will probably dine late."

Captain Nemo ate for a while without saying a word. Then he said to me:

"When I invited you to hunt in my submarine forests, you thought I was mad. You judged me too lightly. You know as well as I do that man can live under water, providing he takes with him a provision of air to breathe. When submarine work has to be done, the workman, clad in an impervious dress, with his head in a metal helmet, receives air from above by means of pumps and regulators."

"Then it is a diving apparatus?"

"Yes, but in one that enables him to get rid of the india-rubber tube attached to the pump. It is the apparatus, invented by two of your countrymen, but which I have brought to perfection for my own use, and which will allow you to risk yourself in the water without suffering. It is composed of a reservoir of thick iron plates, in which I store the air under a pressure of fifty atmospheres. This reservoir is fastened on to the back by means of braces, like a soldier's knapsack; its upper part forms a box, in which the air is kept by means of bellows, and which cannot escape except at its normal tension. Two india-rubber pipes leave this box and join a sort of tent, which imprisons the nose and mouth; one introduces fresh air, the other lets out foul, and the tongue closes either according to the needs of respiration. But I, who encounter great pressure at the bottom of the sea, am obliged to shut my head in a globe of copper, into which the two pipes open."

"Perfectly, Captain Nemo; but the air that you carry with you must soon be used up, for as soon as it only contains fifteen per cent of oxygen, it is no longer fit to breathe."

"I have already told you, M. Aronnax, that the pumps of the *Nautilus* allow me to store up air under considerable pressure, and under these conditions the reservoir of the apparatus can furnish breathable air for nine or ten hours."

"I have no other objection to make," I answered. "I will only ask you one thing, Captain. How do you light your road at the bottom of the ocean?"

"With the Ruhmkorff apparatus, M. Aronnax. It is composed of a Bunsen pile, which I work with sodium. A wire is introduced, which collects the electricity produced, and directs it towards a particularly-made lantern. In this lantern is a spiral glass which contains a small quantity of carbonic gas. When the apparatus is at work the gas becomes luminous, and gives out a white and continuous light. Thus provided, I breathe and see."

"But, Captain Nemo, what sort of a gun do you use?"

"It is not a gun for powder, but an air-gun. I use air under great pressure, which the pumps of the *Nautilus* furnish."

"But this air must be rapidly consumed."

"Well, have I not my Rouquayrol reservoir, which can furnish me with what I need? Besides, you will see for yourself, M. Aronnax, that during these submarine shooting excursions you do not use much air or bullets."

"But it seems to me that in the half-light, and amidst a liquid so much more dense than the atmosphere, bodies cannot be projected far, and are not easily mortal."

"Sir, with these guns every shot is mortal, and as soon as the animal is touched, however slightly, it falls."

"Why?"

"Because they are not ordinary bullets. We use little glass percussion-caps, of which I have a considerable provision. These glass caps, covered with steel, and weighted with a leaden bottom, are little Leyden bottles, in which electricity is forced to a high tension. At the slightest shock they go off, and the animal, however powerful, falls dead. These caps are not larger than the No. 4, and the charge of an ordinary gun could contain ten."

"I will argue no longer," I replied, rising from the table. "The only thing left me is to take my gun. Where you go I will follow."

Captain Nemo then led me aft of the *Nautilus*, and I called my two companions, who followed me immediately. Then we came to a kind of cell, situated near the engine-room, in which we put on our walking dress.

CHAPTER SIXTEEN

AT THE BOTTOM OF THE SEA

THIS CELL was the arsenal and wardrobe of the *Nautilus*. A dozen diving apparatus, hung from the wall, awaited our use.

Ned Land, seeing them, manifested evident repugnance to put one on.

"But, my worthy Ned, I said, "the forests of Crespo Island are only submarine forests!"

"You can do as you please, sir," replied the harpooner, shrugging his shoulders, "but as for me, unless I am forced, I will never get into one."

"No one will force you," said Captain Nemo.

"Does Conseil mean to risk it?" said Ned.

"I shall follow monsieur wherever he goes," answered Conseil.

Two of the ship's crew came to help us on the call of the captain, and we donned the heavy and impervious clothes made of seamless india-rubber and constructed expressly to resist considerable pressure. They looked like a suit of armour, both supple and resisting, and formed trousers and coat; the trousers were finished off with thick boots, furnished with heavy leaden soles. The texture of the coat was held together by bands of copper, which crossed the chest, protecting it from the pressure of the water, and leaving the lungs free to act; the sleeves ended in the form of supple gloves, which in no way restrained the movements of the hands.

Captain Nemo and one of his companions—a sort of Hercules, who must have been of prodigious strength—Conseil and myself were soon enveloped in these dresses. There was nothing left but to put our heads into the metallic globes. But before proceeding with this operation I asked the captain's permission to examine the guns we were to take.

One of the crew gave me a simple gun, the butt end of which, made of steel and hollowed in the interior, was rather large; it served as a reservoir for compressed air, which a valve, worked by a spring, allowed to escape into a metal tube. A box of projectiles, fixed in a groove in the thickness of the butt end, contained about twenty electric bullets, which, by means of a spring, were forced into the barrel of the gun. As soon as one shot was fired another was ready.

Captain Nemo put on his helmet. Conseil and I did the same, not without hearing an ironical "Good sport" from the Canadian. The upper part of our coat was terminated by a copper collar, upon which the metal helmet was screwed. As soon as it was in position the apparatus on our backs began to act, and, for my part, I could breathe with ease.

I found when I was ready, lamp and all, that I could not

move a step. But this was foreseen. I felt myself pushed along a little room contiguous to the wardrobe-room. My companions, tugged along in the same way, followed me. I heard a door, furnished with obturators, close behind us, and we were wrapped in profound darkness.

After some minutes I heard a loud whistling, and felt the cold mount from my feet to my chest. It was evident that they had filled the room in which we were with sea-water by means of a tap. A second door in the side of the *Nautilus* opened then. A faint light appeared. A moment after, our feet were treading the bottom of the sea.

Captain Nemo walked on in front, and his companion followed us some steps behind. Conseil and I remained near one another, as if any exchange of words had been possible through our metallic covering. I no longer felt the weight of my clothes, shoes, air-reservoir, nor of that thick globe in the midst of which my head shook like an almond in its shell.

We were walking on fine even sand, not wrinkled, as it is on a flat shore which keeps the imprint of the billows. This dazzling carpet reflected the rays of the sun with surprising intensity. At that depth of thirty feet I saw as well as in open daylight!

I soon came to some magnificent rocks, carpeted with splendid zoophytes, and I was at first struck by a special effect of this medium.

It was then 10 a.m. The rays of the sun struck the surface of the waves at an oblique angle, and at their contact with the light, composed by a refraction as through a prism, flowers, rocks, plants and polypi were shaded at their edges by the seven solar colours; it was a grand feast for the eyes this complication of tints, a veritable kaleidoscope of green, yellow, orange, violet, indigo and blue—in a word, all the palette of an enthusiastic colourist.

All these wonders I saw in the space of a quarter of a mile. Soon the nature of the soil changed; to the sandy plains succeeded an extent of slimy mud composed of equal parts of siliceous and calcareous shells. Then we travelled over meadows of seaweed so soft to the foot that they would rival the softest carpet made by man.

We had left the *Nautilus* about an hour and a half. It was nearly twelve o'clock. We marched along with a regular step which rang upon the ground with astonishing intensity; the slightest sound is transmitted with a speed to which the ear is not accustomed on the earth.

The ground gradually sloped downwards, and the light took a uniform tint. At this depth of three hundred feet I could still see the rays of the sun, but feebly. To their intense brilliancy had succeeded a reddish-twilight, middle term between day and night. Still we saw sufficiently to guide ourselves, and it was not yet necessary to light our lamps.

At that moment Captain Nemo stopped. He waited for me to come up to him, and with his finger pointed to some obscure masses which stood out of the shade at some little distance.

"It is the forest of Crespo Island," I thought, and I was not mistaken.

CHAPTER SEVENTEEN

A SUBMARINE FOREST

WE HAD at last arrived on the borders of the forest, doubtless one of the most beautiful in the immense domain of Captain Nemo. He looked upon it as his own, and who was there to dispute his right? This forest was composed of arborescent plants, and as soon as we had penetrated under its vast arcades, I was struck at first by the singular disposition of their branches, which I had not observed before.

None of those herbs which carpeted the ground—none of the branches of the larger plants, were either bent, drooped or extended horizontally. There was not a single filament, however thin, that did not keep as upright as a rod of iron. The fusci and llianas grew in rigid perpendicular lines, commanded by the density of the element which had produced them. When I bent them with my hand these plants immediately resumed their first position. It was the reign of perpendicularity.

I noticed that all these productions of the vegetable kingdom had no roots, and only held on to either sand, shell or rock. These plants drew no vitality from anything but the water. The greater number, instead of leaves, shot forth blades of capricious shapes, comprised within a scale of colours—pink, carmine, red, olive, fawn and brown.

About one o'clock Captain Nemo gave the signal to halt. I, for my part, was not sorry, and we stretched ourselves under a thicket of alariæ, the long thin blades of which shot up like arrows.

This short rest seemed delicious to me. Nothing was wanting but the charm of conversation, but it was impossible to speak—I could only approach my large copper head to that of Conseil. I saw the eyes of the worthy fellow shine with contentment, and he moved about in his covering in the most comical way in the world.

After this four hours' walk I was much astonished not to find myself violently hungry, and I cannot tell why, but instead I was intolerably sleepy, as all divers are. My eyes closed behind their thick glass, and I fell into an unavoidable slumber, which the movement of walking had alone prevented up till then. Captain Nemo and his robust companion, lying down in the clear crystal, set us the example.

How long I remained asleep I cannot tell, but when I awoke the sun seemed sinking towards the horizon. Captain Nemo was already on his feet, and I was stretching myself when an unexpected apparition brought me quickly to my feet.

A few steps off an enormous sea-spider, more than a yard high, was looking at me with his squinting eyes, ready to spring upon me. Although my dress was thick enough to defend me against the bite of this animal, I could not restrain a movement of horror. Conseil and the sailor of the *Nautilus* awoke at that moment. Captain Nemo showed his companions the hideous crustacean, and a blow from the butt end of a gun killed it, and I saw its horrible claws writhe in horrible convulsions.

This accident reminded me that other animals, more to be feared, might haunt these obscure depths, and that my diver's dress would not protect me against their attacks. I had not thought of that before, and resolved to be on my guard. I supposed that this halt marked the limit of our excursion, but I was mistaken, and instead of returning to the *Nautilus*, Captain Nemo went on.

The ground still inclined and took us to greater depths. It must have been about three o'clock when we reached a narrow valley between two high cliffs, situated about seventy-five fathoms deep. Thanks to the perfection of our apparatus, we were forty-five fathoms below the limit which Nature seems to have imposed on the submarine excursions of man.

I knew how deep we were because the obscurity became so profound—not an object was visible at ten paces. I walked along groping when I suddenly saw a white light shine out. Captain Nemo had just lighted his electric lamp. His companion imitated him. Conseil and I followed their example. By turning a screw I established the communication between the spool and the glass serpentine, and the sea, lighted up by our four lanterns, was illuminated in a radius of twenty-five yards.

Captain Nemo still kept on plunging into the dark depths of the forest, the trees of which were getting rarer and rarer. I remarked that the vegetable life disappeared sooner than the animal. The medusæ had already left the soil, which had become arid, whilst a prodigious number of animals, zoophytes, articulata, molluscs and fish swarmed there still.

As we walked I thought that the light of our apparatus could not fail to draw some inhabitants from these sombre depths. But if they did approach us they at least kept a respectable distance. Several times I saw Captain Nemo stop and take aim; then, after some minutes' observation, he rose and went on walking.

At last, about four o'clock, this wonderful excursion was ended. A wall of superb rocks rose up before us, enormous granite cliffs impossible to climb. It was the island of Crespo. Captain Nemo stopped suddenly. We stopped at a sign from him. Here ended the domains of the captain.

The return began. Captain Nemo again kept at the head of his little band, and directed his steps without hesitation. I thought I perceived that we were not returning to the *Nautilus* by the road we had come. This new one was very steep, and consequently very painful. We approached the surface of the sea rapidly. But this return to the upper beds was not so sudden as to produce the internal lesions so fatal to divers. Very soon light reappeared and increased, and as the sun was already low on the horizon refraction edged the different objects with a spectral ring.

At that moment I saw the captain put his gun to his shoulder and follow a moving object into the shrubs. He fired, I heard a feeble hissing, and an animal fell a few steps from us.

It was a magnificent sea-otter, the only quadruped which is exclusively marine. This otter was five feet long and must have been very valuable. Its skin, chestnut-brown above and silvery underneath, would have made one of those beautiful furs so sought after in the Russian and Chinese markets; the fineness and lustre of its coat was certainly worth eighty pounds. I admired this curious mammal—its rounded head and short ears, round eyes and white whiskers, like those of a cat, with webbed feet and claws and tufted tail. This precious animal, hunted and tracked by fishermen, is becoming very rare, and it takes refuge principally in the northern parts of the Pacific, where it is likely that its race will soon become extinct. Captain Nemo's companion took up the animal and threw it over his shoulders, and we continued our route.

During the next hour a plain of sand lay stretched before us. Sometimes it rose within two yards and some inches of the surface of the water. I then saw the reflection of our images above us, like us in every point, except that they walked with their heads downwards and their feet in the air.

The thick waves above us looked like clouds above our heads—clouds which were no sooner formed than they vanished rapidly. I even perceived the shadows of the large birds as they floated on the surface of the water.

On this occasion I was witness to one of the finest gun-shots which ever made a hunter's nerve thrill. A large bird, with great breadth of wing, hovered over us. Captain Nemo's companion shouldered his gun and fired when it was only a few yards above the waves. The bird fell dead, and the fall brought it in reach of the skilful hunter's grasp. It was an albatross.

Our march was not interrupted by this incident. I was worn out by fatigue when we at last perceived a faint light half a mile off. Before twenty minutes were over we should be on board and able to breathe with ease, for it seemed to me that my reservoir of air was getting very deficient in oxygen, but I did not reckon upon a meeting which delayed our arrival.

I was about twenty steps behind Captain Nemo when he suddenly turned towards me. With his vigorous hand he threw me to the ground, whilst his companion did the same to Conseil. At first I did not know what to think of this sudden attack, but I was reassured when I saw that the captain lay down beside me and remained perfectly motionless.

I was stretched on the ground just under the shelter of a bush of argæ, when, on raising my head. I perceived enormous masses throwing phosphorescent gleams pass blusteringly by.

My blood froze in my veins. I saw two formidable dog-fish threatening us; they were terrible creatures, with enormous tails and a dull and glassy stare, who threw out phosphorescent beams from holes pierced round their muzzles. Monstrous brutes which would crush a whole man in their jaws! I do not know if Conseil stayed to classify them. For my part, I noticed their silver stomachs and their formidable mouths bristling with teeth from a very unscientific point of view—more as a possible victim than as a naturalist.

Happily, these voracious animals see badly. They passed without perceiving us, brushing us with their brownish fins, and we escaped, as if by a miracle, this danger, certainly greater than the meeting of a tiger in a forest.

Half an hour after, guided by the electric light, we reached the *Nautilus*. The outside door had remained open, and Captain Nemo closed it as soon as we had entered the first cell. Then he pressed a knob. I heard the pumps worked inside the vessel. I felt the water lower around me, and in a few moments the cell was entirely empty. The inner door then opened, and we entered the wardrobe-room.

There our diving-dresses were taken off, and, worn out from want of food and sleep, I returned to my room, lost in wonder at this surprising excursion under the sea.

CHAPTER EIGHTEEN

FOUR THOUSAND LEAGUES UNDER THE PACIFIC

THE NEXT morning I was recovered from my fatigue, and went up on to the platform. The ocean was clear. There was not a sail on the horizon. Crespo Island had disappeared during the night. The sea, absorbing the colours of the solar prism, with the exception of the blue rays, reflected them in every direction, and was of an admirable indigo shade. A large wave was regularly undulating its surface.

I was admiring this magnificent aspect of the sea when Captain Nemo appeared. He did not seem to perceive my presence, and began a series of astronomical observations. Then, when he had ended his operation, he went and leaned against the cage of the watch-light and watched the surface of the ocean.

In the meantime, about twenty sailors from the *Nautilus*, strong and well-built men, ascended the platform. They came to draw in the nets which had been out all night. These sailors evidently belonged to different nations although they were all of the European type, I recognised Irishmen, Frenchmen, some Slavs, one Greek, or a Candiote. These men spoke very little, and only used a strange idiom of which I could not even guess the origin, so that I could not question them.

The nets were hauled in. They were a species of "chaluts," like those used on the Normandy coast, vast pockets which a floating yard and a chain marled into the lower stitches keep half open. These pockets, thus dragged along in their iron gauntlets, swept the bottom of the ocean, and took in all its products on their way.

I reckoned that the haul had brought in more than nine hundredweight of fish. It was a fine haul, but not to be wondered at. We should not want for food.

The fishing ended and the provision of air renewed, the *Nautilus* continued its submarine excursion.

For weeks Captain Nemo was very sparing of his visits. I only saw him at intervals. His mate pricked the ship's course regularly on the chart, and I could always tell the exact route of the *Nautilus*.

During this voyage the sea was prodigal of marvellous spectacles. It varied them infinitely. It changed its scenes and grouping for the pleasure of our eyes, and we were called upon, not only to contemplate the works of the Creator amidst the liquid element, but to penetrate as well the most fearful mysteries of the ocean.

I was reading in the saloon. Ned Land and Conseil were looking at the luminous water through the half-open panels.

The *Nautilus* was stationary; at a depth of 1,000 yards, a region not much inhabited, in which large fish alone make rare appearances.

I was reading at that moment, when Conseil interrupted me.

"Will monsieur come here?" said he in a singular voice.

I rose, went to the window, and looked out. Full in the electric light an enormous black mass, immovable, was suspended in the midst of the waters. I looked at it attentively, trying to make out the nature of this gigantic cetacean. But an idea suddenly came into my mind.

"A vessel!" I cried.

"Yes," replied the Canadian, "a disabled ship sunk perpendicularly."

Land was right. We were close to a vessel of which the tattered shrouds still hung from their chains. The hull seemed to be in good order, and it could not have been wrecked more than a few hours; the vessel had had to sacrifice its mast. It lay on its side, had filled, and was heeling over to port. This skeleton of what it had once been was a sad spectacle under the waves, but sadder still was the sight of the deck, where corpses, bound with rope, were still lying. I counted five; one man was at the helm, and a woman stood by the poop holding an infant in her arms; she was quite young. I could clearly see her features by the light of the *Nautilus*—features which the water had not yet decomposed. In a last effort she had raised the child above her head, and the arms of the little one were round its mother's neck. The sailors looked frightful and seemed to be making a last effort to free themselves from the cords that bound them to the vessel. The helmsman alone, calm, with a clear, grave face, and iron-grey hair glued to his forehead, was clutching the wheel of the helm, and seemed, even then, to be guiding the vessel through the depths of the ocean!

What a scene! It struck us dumb, and our hearts beat faster at the sight of this wreck, photographed at the last moment, and I already saw, advancing towards it with hungry eyes, enormous sharks attracted by the human flesh!

The *Nautilus* just then turned round the submerged vessel, and I read on the stern, " *Florida*, Sunderland."

CHAPTER NINETEEN

VANIKORO

THIS terrible spectacle inaugurated the series of maritime catastrophes which the *Nautilus* was to meet with on her route. Since it had been in more frequented seas we often perceived the hulls of ships—wrecked vessels which were rotting in the midst of the waters, and, deeper down, cannons, bullets, anchors, chains, and other iron objects, which were being eaten up by rust.

I had not seen Captain Nemo for a week, when on the 27th of December, in the morning, he entered the saloon, looking like a man who had seen you five minutes before. I was tracing the route of the *Nautilus* on the planisphere. The captain approached, put his finger on a spot in the map and pronounced this one word:

" Vanikoro."

This name was magical. It was the name of the islands upon which the vessels of La Perouse had been lost. I rose immediately.

" Is the *Nautilus* taking us to Vanikoro?" I asked.

" Yes, Professor," answered the captain.

" And can I visit these celebrated islands where the *Boussole* and *Astrolabe* were lost?"

" If you please, Professor."

" When shall we reach Vanikoro?"

" We are there now, Professor."

Followed by Captain Nemo, I went up to the platform, and from there I looked with avidity round the horizon.

To the NE. emerged two volcanic islands of unequal size,

surrounded by coral reefs. We were in presence of Vanikoro Island, properly so called, to which Dumont d'Urville gave the name of Ile de la Recherche; we were just in front of the little harbour of Vanou. The land seemed covered with verdure from the shore to the summits of the interior, crowned by Mount Kapogo, 3000 feet high.

The *Nautilus*, after having crossed the exterior ring of rocks through a narrow passage, was inside the reefs where the sea is from thirty to forty fathoms deep. Under the verdant shade of some mangroves I perceived several savages, who looked astonished at our approach. Perhaps they took the long body advancing along the surface of the water for some formidable cetacean that they ought to guard themselves against. At that moment Captain Nemo asked me what I knew about the shipwreck of La Perouse.

"What everyone knows, Captain," I answered.

"And can you tell me what everyone knows?" he asked in a slightly ironical tone.

I then related what the last works of Dumont d'Urville had made known: "La Perouse and his second in command, Captain Langle, were sent in 1785, to make a voyage round the world. They equipped the corvettes, the *Boussole* and the *Astrolabe*, neither of which was again heard of."

In 1791 the French Government, uneasy about the fate of the corvettes, equipped the *Recherche* and the *Espérance*, which left Brest, under Bruni d'Entrecasteaux. Two months afterwards it was learnt that the debris of shipwrecked vessels had been seen on the coasts of New Georgia. But d'Entrecasteaux, ignoring this, made for the Admiralty Islands, designated as the scene of La Perouse's shipwreck.

His search was fruitless. The *Espérance* and *Recherche* passed before Vanikoro without stopping there, and this voyage was unfortunate, for it cost the life of d'Entrecasteaux, of two of his mates and several of his crew.

It was an old Pacific seaman, Captain Dillon, who first found traces of the shipwreck. On May 15, 1824, his ship, the *Saint Patrick*, passed near the Tikopia, one of the New Hebrides. There a Lascar, in a pirogue, sold him the silver handle of a sword that had something engraved on it. The Lascar said that six years before, while he was staying at Vanikoro, he had seen two Europeans who belonged to ships wrecked many years before upon the reefs of the island.

Dillon guessed that he referred to the ships of La Perouse, the disappearance of which had troubled the entire world. He wished to reach Vanikoro, where, according to the Lascar, numerous debris of the wrecks were to be found; but contrary winds and currents prevented him. Dillon returned to Calcutta. There he interested the Asiatic Society and the East India Company in his search. A ship, the *Recherche*, was placed at his disposal, and he set out on the 23rd of January, 1827, accompanied by a French agent.

The *Recherche*, anchored before Vanikoro on the 7th of July, 1827, in this same harbour of Vanou where the *Nautilus* is now floating. There he gathered together numerous remains of the wrecks—iron utensils, anchors, pulley-strops, swivel-guns, an 18-lb. shot, debris of astronomical instruments, a piece of taffrail, and a bronze bell, bearing the inscription, *Bazin m'a fait*, the mark of the foundry of Brest Arsenal, about 1785. Doubt was no longer possible.

Dillon, to complete his information, remained upon the scene of the disaster till the month of October. Then he left Vanikoro, made for New Zealand, anchored at Calcutta on the 7th of April, 1828, and returned to France, where he was received warmly by Charles X.

Dumont d'Urville, commander of the *Astrolabe*, had set sail and two months after Dillon had left Vanikoro he anchored before Hobart Town. There he heard of the results obtained by Dillon, and, moreover, he learnt that a certain James Hobbs, mate on board the *Union*, of Calcutta, having landed on an island situated by 80° 18' south lat. and 156° 30' east long., had noticed bars of iron and red stuffs being used by the natives of the place. Dumont d'Urville was perplexed, and did not know if he ought to credit these reports, made by newspapers little worthy of confidence. However, he decided to go on Dillon's track.

On the 10th of February, 1828, the *Astrolabe* anchored

before Tikopia, and took for guide and interpreter a deserter who had taken refuge on that island, set sail for Vanikoro, and anchored inside the barrier, in the harbour of Vanou.

Several officers went round the island and brought back unimportant debris. The natives, adopting denials and evasions, refused to take them to the scene of the disaster. This suspicious conduct led to the belief that they had ill-treated the shipwrecked men, and, in fact, they seemed to fear that Dumont d'Urville and his companions were come to revenge La Perouse.

However, decided by presents, and understanding that they had nothing to fear, they conducted the mate, M. Jacquinot, to the place of shipwreck.

There, in three to four fathoms of water, between the reefs of Pacou and Vanou, lay anchors, cannons, pigs of iron and lead, encrusted in the calcereous concretion. The longboat and the whaler from the *Astrolabe* were sent to this place, and, not without fatigue, their crews succeeded in raising an anchor weighing 800 pounds, an 800-pound brass cannon, some pigs of lead, and two copper swivel guns.

Dumont d'Urville, questioning the natives, learnt also that La Perouse, after having lost his two ships on the reefs of the island, had built a smaller vessel, only to be lost a second time—no one knew where. The commander of the *Astrolabe* then, under a thicket of mangroves, caused a cenotaph to be raised to the memory of the celebrated navigator and his companions. It was a simple quadrangular pyramid on a coral foundation, in which there was no iron to tempt the cupidity of the natives.

"Then," said Captain Nemo, "they do not know where the third vessel, built by the shipwrecked men on Vanikoro, perished?"

"No one knows."

Captain Nemo answered nothing, and made me a sign to follow him to the saloon. The *Nautilus* sank some yards below the surface of the waves, and then the panels were drawn back. I rushed towards the window, and under the crustations of coral covered with fungi, syphonules, alcyons, madrepores, through myriads of fish—I recognised certain objects which the drags could not bring up—iron stirrups, anchors, cannons, capstan fittings, the stem of a ship—all objects from shipwrecked vessels, now carpeted with living flowers. While I was looking upon these sad remnants Captain Nemo said to me in a grave voice:

"La Perouse started with the *Boussole* and the *Astrolabe*. He anchored first in Botany Bay, visited the Friendly Isles, New Caledonia, made for Santa Cruz, and touched at Namouka, one of the Hapai group. Then his ships arrived on the unknown reefs of Vanikoro. The *Boussole*, which went first, struck on the south coast. The *Astrolabe* went to help, and met with the same fate. The former ship was immediately destroyed, but the *Astrolabe* lasted some days. The natives received the shipwrecked men well. They installed themselves on the island, and built a smaller vessel with the remains of the two large ones. Some of the sailors chose to remain at Vanikoro. The others started with La Perouse. They directed their course towards the Solomon Islands. They all perished on the western coast of the principal island of the group, between Capes Deception and Satisfaction."

"And how do you know that?" I exclaimed.

"This is what I found on the spot of the last shipwreck."

Captain Nemo showed me a tin box, stamped with the French arms, and corroded by salt water. He opened it, and I saw a mass of papers, yellow but still readable. They were the instructions of the *Ministre de la Marine* to La Perouse, annotated on the margin in the handwriting of Louis XVI.

"A fine death for a sailor!" said Captain Nemo; "a coral tomb is a tranquil one. Heaven grant that my companions and I may have no other!"

CHAPTER TWENTY

TORRES STRAITS

DURING the night the *Nautilus* left Vanikoro with excessive speed, and in three days it cleared the 750 leagues that separate the group of La Perouse from the south-east point of Papua.

On the 4th of January we sighted the Papuan coasts. On this occasion Captain Nemo informed me that it was his intention to get into the Indian Ocean by Torres Straits. His communication ended there. Ned Land saw with pleasure that this route would take him nearer to the European seas.

The Torres Straits are no less dangerous on account of the reefs with which they bristle than because of the savage inhabitants who frequent their shores. They separate New Holland from the large island of Papua, named also New Guinea.

The Torres Straits are about thirty-four leagues wide, but it is obstructed by an innumerable quantity of islands, reefs and rocks, which make its navigation almost impracticable. Captain Nemo consequently took every precaution to cross it. The *Nautilus*, on a level with the surface of the water, moved slowly along. Its screw like the tail of a cetacean, slowly beat the billows.

Profiting by this situation, my two companions and I took our places on the constantly-deserted platform. Before us rose the helmsman's cage, and I am very much mistaken if Captain Nemo was not there directing his *Nautilus* himself.

Around the *Nautilus* the sea was furiously rough. The current of the waves, which was bearing from SE. to NW. with a speed of two and a half miles, broke over the coral reefs that emerged here and there.

"An ugly sea!" said Ned Land to me.

"Detestable indeed," I answered, "and one that is not suitable to such a vessel as the *Nautilus*."

"That confounded captain must be very certain of his route," answered the Canadian, "for I see coral reefs which would break its keel in a thousand pieces if it only just touched them!"

I was wondering if Captain Nemo, foolishly imprudent, was going to take his vessel into that pass where Dumont d'Urville's two corvettes were stranded, when he changed his direction, and steered for the Island of Gilboa. It was then three o'clock in the afternoon. The ebb tide was just beginning. The *Nautilus* approached this island, which I still think I see with its remarkable border of screw-pines. We were coasting at a distance of two miles.

Suddenly a shock overthrew me. The *Nautilus* had just touched on a reef, and was quite still, laying lightly to port side.

When I rose I saw Captain Nemo and his second on the platform. They were examining the situation of the vessel, and talking in their incomprehensible dialect.

Two miles on the starboard appeared the Island of Gilboa, the coast of which was rounded from N. to W ; like an immense arm towards the S. and E. some heads of coral rocks were jutting, which the ebb tide left uncovered. We had run aground, and in one of the seas where the tides are very slight, an unfortunate circumstance in the floating of the *Nautilus*; however, the vessel had in no wise suffered, its keel was so solidly joined; but although it could neither sink nor split, it ran the risk of being for ever fastened on to these reefs, and then Captain Nemo's submarine apparatus would be done for.

I was reflecting thus, when the captain, cool and calm, appearing neither vexed nor moved, came up.

"An accident?" I asked.

"No, an incident," he answered.

"But an incident," I replied, "which will perhaps again force you to become an inhabitant of the land from which you flee."

Captain Nemo looked at me in a curious manner, and made a negative gesture. It was as much as to say to me that nothing would ever force him to set foot on land again. Then he said:

"The *Nautilus* is not lost. It will yet carry you amid the marvels of the ocean. Our voyage is only just begun, and I do not wish to deprive myself so soon of the honour of your company."

"But, Captain Nemo," I replied, without noticing the irony of his sentence, "the *Nautilus* ran aground at high tide. Now tides are not strong in the Pacific, and if you cannot lighten the *Nautilus* I do not see how it can be floated again."

"Tides are not strong in the Pacific—you are right, Professor," answered Captain Nemo; "but in Torres Straits there is a difference of five feet between the level of high and low tide. To-day is the fourth of January, and in five days the moon will be at the full. I shall be much astonished if this complaisant satellite does not sufficiently raise these masses of water, and render me a service which I wish to owe to her alone."

This said, Captain Nemo went down again into the interior of the *Nautilus*. The vessel remained as immovable as if the coral polypi had already walled it up in their indescructible cement.

"Well, sir?" said Ned Land, who came to me after the departure of the captain.

"Well, friend Ned, we must wait patiently for high tide on the ninth. It appears that the moon will be kind enough to set us afloat again."

"But still we might have a taste of land," replied Land. "There is an island; on that island there are trees; under those trees are animals, bearers of cutlets and roast beef, which I should like to be able to taste."

"There, friend Ned is right," said Conseil, "and I am of his opinion. Could not monsieur obtain from his friend Captain Nemo the permission to be transported to land, if it was only not to lose the habit of treading the solid parts of our planet?"

"I can ask him," I answered, "but he will refuse."

"Let monsieur risk it," said Conseil, "and then we shall know what to think about the captain's amiability."

To my great surprise Captain Nemo gave the permission I asked for, and he gave it me very courteously, without even exacting from me a promise to come back on board. But a flight across the lands of New Guinea would have been very perilous, and I should not have advised Ned Land to attempt it. It was better to be a prisoner on board the *Nautilus* than to fall into the hands of the natives.

The next day, the boat, its deck taken off, was lifted from its niche, and launched from the top of the platform. Two men sufficed for this operation. The oars were in the boat, and we had only to take our place.

At eight o'clock, armed with guns and hatchets, we descended the sides of the *Nautilus*. The sea was pretty calm. A slight breeze was blowing from land. Conseil and I rowed vigorously, and Ned steered in the narrow passages between the breakers.

Land could not contain his joy. He was a prisoner escaped from prison, and did not think of the necessity of going back to it again.

At half-past eight the boat of the *Nautilus* ran softly aground on a strand of sand, after having happily cleared the coral reef which surrounds the island of Gilboa.

CHAPTER TWENTY-ONE

SOME DAYS ON LAND

TOUCHING land again made a great impression on me. Ned Land struck the land with his foot as if to take possession of it. Yet we had only been, according to Captain Nemo's expression, the "passengers of the *Nautilus*" for two months —that is to say, in reality, we had only been the captain's prisoners for two months.

The soil was almost entirely madreporic, but certain dried-up beds of streams, strewed with granitic debris, demonstrated that this island was owing to a primordial formation. All the horizon was hidden by a curtain of admirable forests. Enormous trees, some 200 feet high, with garlands of creepers joining their branches, were real natural hammocks, which were rocked in the slight breeze. They were mimosas, ficus, teak-trees, hibiscus, palm-trees, mixed in profusion; and under the shelter of their verdant vault, grew orchids, leguminous plants, and ferns.

But without noticing all these fine specimens of Papuan flora, the Canadian abandoned the agreeable for the useful. He perceived a coconut tree, brought down some nuts, broke them, and we drank their milk and ate their kernel with a relish that protested against the ordinary fare of the *Nautilus*.

Fortune favoured us in our search after edibles, and one of the most useful products of tropical zones furnished us with a valuable article of food which was wanting on board— I mean the bread-tree, which is very abundant. From its mass of verdure stood out large globular fruit two and a half inches wide, with a rough skin in an hexagonal pattern —a useful vegetable, with which Nature has gratified the regions in which wheat is wanting, and which, without exacting culture, gives fruit for eight months in the year. Land knew this fruit well; he had eaten it before, and he knew how to prepare its edible substance. The sight of it excited his appetite, and he could contain himself no longer.

"Sir," he said to me, "may I die if I don't taste that bread-fruit!"

"Taste, friend Ned—taste as much as you like. We are here to make experiments; let us make them."

"It will not take long," answered the Canadian; and with a burning-glass he lighted a fire of dead wood which crackled joyously.

During this time Conseil and I chose the best fruits. Some were not ripe enough, and their thick skin covered a white but slightly fibrous pulp. There were a great number of others, yellow and gelatinous, ready for gathering.

There was no kernel in this fruit. Conseil took a dozen to Ned Land, who placed them on a fire of cinders, after having cut them into thin slices, during which he kept saying:

"You will see, sir, how good this bread is!"

"Especially when one has been deprived of it for so long, Conseil."

"It is better than bread," added the Canadian; "it is like delicate pastry. Have you never eaten any, sir?"

"No, Ned."

"Well, then, prepare for something good. If you don't return to the charge I am no longer the king of harpooners."

In a short time the side exposed to the fire was quite black. In the interior appeared a white paste and a sort of tender crumb, with a taste something like that of an artichoke.

It must be acknowledged this bread was excellent, and I ate it with great pleasure.

"Unfortunately," I said, "such paste will not keep fresh; and it appears useless to me to make any provision for the vessel."

"Why, sir," cried Ned Land, "you speak like a naturalist, but I am going to act like a baker. Gather some of the fruit, Conseil; we will take it on our return."

"And how do you prepare it?" I asked.

"By making a fermented paste with its pulp, which will keep any length of time. When I wish to use it I will have it cooked in the kitchen on board; and, notwithstanding its slightly acid taste, you will find it excellent."

"Then, Ned, I see that nothing is wanting to this bread."

"Yes, Professor," answered the Canadian; "we want fruit, or at least vegetables."

"Let us seek the fruit and vegetables."

When our gathering was over we set out to complete this terrestrial dinner. Our search was not a vain one, and towards noon we had made an ample provision of bananas.

With these bananas we gathered enormous "jaks" with a very decided taste, savoury mangoes, and pineapples of incredible size. But this took up a great deal of our time, which there was no cause to regret.

Conseil watched Ned continually. The harpooner marched on in front, and during his walk across the forest he gathered with a sure hand the excellent fruit with which to complete his provisions.

"What time is it?" asked the Canadian.

"Two o'clock at least," answered Conseil.

"How the times does go on dry land!" cried Ned Land, with a sigh of regret.

We came back across the forest, and completed our provision by making a razzia of palm cabbages, which we were obliged to gather at the summit of the trees, and little beans which I recognised as being the "abrou" of the Malaysians, and yams.

At last, at five o'clock in the evening, loaded with our riches, we left the shores of the island, and half an hour later reached the *Nautilus*. No one appeared on our arrival. The enormous iron cylinders seemed deserted. When the provisions were embarked I went down to my room. There I found my supper ready. I ate it, and then went to sleep.

The next day there was nothing new on board. No noise in the interior, not a sign of life. The canoe had remained alongside, in the very place where we had left it. We resolved to return to the island. Ned Land hoped to be more fortunate than before from a hunting point of view, and wished to visit another part of the forest.

We set out at sunrise. The boat, carried away by the waves, which were flowing inland, reached the island in a few minutes. We landed, and thinking it was better to trust to the instinct of the Canadian, we followed Ned Land, whose long legs threatened to outdistance us. Ned Land went up the coast westward, and fording some beds of streams, he reached the high plain, bordered by the admirable forests. Some kingfishers were on the banks of the stream, but they would not let themselves be approached; their circumspection proved to me that these fowl knew what to think of bipeds of our sort, and I therefore concluded that, if the island was not inhabited, it was at least frequented by human beings. After having crossed some rich meadow land we reached the borders of a little wood, animated by the song and flight of a great number of birds.

Under the thick foliage of this wood, a whole world of parrots were flying from branch to branch, only waiting for a better education to speak the human language. At present they were screeching in company with paroquets of all colours, grave cockatoos who seemed to be meditating upon some philosophical problem, whilst the lories, of a bright red colour, passed like a morsel of stamen carried off by the breeze, amidst kalaos of noisy flight, papouas, painted with the finest shades of azure, and a whole variety of charming, but generally not edible, birds.

About 11 a.m. we had traversed the first range of mountains that form the centre of the island, and we had killed nothing. Hunger drove us on. The hunters had relied on the products of the chase, and they had done wrong. Fortunately, Conseil, to his great surprise, made a double shot, and secured breakfast. He brought down a white and a wood pigeon, which, quickly plucked and suspended to a skewer, were roasted before a flaming fire of dead wood. Whilst these interesting animals were cooking, Ned had prepared the fruit of the "artocarpus," then the pigeons were devoured to the bones, and pronounced excellent. Nutmegs, with which they are in the habit of stuffing their crops, flavours the flesh and makes it delicious.

"It is like the fowls that eat truffles," said Conseil.

"And now, Ned, what is there wanting?" I asked the Canadian.

"Some four-footed game, M. Aronnax," answered Ned Land. "All these pigeons are only side-dishes and mouthfuls, and until I have killed an animal with cutlets I shall not be content."

"Let us go on with our hunting," answered Conseil, "but towards the sea. We have reached the first declivities of the mountains, and I think we had better regain the forest regions."

It was sensible advice, and was followed. After an hour's walk we reached a veritable forest of sago-trees.

Happily, about two o'clock Ned Land killed a magnificent hog, one of those the natives call "bari-outang." The animal came in time to give us real quadruped meat, and it was well received. Ned Land was very proud of his shot. The hog, struck by the electric bullet, had fallen stone dead.

The Canadian soon skinned and prepared it after having cut half a dozen cutlets to furnish us with grilled meat for our evening meal. Then we went on with the chase that was again to be marked by Ned and Conseil's exploits.

The two friends, by beating the bushes, roused a herd of kangaroos that fled away bounding on their elastic paws. But these animals did not take flight too rapidly for the electric capsule to stop them in their course.

"Ah, Professor," cried Ned Land, excited by the pleasure of hunting, "what excellent game, especially stewed! What provisions for the *Nautilus*! Two, three, five down! And when I think that we shall eat all that meat, and that those imbeciles on board will not have a mouthful!"

I think that in his delight the Canadian, if he had not talked so much, would have slaughtered the whole herd! But he contented himself with a dozen of these interesting marsupians, which, as Conseil informed us, form the first order of agreacentiary mammals.

These animals were small. They belong to a species of kangaroo "rabbits" that live habitually in the hollow of trees, and that are of extraordinary speed; but although they are of middling size, they, at least, furnish excellent meat.

We were very much satisfied with the result of our hunt. The delighted Ned proposed to return the next day to this enchanted island, which he wanted to clear of all its edible quadrupeds. But he reckoned without circumstances.

At 6 p.m. we returned to the shore. Our boat was stranded in its place. The *Nautilus*, like a long rock, emerged from the waves two miles from the island. Ned Land, without more delay, began to prepare the dinner. He understood all about cooking well. The cutlets "bari-outang," grilled on the cinders, soon scented the air with a delicious odour.

But here I perceive that I am walking in the footsteps of the Canadian in delight before grilled pork. May I be pardoned as I have pardoned Ned Land, and from the same motives? In short, the dinner was excellent. Two wood-pigeons completed this extraordinary bill of fare. The sago paste, the artocarpus bread, mangoes, half a dozen pine-apples and the fermented liquor of some cocoa-nuts delighted us. I even think that the ideas of my worthy companions were not so clear as they might be.

"Suppose we do not return to the *Nautilus* this evening," said Conseil.

"Suppose we never return," added Ned Land.

Just then a stone fell at our feet, and cut short the har-pooner's proposition.

CHAPTER TWENTY-TWO

CAPTAIN NEMO'S THUNDERBOLT

WE LOOKED towards the forest without rising, my hand stopping in its movement towards my mouth, Ned Land's completing its office.

"A stone does not fall from the sky," said Conseil, "with-out deserving the name of aërolite."

A second stone, carefully rounded, which struck out of Conseil's hand a savoury pigeon's leg, gave still more weight to his observations.

We all three rose and shouldered our guns, ready to reply to any attack.

"Can they be monkeys?" asked Ned Land.

"Something like them," answered Conseil; "they are savages."

"The boat," said I, making for the sea. In fact, we were obliged to beat a retreat, for about twenty natives, armed with bows and slings, appeared on the skirts of the thicket that hid the horizon one hundred steps off.

Our boat was anchored at about sixty feet from us.

The savages approached us, not running, making most hostile demonstrations. It rained stones and arrows.

Ned Land did not wish to leave his provisions, notwithstanding the imminence of the danger. He went on tolerably fast with his pig on one side and his kangaroos on the other.

In two minutes we were on shore. It was the affair of an instant to load the boat with the provisions and arms, to push it into the sea, and to take the two oars. We had not gone two cables' length when a hundred savages, howling and gesticulating, entered the water up to their waists. I watched to see if their appearance would not attract some men from the *Nautilus* on to the platform.

But no. The enormous machine, lying off, seemed absolutely deserted. Twenty minutes after we ascended the sides; the panels were open. After we had made the boat fast we re-entered the interior of the *Nautilus*.

I went to the saloon, from whence I heard some chords. Captain Nemo was there, bending over his organ, and plunged into a musical ecstasy.

"Captain," I said to him.

He did not hear me.

"Captain," I repeated, touching his hand.

He shuddered and turned.

"Ha, it is you, Professor," he said to me. "Well, have you had good sport? Have you botanised successfully?"

"Yes, Captain," answered I, "but we have, unfortunately, brought back a troop of bipeds, whose neighbourhood appears to me dangerous."

"What bipeds?"

"Savages."

"Savages?" answered Captain Nemo in an ironical tone. "And you are astonished, Professor, that having set foot on one of the lands of this globe, you find savages there? Where are there no savages? Besides, those you call savages, are they worse than others?"

"But, Captain——"

"For my part, sir, I have met with some everywhere."

Well," I answered, "if you do not wish to receive any on board the *Nautilus*, you will do well to take some precautions."

"Make yourself easy, Professor, there is nothing worth troubling about."

"But these natives are numerous."

"How many did you count?"

"A hundred at least."

"M. Aronnax," answered Captain Nemo, who had again placed his fingers on the organ keys, "if all the natives of Papua were gathered together on that shore, the *Nautilus* would have nothing to fear from their attacks."

I went up again on to the platform. Night had already come, for in this low latitude the sun sets rapidly, and there is no twilight. I could only see the island indistinctly. But the numerous fires lighted on the beach showed that the natives did not dream of leaving it.

The night passed without misadventure. The Papuans were, doubtless, frightened by the very sight of the monster stranded in the bay, for the open panels would have given them easy access to the interior of the *Nautilus*.

At 6 a.m., on January 8, I went up on the platform. The morning was breaking. The island soon appeared through the rising mists, its shores first, then its summits.

The natives were still there, more numerous than the day before, perhaps five or six hundred strong. Some of them, taking advantage of the low tide, had come on to the coral heads at less than two cables' length from the *Nautilus*. I easily recognised them. They were real Papuans, of athletic stature, men of fine breed, with wide high foreheads, large, but not broad, and flat noses, and white teeth. Their woolly hair, dyed red, showed off their bodies, black and shining like those of the Nubians. From the cut and distended lobes of their ears hung bone chaplets. These savages were generally naked. Amongst them I remarked some women, dressed from the hips to the knees in a veritable crinoline of herbs, which hung to a vegetable waistband. Some of the chiefs had ornamented their necks with a crescent and collar of red and white glass beads. Nearly all were armed with bows, arrows and shields, carrying on their shoulders a sort of net, containing the rounded stones which they threw with great skill from their slings.

So on that day the boat did not leave the vessel, to the great displeasure of Ned Land, who could not complete his provisions. This skilful Canadian employed his time in preparing the meat and farinaceous substances he had brought from the island of Gilboa. As to the savages, they returned to land about 11 a.m., as soon as the heads of coral began to disappear under the waves of the rising tide. But I saw their number considerably increase on the shore. It was probable that they came from the neighbouring islands, or from Papua proper. However, I had not seen a single native pirogue.

Having nothing better to do, I thought of dragging these limpid waters, under which was a profusion of shells, zoophytes, and marine plants. It was, moreover, the last day the *Nautilus* was to pass in these seas if it was set afloat the next day, according to Captain Nemo's promise.

I therefore called Conseil, who brought me a small light drag, something like those used in the oyster-fisheries.

For two hours our dragging went on actively, but without bringing up any rarity. The drag was filled with Midas-ears, harps, melames, and, particularly, the finest hammers I ever saw. We also took some holothurias, pearl oysters, and a dozen small turtles, which were kept for the pantry on board.

But at the very moment when I expected it least I put my hand on a marvel—I ought to say on a natural deformity —very rarely met with. Conseil had just brought up the drag full of ordinary shells when all at once he saw me thrust my hand into the net, draw out a shell, and utter a conchological cry—that is to say, the most piercing cry that human throat can utter.

"Eh? What is the matter with monsieur?" asked Conseil, much surprised. "Has monsieur been bitten?"

"No, my boy; and yet I would willingly have paid for my discovery with the loss of a finger."

"What discovery?"

"This shell," I said, showing the object of my triumph. "Yes, my boy, it is a sinister shell."

"A sinister shell!" repeated Conseil with a palpitating heart.

"Look at its spiral."

"Ah, monsieur may believe me!" said Conseil, taking the precious shell with a trembling hand, "I have never felt a like emotion!"

And there was cause for emotion! It is well known, as the naturalists have caused to be remarked, that dextrality is a law of Nature. The stars and their satellites in their rotatory movements go from right to left. Man oftener uses his right than his left hand, and consequently his instruments, apparatus, staircases, locks, water-springs, etc., are put together so as to be used from right to left. Nature has generally followed the same law in the spiral of its shells; they are all dexter, with rare exceptions, and when it happens that their spiral is sinister amateurs pay their weight in gold.

Conseil and I were plunged in the contemplation of our treasure, and I was promising myself to enrich the museum with it, when a stone, untowardly hurled by a native, broke the precious object in Conseil's hand.

I uttered a cry of despair! Conseil seized my gun and aimed at a savage who was swinging his sling in the air about ten yards from him. I wished to stop him, but he had fired and broken the bracelet of amulets which hung upon the arm of the native.

"Conseil!" I cried—"Conseil!"

"What, does not monsieur see that this cannibal began the attack?"

"A shell is not worth a man's life," I said.

"Ah, the rascal!" cried Conseil; "I would rather he had broken my arm!"

Conseil was sincere, but I was not of his opinion. However, the situation had changed during the last few minutes, and we had not perceived it. About twenty pirogues then surrounded the *Nautilus*. These pirogues, hollowed in the trunks of trees, long, narrow, and well calculated for speed, were kept in equilibrium by means of double balances of bamboo, which floated on the surface of the water. They were worked by skilful paddlers, half naked, and their approach made me uneasy. It was evident that these Papuans had already had some relations with Europeans, and knew their ships. But what must they have thought of this long iron cylinder, without either masts or funnel? Nothing good, but they kept first at a respectful distance. However, seeing it did not move, they regained confidence by degrees, and tried to familiarise themselves with it. Now it was precisely this familiarity which it was necessary to prevent. Our arms, which made no noise, could only produce an indifferent effect on these natives, who only respect noisy weapons. A thunderbolt without the rolling of thunder would not much frighten men, although the danger exists in the lightning and not in the noise.

At that moment the pirogues approached nearer the *Nautilus*, and a shower of arrows fell upon it.

"Why, it hails," said Conseil, "and perhaps poisoned hail."

"I must tell Captain Nemo," said I, going through the panel.

I went down to the saloon. I found no one there. I ventured to knock at the door of the captain's room.

A "Come in!" answered me.

I entered and found Captain Nemo occupied with a calculation where x and other algebraical signs were plentiful.

"I fear I am disturbing you," said I.

"Yes, M. Aronnax," answered the captain, "but I think you must have serious reasons for seeing me."

"Very serious; we are surrounded by the pirogues of the natives, and in a few minutes we shall certainly be assailed by several hundreds of savages."

"Ah," said Captain Nemo, tranquilly, "so they are here with their pirogues?"

"Yes."

"Well, all we have to do is to shut the panels."

"Precisely, and I came to tell you."

"Nothing is easier," said Captain Nemo.

Pressing an electric bell he transmitted an order to the crew's quarters.

"That's done, sir," said he after a few minutes; "the boat is in its place, and the panels are shut. You do not fear, I imagine, that these gentlemen can break in walls which the balls from your frigate could not touch?"

"No, Captain, but there exists another danger."

"What is that, sir?"

"It is that to-morrow, at the same time, you will be obliged to open the panels to renew the air of the *Nautilus*."

"Certainly, sir, as our vessel breathes like the cetaceans do."

"Now, if at the moment the Papuans occupied the platform, I do not know how you could prevent them entering."

"Then you believe they will get up on the vessel?"

"I am certain of it."

"Well, let them. I see no reason for preventing them. These Papuans are poor devils, and I will not let my visit to Gilboa cost the life of one poor wretch."

That said, I was going to withdraw, but Captain Nemo retained me, and invited me to take a seat near him. He questioned me with interest about our excursions on land and our sport, and he did not seem to understand the need for meat that impassioned the Canadian. Then the conversation touched upon divers subjects, and without being more communicative, Captain Nemo showed himself more amiable.

Amongst other things we spoke of the present position of

the *Nautilus*, abandoned precisely in this strait, where Dumont d'Urville was nearly lost.

"Captain," said I, "there is one point of resemblance between the corvettes of Dumont d'Urville and the *Nautilus*."

"What is that, sir?"

"The *Nautilus* is stranded like them."

"The *Nautilus* is not stranded," replied Captain Nemo, coldly. "The *Nautilus* is made to repose on the bed of the waters, and the difficult work, the manœuvres that d'Urville was obliged to have recourse to, to get his corvettes afloat again, I shall not undertake. The *Astrolabe* and *Zélée* nearly perished, but the *Nautilus* runs no risk. To-morrow, at the said hour, the tide will quietly raise it, and it will recommence its navigation through the seas."

"Captain," I said, "I do not doubt."

"To-morrow," added the captain, rising—"to-morrow at 2.40 p.m. the *Nautilus* will be afloat again, and I will leave without damage Torres Straits."

These words pronounced in a very curt tone, Captain Nemo bowed slightly. It was my dismissal, and I went back to my room.

I was left alone. I went to bed, but slept badly. I heard the savages stamping about on the platform making a deafening noise. The night passed thus without the crew seeming to come out of their habitual inertia. They were not more anxious about the presence of these cannibals than the soldiers of an ironclad fortress would be about the ants that crawl over the iron.

I rose at 6 a.m. The panels had not been opened. The air, therefore, had not been renewed in the interior, but the reservoirs, filled ready for any event, sent some cubic yards of oxygen into the impoverished atmosphere of the *Nautilus*.

I worked in my room till noon without seeing Captain Nemo, even for an instant. There seemed to be no preparation for departure made on board.

I waited for some time longer, and then went into the saloon. The clock was at half past two. In ten minutes the tide would be at its maximum, and if Captain Nemo had not made a boasting promise the *Nautilus* would be immediately set free. If not, many months would pass before it would leave its coral bed.

In the meantime several shocks were felt in the hull of the vessel. I heard its sides grate against the calcareous asperities of the coral.

At 2.35 p.m. Captain Nemo appeared in the saloon.

"We are going to start," said he.

"Ah!" I said.

"I have given orders to have the panels opened."

"What about the Papuans?"

"The Papuans?" answered Captain Nemo, slightly raising his shoulders.

"Will they not penetrate into the interior of the *Nautilus*?"

"How can they?"

"Through the panels you have had opened."

"M. Aronnax," answered Captain Nemo tranquilly, "it is not so easy to enter the *Nautilus* through its panels, even when they are opened."

I looked at the captain.

"You do not understand?" he asked.

"Not at all."

"Well, come, and you will see."

I went towards the central staircase. There Ned Land and Conseil, much puzzled, were looking at some of the crew, who were opening the panels, whilst cries of rage and fearful vociferations resounded outside.

The lids were opened on the outside. Seventy horrible faces appeared. But the first of the natives who put his hand on the balustrade, thrown backwards by some invisible force, fled, howling and making extraordinary gambols.

Ten of his companions succeeded him. Ten had the same fate.

Conseil was in ecstasies. Ned Land, carried away by his violent instincts, sprang up the staircase. But as soon as he had seized the handrail with both hands he was overthrown in his turn.

"Malediction!" he cried. "I am thunderstruck."

That word explained it all to me. It was no longer a handrail but a metal cable, charged with electricity. Whoever touched it felt a formidable shock, and that shock would have been mortal if Captain Nemo had thrown all the current of his apparatus into this conductor. It may be truly said that between his assailants and himself he had hung an electric barrier that no one could cross with impunity.

In the meantime the frightened Papuans had beaten a retreat, maddened with terror. We, half laughing, consoled and frictioned the unfortunate Ned Land, who was swearing like one possessed.

But at that moment the *Nautilus*, raised by the last tidal waves, left its coral bed at that fortieth minute exactly fixed by the captain. Its screw beat the waves with majestic slowness. Its speed increased by degrees, and navigating on the surface of the ocean, it left safe and sound the dangerous passages of Torres Straits.

CHAPTER TWENTY-THREE

ÆGRI SOMNIA

THE following day the *Nautilus* resumed its course under the water, but at a remarkable speed, which I could not estimate at less than thirty-five miles an hour. The rapidity of its screw was such that I could neither follow its turns nor count them.

On the 18th of January the *Nautilus* was in longitude 105°, in S. lat. 15°. The weather was threatening, the sea rough. The wind was blowing a strong gale from the east. The barometer, which had been going down for some days, announced an approaching war of the elements.

I had gone up on to the platform at the moment the first officer was taking his bearings. Almost immediately I saw Captain Nemo appear and sweep the horizon with a telescope.

For some minutes the captain remained immovable, without leaving the point enclosed in the field of his object glass. Then he lowered his telescope and exchanged about ten words with his officer, who seemed to be a prey to an emotion that he tried in vain to suppress.

Captain Nemo, more master of himself, remained calm. He appeared, besides, to make certain objections, to which the officer answered by formal assurances—at least, I understood them thus by the difference of their tone and gestures.

I looked carefully in the direction they were observing without perceiving anything. Sky and water mixed in a perfectly clear horizon.

In the meantime Captain Nemo walked up and down the platform without looking at me, perhaps without seeing me. His step was assured, but less regular than usual. Sometimes he stopped, folded his arms, and looked at the sea. What was he seeking in that immense space? The *Nautilus* was then some hundreds of miles from the nearest coast.

The first officer had taken up his telescope again, and was obstinately interrogating the horizon, going and coming, stamping, and contrasting with his chief by his nervous excitement.

This mystery must necessarily be soon cleared up, for, obeying an order of Captain Nemo's, the machine, increasing its propelling power, gave a more rapid rotatory movement to the screw.

At that moment the officer again attracted the Captain's attention, who stopped his walk and directed his telescope towards the point indicated. He observed it for a long time. I, feeling very curious about it, went down to the saloon and brought up an excellent telescope that I generally used. Then leaning it against the lantern cage that jutted in front of the platform, I prepared to sweep all the line of sky and sea. But I had not placed my eye to it when the instrument was quickly snatched out of my hands.

I turned. Captain Nemo was before me, but I hardly knew him. His physiognomy was transfigured. His eyes shone with sombre fire under his frowning eyebrows. His teeth glittered between his firm-set lips. His stiffened body, closed fists, and head set hard on his shoulders, showed the violent hatred breathed by his whole appearance. He did not move. My telescope, fallen from his hand, had rolled to his feet.

Had I, then, unintentionally provoked this angry attitude? Did the incomprehensible personage imagine that I had surprised some secret interdicted to the guests of the *Nautilus*?

No! I was not the object of this hatred, for he was not looking at me; his eyes remained fixed on the impenetrable point of the horizon.

At last Captain Nemo recovered his self-possession. His face, so profoundly excited, resumed its habitual calmness. He addressed some words in a foreign tongue to his officer, and then turned towards me again.

"M. Aronnax," said he in a rather imperious tone, "I require from you the fulfilment of one of the engagements that bind me to you."

"What is that, Captain?"

"To let yourself be shut up—you and your companions—until I shall think proper to set you at liberty again."

"You are master here," I answered, looking at him fixedly. "But may I ask you one question?"

"No, sir, not one!"

After that I had nothing to do but obey, as all resistance would have been impossible.

I went down to the cabin occupied by Ned Land and Conseil, and I told them of the captain's determination. I leave it to be imagined how that communication was received by the Canadian. Besides, there was no time for any explanation. Four of the crew were waiting at the door, and they conducted us to the cell where we had passed our first night on board the *Nautilus*.

Ned Land wanted to expostulate, but for all answer the door was shut upon him.

"Will monsieur tell me what this means?" asked Conseil.

I related what had happened to my companions. They were as astonished as I, and not more enlightened.

I was overwhelmed with reflections, and the strange look on Captain Nemo's face would not go out of my head. I was incapable of putting two logical ideas together, and was losing myself in the most absurd hypotheses, when I was aroused by these words of Ned Land:

"Why, they have laid breakfast for us!"

In fact, the table was laid. It was evident that Captain Nemo had given this order at the same time that he caused the speed of the *Nautilus* to be hastened.

"Will monsieur allow me to recommend something to him?" asked Conseil.

"Yes, my boy," I replied.

"It is that monsieur should breakfast. It would be prudent, for we do not know what may happen."

"You are right, Conseil."

"Unfortunately," said Ned Land, "they have only given us the usual fare on board."

"Friend Ned," replied Conseil, "what should you say if you had had no breakfast at all?"

That observation cut short the harpooner's grumbling.

We sat down to breakfast. The meal was eaten in silence. I ate little. Conseil forced himself to eat for prudence sake, and Ned Land ate as usual. Then, breakfast over, we each made ourselves comfortable in a corner.

At that moment a luminous globe that had been lighting us went out and left us in profound darkness. Ned Land soon went to sleep, and, what astonished me, Conseil went off into a heavy slumber. I was asking myself what could have provoked in him so imperious a need of sleep, when I felt heaviness creep over my own brain. My eyes, which I wished to keep open, closed in spite of my efforts. I became a prey to painful hallucinations. It was evident that soporific substances had been mixed with the food we had just eaten. Imprisonment, then, was not enough to conceal Captain Nemo's project from us; we must have sleep as well.

I heard the panels closed. The undulations of the sea, that

of a slight rolling motion, ceased. Had the *Nautilus*, then, left the surface of the ocean? Had it again sunk to the motionless depth?

I wished to resist sleep. It was impossible. My breathing became weaker. I felt a deathlike coldness freeze and paralyse my limbs. My eyelids fell like leaden coverings over my eyes. I could not raise them. A morbid slumber, full of hallucinations, took possession of my whole being. Then the visions disappeared and left me in complete insensibility.

CHAPTER TWENTY-FOUR

THE CORAL KINGDOM

THE NEXT day I woke with my faculties singularly clear. To my great surprise I was in my own room. My companions had doubtless been carried to their cabin without being more aware of it than I. They knew no more what had happened during the night than I, and to unveil the mystery I only depended on the hazards of the future.

I then thought of leaving my room. Was I once more free or a prisoner? Entirely free. I opened the door, went through the waist, and climbed the central staircase. The panels, closed the night before, were opened. I stepped on to the platform.

Ned Land and Conseil were awaiting me there. I questioned them; they knew nothing. They had slept a dreamless sleep, and had been much surprised to find themselves in their cabin on awaking.

As to the *Nautilus*, it appeared to us tranquil and mysterious as usual. It was floating on the surface of the waves at a moderate speed. Nothing on board seemed changed.

Ned Land watched the sea with his penetrating eyes.

It was deserted. The Canadian signalled nothing fresh on the horizon—neither sail nor land. There was a stiff west breeze blowing, and the vessel was rolling under the influence of long waves raised by the wind.

The *Nautilus*, after its air had been renewed, was kept at an average depth of fifteen yards, so as to rise promptly, if necessary, to the surface of the waves, an operation which, contrary to custom, was performed several times during that day of January 19th. The second then went up on the platform, and the accustomed sentence was heard in the interior of the vessel.

Captain Nemo did not appear. Of the men on board I only saw the impassible steward, who served me with his usual exactitude and speechlessness.

About 2 p.m. I was in the saloon occupied in classifying my notes, when the captain opened the door and appeared.

"Are you a doctor, M. Aronnax?"

"Yes," I said; "I am doctor and surgeon. I was in practice for several years before entering the museum."

"That is well."

My answer had evidently satisfied Captain Nemo, but not knowing what he wanted, I awaited fresh questions, meaning to answer according to circumstances.

"M. Aronnax," said the captain, "will you consent to prescribe for a sick man?"

"There is someone ill on board?"

"Yes."

"I am ready to follow you."

"Come."

I must acknowledge that my heart beat faster. I do not know why I saw some connection between the illness of this man of the crew and the events of the night before, and this mystery preoccupied me at least as much as the sick man.

Captain Nemo conducted me aft of the *Nautilus*, and made me enter a cabin situated in the crew's quarters.

There, upon a bed, a man of some forty years, with an energetic face and true Anglo-Saxon type, was reposing.

I bent over him. He was not only a sick man but a wounded one too. His head, wrapped in bandages, was resting on a double pillow. I undid the bandages, and the wounded man, looking with his large fixed eyes, let me do it without uttering a single complaint.

The wound was horrible. The skull, crushed by some blunt instrument, showed the brain, and the cerebral substance had sustained profound attrition. The breathing of the sick man was slow, and spasmodic movements of the muscles agitated his face.

I felt the pulse; it was intermittent. The extremities were already growing cold, and I saw that death was approaching without any possibility of my preventing it. After dressing the wound I bandaged it again, and turned towards Captain Nemo.

"He will be dead in two hours."

"Can nothing save him?"

"Nothing."

Captain Nemo clenched his hand, and his eyes, which I did not think made for weeping, filled with tears.

For some time I still watched the dying man, whose life seemed gradually ebbing. He looked still paler under the electric light that bathed his deathbed. I looked at his intelligent head, furrowed with premature lines which misfortune, misery perhaps, had long ago placed there. I tried to learn the secret of his life in the last words that escaped from his mouth.

"You can go now, M. Aronnax," said Captain Nemo.

I left the captain in the room of the dying man, and went back to my room much moved by this scene. During the whole day I was agitated by sinister presentiments. I slept badly that night, and, amidst my frequently interrupted dreams, I thought I heard distant sighs and a sound like funeral chants. Was it the prayer for the dead murmured in that language which I could not understand?

The next morning I went upon deck. Captain Nemo had preceded me there. As soon as he perceived me he came to me.

"Professor," said he, "would it suit you to make a submarine excursion to-day?"

"With my companions?" I asked.

"If they like."

"We are at your disposition, Captain."

"Then please put on your diving-dresses."

Of the dying or dead there was no question. I went to Ned Land and Conseil and told them of Captain Nemo's proposal. Conseil accepted it immediately, and this time the Canadian seemed quite ready to go with us.

It was 8 a.m. At half past we were clothed for our walk and furnished with our breathing and lighting apparatus. The double door was opened, and accompanied by Captain Nemo, who was followed by a dozen men of the crew, we set foot at a depth of ten yards on the firm ground where the *Nautilus* was stationed.

A slight incline brought us to an undulated stretch of ground at about fifteen fathoms depth. This ground differed completely from any I saw during my first excursion under the waters of the Pacific Ocean. Here there was no fine sand, no submarine meadows, no seaweed forests. I immediately recognised this region of which Captain Nemo was doing the honours. It was the kingdom of coral.

The Ruhmkorff apparatus was set going, and we followed a coral bank in process of formation, which, helped by time, would one day close in that portion of the Indian Ocean. The route was bordered by inextricable bushes formed by the entanglement of shrubs that the little white-starred flowers covered. Sometimes, contrary to the land plants, these arborisations, rooted to the rocks, grew from top to bottom.

At last, after two hours' walking, we reached a depth of about 150 fathoms—that is to say, the extreme limit that coral begins to form itself. But there it was no longer the isolated shrub nor the modest thicket of low brushwood. It was the immense forest, the great mineral vegetations, the enormous petrified trees, united by garlands of elegant plumarias, sea-bindweed, all decked off with colours and shades. We passed freely under their high branches lost in the depths of the water above, whilst, at our feet the tubipores, meandrines, stars, fungi, and caryophyllidæ formed a carpet of flowers strewed with dazzling gems.

In the meantime Captain Nemo had stopped. My companions and I imitated him, and turning round, I saw that his men had formed a semi-circle round their chief. Looking with more attention, I noticed that four of them were carrying an object of oblong form on their shoulders.

We were then in the centre of a vast open space surrounded by high arborisations of the submarine forest. Our lamps lighted up the space with a sort of twilight which immoderately lengthened the shadows on the ground. At the limit of the open space darkness again became profound, and was only "made visible" by little sparks reflected in the projections of the coral.

Ned Land and Conseil were near me. We looked on, and the thought that I was going to assist at a strange scene came into my mind. As I looked at the ground I saw that it was raised in certain places by slight excrescences encrusted with calcareous deposits, and laid out with a regularity that betrayed the hand of man.

In the centre of the open space, on a pedestal of rocks roughly piled together, rose a coral cross, which extended its long arms that one might have said were made of petrified blood.

Upon a sign from Captain Nemo one of his men came forward, and at some feet distance from the cross began to dig a hole with a pickaxe that he took from his belt.

I then understood it all! This space was a cemetery; this hole a grave; this oblong object the body of the man who had died during the night! Captain Nemo and his men came to inter their companion in this common resting-place in the depths of the inaccessible ocean!

My mind was never so much excited before. More impressionable ideas had never invaded my brain! I would not see what my eyes were looking at!

In the meantime the tomb was being slowly dug. Fish fled hither and thither as their retreat was troubled. I heard on the calcareous soil the ring of the iron pickaxe that sparkled when it struck some flint lost at the bottom of the sea. The hole grew larger and wider, and was soon deep enough to receive the body.

Then the bearers approached. The body, wrapped in a tissue of white byssus, was lowered into its watery tomb. Captain Nemo, with his arms crossed on his chest, and all the friends of the man who had loved them, knelt in the attitude of prayer. My two companions and I bent religiously.

The tomb was then filled with the matter dug from the soil, and formed a slight excrescence.

When this was done Captain Nemo and his men rose; then collecting round the tomb, all knelt again, and extended their hands in sign of supreme adieu.

Then the funeral procession set out for the *Nautilus* again, repassing under the arcades of the forest, amidst the thickets by the side of the coral bushes, going uphill all the way.

At last the lights on board appeared. Their luminous track guided us to the *Nautilus*. We were back at one o'clock.

As soon as I had changed my clothes I went up on to the platform, and, a prey to a terrible conflict of emotions, I went and seated myself near the lantern cage.

Captain Nemo joined me there. I rose and said:

"Then, as I foresaw, that man died in the night?"

"Yes, M. Aronnax," answered Captain Nemo.

"And now he is resting by the side of his companions in the coral cemetery?"

"Yes, forgotten by everyone but us! We dig the grave, and the polypi take the trouble of sealing our dead therein for eternity?"

And hiding his face in his hands with a brusque gesture, the captain tried in vain to suppress a sob. Then he added:

"That is our peaceful cemetery, at some hundreds of feet below the surface of the waves!"

"Your dead sleep, at least, tranquil, Captain, out of reach of the sharks!"

"Yes, sir," answered Captain Nemo gravely, "of sharks and men!"

CHAPTER TWENTY-FIVE

THE INDIAN OCEAN

WHEN THE *Nautilus* was prepared to continue her submarine journey, I went down to the saloon. The panels were closed, and our course was directly west.

We were ploughing then through the waves of the Indian Ocean, a vast liquid plain of 1,200,000,000 acres' extent, the waters of which are so transparent that they make anyone looking into their depths quite giddy. The *Nautilus* generally floated in a depth of between a hundred and two hundred fathoms. We went on thus for several days. To any other than myself, who had a great love for the sea, the hours would have seemed long and monotonous; but my daily walks upon the platform, when I acquired new strength in the reviving air of the ocean, the sight of these rich waters through the window of the saloon, reading, and the compiling of my memoirs, took up all my time, and did not leave me an idle or weary moment.

The health of all on board kept in a very satisfactory state. The fare on board suited us perfectly, and, for my own part, I could have dispensed with the variations which Ned Land, through spirit of protestation, was ingenious in making to it. More, in so constant a temperature there were no colds to fear; besides, the madrepore *Dendrophyllæ*, known in Provence as "sea-samphire," and of which there existed a reserve on board, would have furnished with the dissolving flesh of its polypi an excellent remedy for coughs.

From the 21st to the 23rd of January the *Nautilus* went at the rate of 250 leagues in 24 hours, or 22 miles an hour. Many different varieties of fish, attracted by the electric light, tried to accompany us; the greater number, distanced by our speed, remained behind. Some of them, however, kept their place for a certain time in the waters of the *Nautilus*.

On the morning of the 24th we sighted Keeling Island, a madrepore formation, planted with magnificent cocoas. The *Nautilus* kept along the shores of this desert island for some little distance.

From Keeling Island our progress became slower, our route more varied, and we often went to great depths. Inclined planes, which were placed by levers obliquely to the water-line, were made use of several times. We went thus about two miles, but without ever ascertaining the greatest depths of the Indian Ocean, the bottom of which has never been reached even by soundings of seven thousand fathoms. As to the temperature in the deepest waters, the thermometer invariably indicated 4° above zero. I observed that the water is always colder on the higher than on the lower levels of the sea.

On the 25th of January, the ocean being entirely deserted, the *Nautilus* passed the day on the surface, beating the waves with her powerful screw and making them rebound to a great height. In these conditions how much the *Nautilus* must have looked like a gigantic cetacean; I passed three-quarters of this day upon the platform. I looked at the sea. Nothing to be seen on the horizon till, about four o'clock, a steamer appeared, going westward. Her masts were visible for an instant, but she could not see the *Nautilus*, as she was too low in the water.

The next day we cut the Equator at the eighty-second meridian and entered into the northern hemisphere.

During this day a formidable shoal of sharks accompanied us—terrible creatures which swarm in these seas and make them very dangerous.

These were "cestracio philippi"—sharks with brown backs

and whitish bellies, armed with eleven rows of teeth, and having their necks marked with a great black spot surrounded with white, which look like an eye. There were some sharks with rounded muzzles and marked with dark spots. These powerful animals often dashed themselves against the windows of the saloon with an amount of violence that made us tremble. At such times Ned Land was no longer master of himself. He was impatient to go to the surface of the water and harpoon these monsters, especially some that had their jaws studded with teeth like a mosaic; and large tiger-sharks, about six yards long, which provoked him particularly. But soon the *Nautilus* increased her speed, and quickly left behind the most rapid of these monsters.

On the 27th of January, at the entrance of the vast bay of Bengal, we frequently met with a horrible spectacle—dead bodies which floated on the surface of the water! These were the dead of the Indian villages, drifted by the Ganges to the open sea, and which the vultures, the only undertakers of the country, had not yet been able to devour. But the sharks did not fail to help them in their horrible task.

CHAPTER TWENTY-SIX

A FRESH PROPOSITION OF CAPTAIN NEMO'S

WHEN THE *Nautilus* returned at noon on the 28th of February to the surface of the sea in 9° 4′ north latitude, we could see land about eight miles to westward. The first thing I saw was a group of mountains about 2000 feet high, the forms of which were very peculiar. I found when the bearings had been taken that we were near the Island of Ceylon, that pearl which hangs from the ear of the Indian peninsula.

I went to look in the library for a book giving an account of this island, one of the most fertile on the globe. At this moment Captain Nemo and the mate appeared. The captain glanced at the map, then turned towards me.

"The Island of Ceylon," said he, "is very celebrated for its pearl fisheries. Would you like to see one of them, M. Aronnax?"

"I should, indeed, Captain."

"Well, that will be easy enough. Only if we see the fisheries we shall not see the fishermen. The annual working of the pearl fisheries has not yet begun. But that does not matter. I will give orders to make for the Gulf of Manaar, where we shall arrive during the night."

The captain said a few words to his first officer, who went out immediately. The *Nautilus* soon returned to her liquid element, and the manometer indicated that we were at a depth of thirty feet.

"Professor," then said Captain Nemo, "there are pearl fisheries in the Bay of Bengal, in the Indian Ocean, in the seas of China and Japan, in the Bay of Panama and the Gulf of California, but nowhere are such results obtained as at Ceylon. We shall arrive a little too soon, no doubt. The divers do not assemble till March in the Gulf of Manaar, and there for thirty days they give themselves up to this lucrative employment. There are about three hundred boats, and each boat has ten rowers and ten divers. These divers, divided into two groups, plunge into the sea alternately, diving to a depth of about thirteen yards by means of a heavy stone, which they hold between their feet, and a cord fastened to the boat."

"Then," said I, "the primitive method is still in use?"

"Yes," answered Captain Nemo, "although these fisheries belong to the most industrious nation in the world, to England."

"It seems to me, however, that a diving dress, such as you use, would be of great service in such an operation."

"Yes, for the unfortunate divers cannot remain long under water. The Englishman Percival, in his voyage to Ceylon, does speak of a Caffre who remained five minutes without rising to the surface, but I can hardly believe it. I know there are some divers who can stay under for fifty-seven seconds, and some as long as eighty-seven, but these cases are rare, and when the poor creatures return to the boats they bleed from ears and nose. I believe the usual time that divers can stay under is thirty seconds, and during this time they hasten to fill a small bag with the pearl oysters. These divers do not live to be old; their sight becomes weakened, and their eyes ulcerated; sores break out on their bodies, and very frequently they are seized with apoplexy at the bottom of the sea."

"Ah," said I, "it is a miserable occupation, and only serves for the gratification of vanity and caprice. But tell me, Captain, what quantity of oysters can one boat take in a day?"

"From about forty to fifty thousand. They even say that in 1814 the English Government, fishing on its own account, its divers in twenty days' work brought up seventy-six millions of oysters."

"But at least these divers are sufficiently remunerated?" I asked.

"Scarcely, Professor. At Panama they only earn one dollar a week. And they oftener only earn one sol for each oyster that contains a pearl, and how many they bring up that contain none!"

"One sol only to the poor fellows who enrich their masters! It is odious!"

"Thus, then, Professor," added the captain, "you and your companions shall see the oyster bank of Manaar, and if by chance some early diver should be found there, we shall see him at work."

"Agreed, Captain."

"But, M. Aronnax, you are not afraid of sharks?"

"I confess, Captain, that I am not yet quite at home with that kind of fish."

"We are used to them," answered Captain Nemo, "and in time you will be so also. However, we shall be armed, and on the road we may have a shark-hunt. So good-bye till to-morrow, sir, and early in the morning."

This said in a careless tone, Captain Nemo left the saloon.

"I must reflect and take time," I said to myself. "To hunt otters in submarine forests, as we did in the forests of Crespo Island, is one thing, but to walk along the bottom of the sea when you are pretty sure of meeting with sharks is another! I am aware that in certain countries, especially in the Andaman Islands, the negroes do not hesitate to attack them with a dagger in one hand and a noose in the other, but I know, too, that many who affront these creatures do not return alive. Besides, I am not a negro, and if I were a negro I think a slight hesitation on my part would not be out of place."

CHAPTER TWENTY-SEVEN

A PEARL WORTH TEN MILLIONS

NIGHT CAME. I went to bed and slept badly. Sharks played an important part in my dreams, and I found the etymology both just and unjust that made *requin*, the French for shark, come from the word "requiem."

The next day, at 4 a.m., I was awakened by the steward, whom Captain Nemo had specially placed at my service. I rose rapidly, dressed, and went into the saloon. Captain Nemo was waiting for me there.

"Are you ready to start, M. Aronnax?"

"I am ready."

"Then follow me, please."

"And my companions, Captain?"

"They are waiting for us."

"Are we to put on our diving dresses?"

"Not yet. I have not allowed the *Nautilus* to come too near this coast, and we are still some way off Manaar Bank but I have ordered the boat to be got ready, and it will take us to the exact point for landing, which will save us a rather long journey. It will have on board our diving dresses, and we shall put them on as soon as our submarine exploration begins."

Captain Nemo accompanied me to the central staircase, which led to the platform. Ned and Conseil were there, delighted at the notion of the pleasure party which was being prepared. Five sailors from the *Nautilus*, oars in hand, awaited us in the boat, which had been made fast against the side.

The night was yet dark. Heavy clouds covered the sky, and scarcely allowed a star to be seen. I looked towards the land, but saw nothing but a faint line enclosing three-quarters of the horizon from south-west to north-west. The *Nautilus* having moved up the western coast of Ceylon during the night, was now on the west of the bay, or rather gulf, formed by the land and the Island of Mannar.

There under the dark waters stretched the oyster-bank, an inexhaustible field of pearls, the length of which is more than twenty miles.

Captain Nemo, Conseil, Ned Land and I took our places in the stern of the boat, and we moved off.

About half-past five the first streaks of daylight showed more clearly the upper line of the coast. Flat enough in the east, it rose a little towards the south. Five miles still separated us from it, and the shore was indistinct, owing to the mist on the water. There was not a boat or a diver to be seen. It was evident, as Captain Nemo had warned me, that we had come a month too soon.

At 6 a.m. it became daylight suddenly, with that rapidity peculiar to the tropical regions, which have neither dawn nor twilight. I saw the land distinctly, with a few trees scattered here and there. The boat neared Manaar Island; Captain Nemo rose from his seat and watched the sea.

At a sign from him the anchor was dropped, but it had but a little distance to fall, for it was scarcely more than a yard to the bottom, and this was one of the highest points of the oyster-bank.

"Now, M. Aronnax," said Captain Nemo, "here we are. In a month numerous boats will be assembled here, and these are the waters that the divers explore so boldly. This bay is well placed for the purpose; it is sheltered from the high winds, the sea is never very rough here which is highly favourable for divers' work. We will now put on our diving dresses and begin our investigations."

Aided by the sailors, I began to put on my heavy dress. Captain Nemo and my two companions also dressed themselves. None of the sailors from the *Nautilus* were to accompany us.

"Our weapons?" I asked, "our guns?"

"Guns! What for? Do not the mountaineers attack the bear dagger in hand, and is not steel surer than lead? Here is a stout blade; put it in your belt, and we will start."

I looked at my companions. They were armed like us, and more than this, Ned Land brandished an enormous harpoon which he had put into the boat before leaving the *Nautilus*.

Then, following the example of the captain, I let them put on my heavy copper helmet, and the air reservoirs were at once put in activity. Directly afterwards we were landed in about five feet of water upon a firm sand. Captain Nemo gave us a sign with his hand. We followed him, and going down a gentle slope, we disappeared under the waves.

There the ideas which had previously disturbed me left me. I became astonishingly calm. The ease of my movements increased my confidence, and the strangeness of the sight captivated my imagination.

The sun already sent a sufficient light under the water. The least object could be distinctly seen. After ten minutes' walk we were about sixteen feet under water, and the ground became nearly level.

About seven o'clock we were at last on the bank of pintadines, where the pearl oysters breed by millions. These precious molluscs adhered to the rocks, strongly fastened to them by brown-coloured byssus that prevents them moving.

In that these oysters are inferior to mussels for Nature has not refused to them all faculty of locomotion.

But we could not stop. We were obliged to follow the captain, who appeared to choose paths known only to himself. The ground rose sensibly, and sometimes, when I raised my arm, it was above the surface of the sea. Then the level of the bank sank capriciously. Sometimes we rounded high rocks in the form of pyramids. In their dark fractures immense crustacea, reared up on their high paws like some war-machine, looked at us with fixed eyes, and under our feet crawled annelides and other curious creatures.

At this moment there opened before us a vast grotto, hollowed in a picturesque cluster of rocks, and carpeted with seaweed. At first this grotto appeared very dark to me. The solar rays seemed to die out there in successive gradations. The clear light became drowned light.

Captain Nemo entered. We followed him. My eyes soon became accustomed to the relative darkness. I saw the springing of the vault so capriciously distorted, supported by natural pillars, widely seated on their granitic bases, like the heavy columns of Tuscan architecture. Why did our incomprehensible guide lead us into the depths of this submarine crypt? I should soon know.

After descending a rather steep incline we were at the bottom of a sort of circular well. There Captain Nemo stopped and pointed to an object we had not perceived before.

It was an oyster of extraordinary dimensions, a gigantic tridacne, a font that would have contained a lake of holy water, a vase more than two yards across, and consequently larger than the one in the saloon of the *Nautilus*.

I approached this unparalleled mollusc. It was adhering by its byssus to a granite slab, and there it was developing itself in isolation amidst the calm waters of the grotto. I estimated the weight of this tridacne at 600 lbs. Now such an oyster contains 30 lbs. of meat, and it would take the stomach of a Gargantua to absorb some dozens.

Captain Nemo evidently knew of the existence of this

bivalve. It was not the first visit he had paid to it, and I thought that in conducting us to that place he merely wished to show us a natural curiosity. I was mistaken. Captain Nemo had an interest in seeing the actual condition of this tridacne.

The two valves of the mollusc were half open. The captain went up to them and put his dagger between them to prevent them shutting, then with his hand he raised the membranous tunic, fringed at the border, that formed the animal's mantle.

There, amidst its foliated pleats, I saw a pearl as large as a coconut. Its globular form, perfect limpidity, and admirable water made it a jewel of inestimable price. Carried away by curiosity, I stretched out my hand to take it, weigh it, feel it. But the captain stopped me, made a sign in the negative, and drawing back his dagger by a rapid movement, he let the two valves fall together.

I then understood the purpose of Captain Nemo. By leaving this pearl wrapped up in the mantle of the tridacne he allowed it to grow insensibly. With each year the secretion of the mollusc added fresh concentric layers to it. The captain alone knew of this grotto where this admirable fruit of Nature was ripening; he alone was raising it, thus to speak, in order one day to transport it to his precious museum. Perhaps even, following the example of the Chinese and Indians, he had determined the production of this pearl by introducing under the folds of the mollusc some piece of glass and metal which was gradually being covered with the pearly matter. In any case, comparing this pearl with those I already knew, and those that shone in the captain's collection, I estimated its value at ten millions of francs at least. It was a superb natural curiosity, and not a jewel *de luxe*, for I do not know what feminine ears could have supported it.

The visit to the opulent tridacne was over. Captain Nemo left the grotto, and we went up on to the bank of pintadines again, amidst the clear waters that were not yet troubled by the work of the divers.

We walked separately, stopping or going on according to our pleasure. For my own part I had forgotten the dangers that my imagination had so ridiculously exaggerated. The bottom of the sea sensibly approached its surface, and soon my head passed above the oceanic level. Conseil joined me, and placing his glass plate next to mine, gave me a friendly salutation with his eyes. But this elevated plateau was only some yards long, and we were soon back again in our own element. I think I have now the right of calling it thus.

Ten minutes afterwards Captain Nemo suddenly stopped. I thought he was making a halt before going back. But no; with a gesture he ordered us to squat down near him on a large confractuosity. He was pointing to a point of the liquid mass, and I looked attentively.

At five yards from me a shade appeared and bent to the ground. The uneasy idea of sharks came into my mind. But I was mistaken, and this time we had not to do with any oceanic monster. It was a man, a living man, a black Indian, a diver, a poor fellow, no doubt, come to glean before the harvest. I perceived the bottom of his canoe anchored at some feet above his head. He plunged and went up again successively. A stone cut in the form of a sugar-loaf which he had tied to his foot, whilst a cord fastened him to the boat, made him descend more rapidly to the bottom. That was all his stock-in-trade. Arrived on the ground by about three fathoms' depth he threw himself on his knees and filled his bag with pintadines picked up at random. Then he went up again, emptied his bag, put on his stone again, and recommenced the operation that only lasted thirty seconds.

The diver did not see us. The shadow of the rock hid us from him. And, besides, how could a poor Indian ever suppose that men, beings like him, were there under the water, watching his movements, and losing no detail of his work?

He went up and plunged again several times. He did not bring up more than ten pintadines at each plunge, for he was obliged to tear them from the bank to which they were fastened by their strong byssus. And how many of these oysters for which he risked his life were destitute of pearls!

I watched him with profound attention. His work was done regularly, and for half an hour no danger seemed to threaten him. I was, therefore, getting familiar with the spectacle of this interesting fishery when all at once, at the moment when the Indian was kneeling on the ground, I saw him make a movement of terror, get up, and spring to remount to the surface of the waves.

I understood this fear. A gigantic shadow appeared above the unfortunate plunger. It was an enormous shark advancing diagonally, with eyes on fire and open jaws. I was mute with terror, incapable of making a movement.

The voracious animal, with a vigorous stroke of his fin, was springing towards the Indian, who threw himself on one side and avoided the bite of the shark, but not the stroke of his tail, for that tail, striking him on the chest, stretched him on the ground.

This scene had hardly lasted some seconds. The shark returned to the charge, and turning on his back, it was prepared to cut the Indian in two, when I felt Captain Nemo, who was near me, suddenly rise. Then, his dagger in hand, he walked straight up to the monster, ready for a hand-to-hand struggle with him.

The shark, at the moment he was going to nab the unfortunate diver, perceived his fresh adversary, and going over on to its stomach again, directed itself rapidly towards him.

I still see the attitude of Captain Nemo. Thrown backwards, he was waiting with admirable *sang-froid* the formidable shark; when it threw itself upon him he threw himself on one side with prodigious agility, avoided the shock, and thrust his dagger into its stomach. But that was not the end. A terrible combat took place.

The shark reddened, thus to speak. The blood flowed in streams from its wounds. The sea was dyed red, and across this opaque liquid I saw no more until it cleared a little, and I perceived the audacious captain holding on to one of the animal's fins, struggling hand-to-hand with the monster, belabouring its body with dagger thrusts without being able to reach the heart, where blows are mortal. The shark in the struggle made such a commotion in the water that the eddies threatened to overthrow me.

I wanted to run to the captain's aid. But, nailed down by horror, I could not move.

I looked on with haggard eyes. I saw the phases of the struggle change. The captain fell on the ground, over-thrown by the enormous mass that was bearing him down. Then the jaws of the shark opened inordinately, and all would have been over for the captain, if, prompt as thought, harpoon in hand, Ned Land, rushing towards the shark, had not struck it with its terrible point. The waves became impregnated with a mass of blood. They were agitated by the movements of the shark that beat them with indescrib-able fury. Ned Land had not missed his aim. It was the death-rattle of the monster. Struck in the heart it struggled in fearful spasms, the rebound of which knocked over Conseil.

In the meantime Ned Land had set free the captain, who rose unhurt, went straight to the Indian, quickly cut the cord which fastened him to the stone, took him in his arms, and with a vigorous kick, he went up to the surface of the sea. We all three followed him, and in a short time, miracu-lously saved, we reached the diver's boat.

Captain Nemo's first care was to recall the unfortunate man to life. I did not know if he would succeed. I hoped so, for the immersion of the poor fellow had not been long. But the blow from the shark's tail might have killed him. Happily, under the vigorous friction of Conseil and the captain, I saw the drowned man gradually recover his senses. He opened his eyes. What must have been his surprise, terror even, at seeing four large brass heads leaning over him! And, above all, what must he have thought, when Captain Nemo, drawing from a pocket in his garment a bag of pearls, put it into his hand! This magnificent gift from the man of the sea to the poor Indian of Ceylon was accepted by him with a trembling hand. His frightened eyes showed that he did not know to what superhuman beings he owed at the same time his fortune and his life.

At a sign from the captain we went back to the bank of pintadines, and following the road we had already come along, half an hour's walking brought us to the anchor that fastened the boat of the *Nautilus* to the ground.

Once embarked, we each, with the help of the sailors, took off our heavy brass carapaces.

Captain Nemo's first word was for the Canadian.

"Thank you, Land," he said.

"It was by way of retaliation, Captain," answered Ned Land. "I owed it you."

A pale smile glided over the captain's lips, and that was all.

"To the *Nautilus*," he said.

At half-past eight we were back on the *Nautilus*.

Then I began to reflect on the incidents of our excursion to the Manaar Bank. Two observations naturally resulted from it. One was upon the unparalleled audacity of Captain Nemo, the other was his devoting his own life to saving a human being, one of the representatives of that race he was flying from under the seas. Whatever he might say, that man had not succeeded in entirely killing his own heart.

When I said as much to him, he answered me in a slightly moved tone:

"That Indian, Professor, is an inhabitant of an oppressed country, and I am, and until my last breath shall be, the same."

CHAPTER TWENTY-EIGHT

THE RED SEA

DURING THE day the Island of Ceylon disappeared upon the horizon, and the *Nautilus*, at a speed of twenty miles an hour, glided amongst that labyrinth of canals that separate the Maldives from the Laccadives.

The next day—the 30th of January—when the *Nautilus* went up to the surface of the ocean, there was no longer any land in sight. It was going NNW., and directing its course towards that Sea of Oman, situated between Arabia and the Indian peninsula, into which the Persian Gulf flows.

For four days, until the 3rd of February, the *Nautilus* was in the Gulf of Oman, at different depths and various speeds. It seemed to move about at random, as if hesitating upon what route to follow, but it never crossed the tropic of Cancer.

Upon leaving this sea we saw for an instant Muscat, the most important town of the country of Oman. I admired its strange aspect in the midst of the black rocks that surround it, and that show up its white houses and fortresses. I perceived the round domes of its mosques, the elegant point of its minarets, its fresh and verdant terraces. But it was only a vision, and the *Nautilus* soon sank under the sombre waves of its shores.

Then it coasted, at a distance of six miles, the Arabic coasts of Mahrah and Hadramaut, and its undulating line of mountains, relieved by ancient ruins. On the 5th of February we at last entered the Gulf of Aden, a veritable funnel put into the bottle neck of Bab-el-Mandeb, which pours the Indian waters into the Red Sea.

On the 6th of February the *Nautilus* was floating in sight of Aden, perched on a promontory which a narrow isthmus joins to the continent, a sort of inaccessible Gibraltar that the English fortified afresh after taking it in 1839. I caught sight of the rich octagon minarets of that town, which was formerly the richest and most commercial place on the coast, if we are to believe the historian Edrisi.

The next day, the 7th of February, we entered the Straits of Babel-Mandeb, the name of which means "Gate of Tears" in Arabic. It is twenty miles wide, and only thirty long, and for the *Nautilus*, at full speed, it was hardly the business of an hour. But I saw nothing, not even the Island of Perim, with which the British Government has fortified the position of Aden. Too many English or French steamers of the lines between Suez and Bombay, Calcutta, Melbourne, Bourbon, Mauritius, ploughed the narrow passage for the *Nautilus* to venture to show itself. So it kept prudently at a good depth. At last, at noon, we were ploughing the waves of the Red Sea.

I would not even seek to understand the caprice of Captain Nemo that took us into this gulf. But I unfeignedly approved of the *Nautilus* entering it. It went at an average speed, sometimes keeping on the surface, sometimes plunging to avoid some ship. I could thus observe the inside and outside of this curious sea.

On the 8th of February, at early dawn, Mocha appeared, a town now in ruins, the walls of which fall even at the noise of cannon, and which shelter here and there verdant date-trees. It was formerly an important city, enclosing six public markets, 26 mosques, and to which its walls, defended by 14 forts, made a belt of 3 kilometres.

On the 9th of February the *Nautilus* was floating in that wide part of the Red Sea that is comprised between Suakin on the West Coast and Guonfodah on the East Coast, on a diameter of one hundred and ninety miles.

That day, at noon, after the position was taken, Captain Nemo came up on to the platform where I happened to be, I promised myself not to let him go down again without having at least made an attempt to ascertain his ulterior projects. He came to me as soon as he saw me, gracefully offered me a cigar, and said:

"The day after to-morrow we shall be in the Mediter-ranean."

"In the Mediterranean?" I cried.

"Yes, Professor. Does that astonish you?"

"What astonishes me is that we shall be there the day after to-morrow."

"Really?"

"Yes, Captain, although I ought to be accustomed to being astonished at nothing on board your vessel."

"But why are you surprised now?"

"At the frightful speed your *Nautilus* must reach to find itself to-morrow in full Mediterranean, having made the tour of Africa and doubled the Cape of Good Hope."

"And who told you it would make the tour of Africa, Professor? Who spoke of doubling the Cape of Good Hope?"

"Unless the *Nautilus* can move along *terra firma* and passes over the isthmus——"

"Or underneath, M. Aronnax."

"Underneath?"

"Certainly," answered Captain Nemo tranquilly. "It is a long time since Nature has done under that tongue of land what men are now doing on its surface."

"What! There exists a passage!"

"Yes, a subterranean passage that I have named Abraham Tunnel. It begins above Suez and ends in the Gulf of Pelusium."

"But the isthmus is only formed of moving sand."

"To a certain depth. But at a depth of fifty yards only there is a stratum of rock."

"And did you discover that passage by accident?" I asked, more and more surprised.

"By accident and reasoning, Professor, and by reasoning more than by accident."

"Captain, I hear you, but my ear resists what it hears."

"Ah, sir! *Aures habent et non audient* belongs to all time. Not only does this passage exist, but I have passed by it several times. But for that I should not have adventured to-day into the impassable Red Sea."

"Would it be indiscreet to ask you how you discovered this tunnel?"

"Sir," answered the captain, "there can be no secret between people who are never to leave each other again."

I paid no attention to the insinuation, and awaited Captain's Nemo's communication.

"Professor," said he, "it was a naturalist's reasoning that led me to discover this passage, which I alone know about.

I had noticed that in the Red Sea and the Mediterranean there existed a certain number of fish of absolutely identical species—ophidia, fiatoles, girelles, exocœti. Certain of this fact, I asked myself if there existed no communication between the two seas. If one did exist, the subterranean current must necessarily flow from the Red Sea to the Mediterranean on account of the different levels. I therefore took a great number of fish in the neighbourhood of Suez. I put a brass ring on their tails, and threw them back into the sea. A few months later, on the coast of Syria, I again took some specimens of my fish with their tell-tale ornaments. The communication between the two seas was then demonstrated. I looked for it with my *Nautilus*, discovered it, ventured into it, and before long, Professor, you too will have been through my Arabic tunnel."

CHAPTER TWENTY-NINE

THE ARABIAN TUNNEL

THE NEXT day, the 10th of February, several ships appeared to windward. The *Nautilus* went on with her submarine navigation; but at noon, when her bearings were taken, the sea being deserted, she went up to the sea-level.

Accompanied by Ned and Conseil, I went to sit down on the platform. The coast on the east was outlined in a damp fog.

Leaning on the sides of the vessel, we were talking about various things, when Ned Land, pointing towards a point in the sea, said:

"Do you see anything there, Professor?"

"No, Ned," I replied; "but my eyes are not yours, you know."

"Look well," said Land, "over there on the starboard beam, about the height of the lantern. Don't you see a mass that moves?"

"Yes," said I, after an attentive examination. "I perceive a long black body on the surface of the water."

"Another *Nautilus*?" said Conseil.

The long black object was soon not a mile from us. It looked like a great rock deposited in the open sea. What was it? I could not yet determine.

"Ah, it is moving! It plunges!" cried Ned Land. "What animal can it be? It has not even a forked tail like whales or cachalots, and its fins look like stumps."

"Then——" I began.

"It is on its back now," resumed the Canadian, "and it raises its udders in the air!"

"It's a syren," cried Conseil, "a veritable syren!"

The name of syren set me on its track, and I understood that this animal belonged to the order of marine animals of which fable has made syrens—half women, half fishes.

"No," said I to Conseil, "it is not a syren, but a curious animal of which there only remain a few specimens in the Red Sea. It is a dugong."

In the meantime Ned Land was still looking. His eyes shone covetously at the sight of this animal. His hand seemed ready to harpoon it. Anyone would have thought he was awaiting the moment to throw himself into the sea to attack it in its own element.

"Oh, sir!" he said in a voice trembling with emotion, "I have never killed any of ' that.'"

All the harpooner was in that word.

At that instant Captain Nemo appeared on the platform. He perceived the dugong, understood the Canadian's attitude and said to him:

"If you held a harpoon, Mr. Land, would it not burn your hand?"

"That it would!"

"And you would not be sorry to take up your old trade again for one day, and add that cetacean to the list of those you have already struck?"

"No, I shouldn't be sorry."

"Well, you may try."

"Thank you, sir," answered Ned Land, with eyes aflame.

"Only," continued the captain, "I advise you, in your own interest, not to miss that animal."

"Is the dugong dangerous to attack?" I asked, in spite of the Canadian's contemptuous shrug.

"Yes, sometimes," answered the captain. "That animal turns on its assailants and wrecks their boats. But for Ned Land that danger is not to be feared. His glance is prompt, his hand sure. If I recommend him not to miss the dugong it is because it is justly considered fine game, and I know that Ned Land likes good meat."

"Ah!" said the Canadian, "so that animal gives himself the luxury of being good to eat?"

"Yes, Mr. Land. Its flesh, a veritable meat, is much esteemed, and in all Malasia it is kept for princes' tables. This animal is so much hunted, that, like the lamantin, or sea-cow, it becomes more and more rare."

"Then, sir captain," said Conseil seriously, "if this one should be the last of its race, ought it not, in the interest of science, to be spared?"

"Perhaps," replied the Canadian; "but in the interest of our table it is better to pursue it."

"Do it, then, Mr. Land," answered Captain Nemo.

At that moment seven of the crew, mute and impassible as usual, came upon the platform. One was carrying a harpoon and a line similar to those employed by whale-fishers. The deck was taken off the boat, which was lifted from its niche and thrown into the sea. Six rowers took their places on the seats, and the coxswain at the helm. Ned, Conseil, and I seated ourselves aft.

"Are you not coming, Captain?" I asked.

"No, sir, but I wish you much success."

The boat, rowed vigorously, went rapidly towards the dugong, which was then floating about two miles from the *Nautilus*.

When it arrived within a few cables' length of the cetacean it slackened speed, and the oars dipped noiselessly into the tranquil waters. Ned Land, harpoon in hand, went and stood at the prow. The whale-harpoon is generally fastened to a very long cord that rapidly unwinds as the wounded animal drags it away. But here the cord was not more than ten cables long, and its extremity only fastened to a little barrel to float on the surface and indicate the course of the dugong under water.

I rose and distinctly observed the Canadian's adversary. The dugong was very much like a lamantin. Its oblong body terminated in a much-elongated tail, and its lateral fins by veritable claws. The difference between it and the lamantin was that its upper jaw was armed with two long and pointed teeth that formed divergent defences on either side.

The dugong that Ned Land was preparing to attack was of colossal dimensions, not less than eight yards long. It was not moving, and seemed to be sleeping on the surface of the water, a circumstance that made its capture easier.

The boat prudently approached to within three cables' length of the animal. The oars remained suspended on their rowlocks. I half rose. Ned Land, his body thrown slightly backward, brandished his harpoon in his experienced hand.

Suddenly a hissing sound was heard, and the dugong disappeared. The harpoon, launched with force, had doubtless only struck the water.

"The devil!" cried the Canadian in a rage. "I have missed it!"

"No," I said, "the animal is wounded; there is its blood, but your instrument did not remain in its body."

"My harpoon! My harpoon!" cried Ned Land.

The sailors rowed vigorously, and the coxswain guided the boat towards the floating barrel. When the harpoon was fished up again the boat began to pursue the animal.

The dugong came up to the surface of the sea to breathe from time to time. Its wound had not weakened it, for it moved along with extreme rapidity. The boat, rowed by vigorous arms, flew on its track. Several times it approached to within a few cables, and the Canadian made ready to strike; but the dugong escaped by a rapid plunge, and it was impossible to reach it.

Ned Land's anger may be imagined. He launched the most energetic oaths in the English language at the animal.

They pursued it thus without ceasing for an hour, and I was beginning to believe that it would be very difficult to catch it, when the animal was taken with an unfortunate idea of vengeance that it was destined to repent. He turned upon the boat to assail it in return.

This manœuvre did not escape the Canadian.

"Attention!" said he.

The coxswain pronounced several words in his strange language, and he was doubtless warning his men to keep on their guard.

The dugong stopped within twenty feet of the boat, roughly took in air with his vast nostrils, situated, not at the extremity, but at the upper part of its snout; then, taking a spring, he rushed upon us.

The boat could not avoid the shock; half overturned, it embarked one or two tons of water we were obliged to empty; but thanks to the skill of the coxswain, it righted itself. Ned Land, clinging to the bows, belaboured the gigantic animal with blows from his harpoon; the creature's teeth were buried in the gunwale, and it lifted the whole thing out of the water like a lion can a roebuck. We were thrown over one another, and I hardly know how the adventure would have ended had not the Canadian still enraged with the beast, at last struck it in the heart. I heard its teeth grind on the iron plate, and the dugong disappeared dragging the harpoon with it. But the barrel soon returned to the surface, and a few instants afterwards the body of the animal appeared, turned over on its back. The boat went up to it, took it in tow, and rowed towards the *Nautilus*.

They were obliged to use tackle of enormous strength to hoist up the dugong on to the platform. It weighed 10,000 lbs. They cut it up under the eyes of the Canadian, who wanted to follow all the details of the operation. The same day the steward served me at dinner with some slices of the flesh skilfully prepared by the ship's cook. I thought it excellent, superior to veal, if not to beef.

About 5 p.m. we sighted the Cape of Ras-Mohammed. It is the cape that forms the extremity of Arabia Petræa, lying between the Gulf of Suez and the Gulf of Acabah. The *Nautilus* entered the Straits of Jubal, that lead to the Gulf of Suez. I distinctly perceived a high mountain between the two gulfs. It was Mount Horeb, the Sinai at the top of which Moses saw God face to face, and which the mind pictures as incessantly crowned with lightning.

At 6 p.m. the *Nautilus*, sometimes floating, sometimes submerged, passed by Tor, seated on a bay, the waters of which seemed of a reddish tint, as Captain Nemo had said. Then night fell in the midst of a deep silence, sometimes broken by the cries of the pelican and other night birds, the noise of the waves beating on the rocks, or the far-off panting of some steamer beating the waters of the gulf with its noisy paddles.

From eight to nine o'clock the *Nautilus* kept at some yards below the water. According to my calculations we were very near Suez. Through the panels of the saloon I perceived the rocks lighted up by our electric light. It seemed to me that the passage grew gradually narrower.

At a quarter past nine the boat went up again to the surface, and I ascended to the platform. Impatient to go through the captain's tunnel, I could not keep still, and wanted to breathe the fresh air of night.

Soon, in the darkness, I perceived a pale light, half-discoloured by the mist, shining about a mile off.

"A lightship," said someone near me.

I turned and recognised the captain.

"It is the Suez lightship," he continued. "We shall not be long before we reach the orifice of the tunnel."

"It cannot be very easy to enter it."

"No. And I am in the habit of keeping in the helmsman's cage to direct the manœuvre myself. And now, if you will go down, M. Aronnax, the *Nautilus* will sink under the waves, and will not come up to the surface again till it has been through the Arabian tunnel."

I followed Captain Nemo. The panels were shut, the reservoirs of water filled, and the apparatus sank about thirty feet. As I was about to enter my room the captain stopped me.

"Professor," said he, "should you like to accompany me in the pilot's cage?"

"I dared not ask it of you," I answered.

"Come, then. You will thus see all that can be seen of that navigation at the same time subterrestrial and submarine."

Captain Nemo conducted me to the central staircase. About half-way up he opened a door, went along the upper waist, and arrived at the pilot's cage, which, my readers know, rose from one end of the platform.

It was a cabin, six feet square, something like those occupied by the helmsmen of the Mississippi or Hudson steamboats. In the midst was a wheel, vertically stationed, working into the truss of the helm that ran as far as the aft of the *Nautilus*. Four light ports made of lenticular glasses, were fixed in the sides of the cabin, and allowed the man at the helm to see in every direction.

This cabin was dark, but my eyes soon became accustomed to the obscurity, and I perceived the pilot, a vigorous man, whose hands were leaning on the fellies of the wheel. Outside the sea seemed brilliantly lighted up by the lantern that was shining behind the cabin at the other extremity of the platform.

"Now," said Captain Nemo, "we must seek our passage."

Electric wires put the helmsman's cage into communication with the engine-room, and from thence the captain could give simultaneously to his *Nautilus* both direction and movement. He pressed a metal knob, and immediately the speed of the screw was much diminished.

I watched in silence the high wall that we were moving along at that moment; it was the immovable foundation of the sand-bed on the coast. We followed it thus for an hour at some yards distance only. Captain Nemo did not look away from the compass, hung by two concentric circles in the midst of the cabin. At a sign the helmsman modified every instant the direction of the *Nautilus*.

I had placed myself at the triboard port-glass, and perceived magnificent substructures of coral, zoophytes, seawrack, and crustaceans waving their enormous claws that they passed out from the confractuosities of the rock.

At 10.15 p.m. Captain Nemo took the helm himself. A wide gallery, black and deep, opened before us. The *Nautilus* entered it boldly. An unaccustomed rumbling was heard along the sides. It was the waters of the Red Sea that the slope of the tunnel was precipitating into the Mediterranean. The *Nautilus* followed the torrent with the speed of an arrow, notwithstanding the efforts of the machine that, in order to resist it, beat the waves backwards.

On the narrow walls of the passage I saw nothing but brilliant lines, furrows of fire traced by the speed under the electric light. My heart beat wildly, and I pressed my hand to it to stay its palpitations.

At 10.35 p.m. Captain Nemo let go the helm, and, turning towards me:

"The Mediterranean!" said he.

In less than twenty minutes the *Nautilus*, carried along by the torrent, had cleared the Isthmus of Suez.

CHAPTER THIRTY

THE GRECIAN ARCHIPELAGO

THE NEXT day, the 12th of February, at daybreak, the *Nautilus* went up to the surface of the sea. I rushed up to the platform. At three miles to the south was the vague outline of Pelusium. A torrent had carried us from one sea to another. But the tunnel, so easy to descend, must be impossible to ascend.

About seven o'clock Ned and Conseil joined me. These two inseparable companions had slept tranquilly, thinking no more of the *Nautilus's* feat.

"Well, Mr. Naturalist," asked the Canadian in a slightly jeering tone, "what about the Mediterranean?"

"We are on its surface, friend Ned."

"What!" said Conseil, "last night——"

"Yes, last night itself, in a few minutes, we cleared the insuperable isthmus."

"I don't believe it," said the Canadian.

"And you are wrong, Land," I resumed. "The low coast rounding off towards the south is the Egyptian coast."

"You won't take me in," said the obstinate Canadian.

"But it must be true," said Conseil, "or monsieur would not say so."

"Besides, Ned, Captain Nemo did the honours of his tunnel, and I was near him in the helmsman's cage whilst he guided the *Nautilus* through the narrow passage himself."

"You hear, Ned?" said Conseil.

"And you who have such good eyes," I added—"you, Ned, can see the piers of Port Said stretching out into the sea."

The Canadian looked attentively.

"Yes," said he, "you are right, Professor, and your captain is a clever man. We are in the Mediterranean. Good. Well, now let us talk, if you please, about our own concerns, but so that no one can hear."

I saw very well what the Canadian was coming to. In any case I thought it better to talk about it, as he desired, and we all three went and sat down near the lantern house, where we were less exposed to be wet by the spray from the waves.

"Now, Ned, we are ready to hear you," said I. "What have you to tell us?"

"What I have to tell you is very simple," answered the Canadian. "We are in Europe, and before Captain Nemo's caprice drags us to the bottom of the Polar Seas, or takes us back to Oceania, I want to leave the *Nautilus*."

I must acknowledge that a discussion with the Canadian on the subject always embarrassed me.

I did not wish to trammel the liberty of my companions in any way, and yet I felt no desire to leave Captain Nemo. Thanks to him and his apparatus, I was each day completing my submarine studies, and I was writing my book on submarine depths again in the very midst of its element. Should I ever again meet with such an opportunity of observing the marvels of the ocean? No, certainly. I could not, therefore, reconcile myself to the idea of leaving the *Nautilus* before our cycle of investigations was accomplished.

"Friend Ned," I said, "answer me frankly. Are you dull here? Do you regret the destiny that has thrown you into the hands of Captain Nemo?"

The Canadian remained for some moments without answering. Then crossing his arms:

"Frankly," he said, "I do not regret this voyage under the seas. I shall be glad to have made it; but to have made it, it must come to an end. That is my opinion."

"It will come to an end, Ned."

"Where and when?"

"I do not know where, and I can't say when, or rather I suppose it will end when these seas have nothing further to teach us. All that begins has necessarily an end in this world."

"I think like monsieur," answered Conseil, "and it is quite possible that after going over all the seas of the globe Captain Nemo will give us our discharge."

"Our discharge! (*la volée*)," cried the Canadian. "A drubbing (*une volée*) you mean!"

"We must not exaggerate, Land," I resumed. "We have nothing to fear from the captain, but I am not of Conseil's opinion either. We are acquainted with the secrets of the *Nautilus*, and I have no hope that its commander, in order to set us at liberty, will resign himself to the idea of our taking them about the world with us."

"Then what do you hope?" asked the Canadian.

"That circumstances will happen of which we can and

ought to take advantage, as well in six months' time as now."

"Phew!" said Ned Land. "And where shall we be in six months, if you please, Mr. Naturalist?"

"Perhaps here, perhaps in China. You know that the *Nautilus* is a quick sailer. It crosses oceans like a swallow the air, or an express a continent. It does not fear frequented seas. How do we know that it will not rally round the coasts of France, England, or America, where we can attempt to escape as advantageously as here?"

"M. Aronnax," answered the Canadian, "your premises are bad. You speak in the future tense; 'We shall be there! We shall be here!' I speak in the present. 'We are here, and we must take advantage of it.'"

I was closely hemmed in by Ned Land's logic, and felt myself beaten on that ground. I no longer knew what arguments to use.

"Sir," Ned went on, "let us suppose, for the sake of argument, that Captain Nemo were to offer you your liberty to-day, should you accept it?"

"I do not know," I replied.

"And if he were to add that the offer he makes to-day he would not renew later on, should you accept?"

I did not answer.

"And what do you think about it, friend Conseil?" asked Ned Land.

"I have nothing to say. I am absolutely disinterested in the question. Like my master and Ned, I am a bachelor. No wife, relations, nor children expect my return. I am at monsieur's service. I think like monsieur, I say what monsieur says, and you must not depend upon me to make a majority. Two persons only are concerned; monsieur on one side, Ned Land on the other. That said, I listen, and am ready to count for either."

I could not help smiling at seeing Conseil annihilate his personality so completely. The Canadian must have been enchanted not to have him against him.

"Then, sir," said Ned Land, "as Conseil does not exist, we

have only to speak to each other. I have spoken, you have heard me. What have you to answer?"

It was evident that I must sum up, and subterfuges were repugnant to me.

"Friend Ned," I said, "this is my answer. You are right and I am wrong. We must not depend upon Captain Nemo's goodwill. The commonest prudence forbids him to set us at liberty. On the other hand, prudence tells us that we must profit by the first opportunity of leaving the *Nautilus*."

"Very well, M. Aronnax, that is wisely spoken."

"Only," I said, "I have but one observation to make—the occasion must be serious. Our first attempt must succeed, for if it fail we shall not find another opportunity of attempting it again, and Captain Nemo will not forgive us."

"That's true enough," answered the Canadian. "But your observation applies to every attempt at flight, whether it be made in two years' or two days' time. Therefore the question is still the same; if a favourable opportunity occurs, we must seize it."

"Agreed. And now, friend Ned, will you tell me what you mean by a favourable opportunity?"

"For instance, a dark night when the *Nautilus* would be only a short distance from some European coast."

"Then you would attempt to escape by swimming?"

"Yes, if we were sufficiently near the coast, and the vessel were on the surface; but if we were far off, or if the vessel were under water——"

"And in that case?"

"In that case I should try to take possession of the boat. I know how it is worked. We could get into the interior of it, undo the bolts, and get up to the surface without even the helmsman seeing us."

"Well, Ned, look out for that opportunity; but do not forget that a failure would be fatal to us."

"I will not forget it, sir."

"And now, Ned, should you like to know what I think of your plan?"

"Yes, M. Aronnax."

"Well, I think—I do not say I hope—that so favourable an opportunity will not occur."

"Why?"

"Because Captain Nemo cannot be unaware that we have not renounced the hope of recovering our liberty, and will keep watch above all in European seas."

"I am of monsieur's opinion," said Conseil.

"We shall see," answered Ned Land, shaking his head in a determined manner.

"And now, Ned Land," I added, "we must leave it there. Not another word on this subject. The day you are ready you will inform us and we shall follow you. I leave it entirely to you."

This conversation, that was destined to have such grave consequences later on, ended thus. I ought now to say that facts seemed to confirm my previsions, to the Canadian's great despair. Did Captain Nemo distrust us in these frequented seas, or did he merely wish to keep out of sight of the numerous ships of all nations that plough the Mediterranean? I do not know, but he generally kept under water and a good distance from land. When the *Nautilus* rose to the surface nothing but the helmsman's cage emerged, and it went to great depths, for between the Grecian Archipelago and Asia Minor the sea is more than 2,000 yards deep.

I only made acquaintance with the Island of Carpathos, one of the Sporades, by these lines of Virgil that Captain Nemo quoted to me whilst placing his finger on a point of the planisphere:

"Est in Carpathio Neptuni gurgite vates,
    Cæruleus Proteus——"

It was, in fact, the ancient sojourn of Proteus, the old shepherd of Neptune's flocks, now the Island of Scarpanto, situated between Rhodes and Crete. I only saw its granite substructure through the saloon windows.

The next day, the 14th of February, I resolved to spend

some hours in studying the fish of the archipelago; but for some motive or other the panels remained hermetically closed. By taking the direction of the *Nautilus*, I saw that it was making towards the Island of Crete. At the epoch I had embarked on board the *Abraham Lincoln*, that island had just revolted against Turkish despotism. But what had become of the insurrection since I knew nothing, and Captain Nemo, cut off as he was from all communication with land, could not inform me.

I therefore made no allusion to this event when in the evening I was alone with him in the saloon. Besides, he seemed taciturn and preoccupied. Then, contrary to his custom, he ordered the panels of the saloon to be opened, and going from one to another he attentively observed the mass of water, for what purpose I could not guess, and on my side I employed my time in studying the fish that passed before my eyes.

I could not take my eyes off these wonders of the sea, when they were suddenly struck with an unexpected apparition. In the midst of the waters a man appeared, a diver, wearing in his belt a leather purse. It was a living man, swimming vigorously, occasionally disappearing to take breath on the surface, then plunging again immediately. I turned to Captain Nemo, and exclaimed in an agitated voice:

"A man! A shipwrecked man! He must be saved at any price!"

The captain did not answer, but came and leaned against the window.

The man had approached, and with his face flattened against the glass, he was looking at us.

To my profound stupefaction Captain Nemo made a sign to him. The diver answered him with his hand, immediately went up again to the surface of the sea, and did not appear again.

"Don't be uneasy," said the captain to me. "It is Nicholas of Cape Matapan, surnamed the Pesce. He is well known in all the Cyclades. A bold diver! Water is his element, and he lives in it more than on land, going constantly from one island to another, and even as far as Crete."

"Do you know him, Captain?"

"Why not, M. Aronnax?"

That said, Captain Nemo went towards a piece of furniture placed near the left panel of the saloon. Near this piece of furniture I saw an iron safe, on the lid of which was a brass plate with the initials of the *Nautilis*, and its motto, "*Mobilis in Mobile*," upon it.

At that moment the captain, without taking further notice of my presence, opened the piece of furniture, which contained a great number of ingots.

They were ingots of gold. From whence came this precious metal that represented an enormous sum? Where did the captain get this gold, and what was he going to do with it?"

I did not speak a word. I looked. Captain Nemo took these ingots, one by one, and arranged them methodically in the safe, which he entirely filled. I estimated that it then contained more than 2000 lb. weight of gold—that is to say, nearly £200,000.

The safe was securely fastened, and the captain wrote an address on the lid in what must have been modern Greek characters.

This done, Captain Nemo pressed a knob, the wire of which communicated with the quarters of the crew. Four men appeared, and, not without some trouble, pushed the safe out of the saloon. Then I heard them pulling it up the iron staircase with pulleys.

Then Captain Nemo turned to me.

"Did you speak, Professor?"

"No, Captain."

"Then, sir, if you allow me, I will wish you good night." Upon which Captain Nemo left the saloon.

I went back to my room very curious, as may be believed. I tried in vain to sleep. I tried to find what connection there could be between the diver and the safe filled with gold. I soon felt by its pitching and tossing that the *Nautilus* was back on the surface of the water.

Then I heard a noise of steps on the platform. I understood that they were unloosening the boat and launching it on the sea. It struck for an instant against the sides of the *Nautilus*, and then the noise ceased.

Two hours afterwards the same noise, the same movements, were repeated. The boat, hoisted on board, was replaced in its socket, and the *Nautilus* sank again under the waves.

Thus, then, the gold had been sent to its address. To what point of the continent? Who was Captain Nemo's correspondent?"

The next day, the 16th of February, the *Nautilus*, passing within sight of Cerigo, left the Grecian Archipelago after doubling Cape Matapan.

CHAPTER THIRTY-ONE

THE MEDITERRANEAN IN FORTY-EIGHT HOURS

THE MEDITERRANEAN, the blue sea *par excellence*, "the great sea" of the Hebrews, the "sea" of the Greeks, the *mare nostrum* of the Romans, bordered with orange trees, aloes, cactus, maritime pines, made fragrant with the perfume of myrtles, framed in rude mountains, saturated with a pure and transparent air, but inceassantly worked by underground fires, is a perfect battlefield, in which Neptune and Pluto still dispute the empire of the world. It is there, upon its banks and waters, says Michelet, that man is renewed in one of the most powerful climates of the world. But, although it is so beautiful, I could only take a rapid glance at its basin, which covers a superficial area of two millions of square kilometres. Even Captain Nemo's knowledge was lost to me, for the enigmatical personage did not once appear during our rapid passage. I estimated at about six hundred leagues the course of the *Nautilus* under the waves of this sea, and it accomplished this voyage in twice twenty-four hours. Starting on the morning of the 16th of February from the Grecian seas, we had cleared the Straits of Gibraltar by sunrise on the 18th.

It was evident to me that this Mediterranean, enclosed by the countries which he wished to avoid, was distasteful to Captain Nemo. Its waves and breezes recalled too many memories, if not too many regrets. He had not here that liberty of movement, that independence of manœuvre, that he had in the ocean, and his *Nautilus* was cramped between the shores of Africa and Europe.

Our speed was now twenty-five miles an hour, or twelve leagues of four kilometres. It is useless to say that Ned Land, notwithstanding his great wish, was obliged to renounce his projects of flight. He could not use a boat that was being dragged along at the rate of thirteen yards a second. To leave the *Nautilus* then would be like jumping out of a train going at the same speed, as imprudent a thing as could possibly be attempted. Besides, our apparatus only went up to the surface at night in order to renew its provision of air, and it was guided entirely by the compass and log.

I therefore only saw of the Mediterranean what passengers by an express see of the country that is flying before their eyes—that is to say, the distant horizon, and not the nearer objects which pass like a flash of lightning.

During the night between the 16th and 17th of February we entered the second Mediterranean basin, the greatest depths of which are found at 1,500 fathoms. The *Nautilus*, under the action of its screw, gliding over its inclined planes, sank into the lowest depths of the sea.

There, instead of natural marvels, the mass of waters offered me many touching and terrible scenes. In fact, we were then crossing all that part of the Mediterranean so fertile in disasters. From the Algerian coast to the shores of Provence, how many vessels have been wrecked, how many ships have disappeared! The Mediterranean is only a lake compared to the vast liquid plains of the Pacific, but it is a capricious lake with changing waters, to-day propitious and caressing to the fragile tartan that seems to float between the double ultramarine of sea and sky, to-morrow tempestuous, agitated by winds, breaking up the strongest ships by the precipitated blows of its short waves.

In that rapid course across the great depths what wrecks I saw lying on the ground! Some already encrusted with coral. Others simply covered with a layer of rust, anchors, cannons, bullets, iron tackle, screws, pieces of engines, broken cylinders, crushed boilers, and hulls floating in mid-water, some upright, some overturned.

I observed that the bottom of the Mediterranean was more encumbered with these wrecks as the *Nautilus* approached the Straits of Gibraltar. The coasts of Africa and Europe are then nearer each other, and in the narrow space collisions are frequent. I saw there numerous iron keels, the fantastic ruins of steamers, some lying down, others upright, like formidable animals. One of these boats with open sides, bent funnel, wheels of which only the mounting remained, the helm separated from the sternpost, and still held by an iron chain, its stern eaten away by marine salts, presented a terrible spectacle! How many existences did this shipwreck destroy! How many victims swallowed up by the waves! Had any sailor on board survived to relate the terrible disaster, or did the waves still keep the fatal secret. I do not know why, but it came into my head that this boat must be the *Atlas* that had totally disappeared for twenty years, and of which nothing had ever been heard! Ah, what a fatal history would be that of these Mediterranean depths, this vast charnel house where so many riches have been lost, and so many victims have met with their death!

In the meantime the *Nautilus*, indifferent and rapid, journeyed at full speed amidst these ruins. On the 18th of February, about 3 a.m., it was at the entrance to the Straits of Gibraltar.

There two currents exist—an upper current, long since

known, that conveys the waters of the ocean into the Mediterranean basin, and a lower counter-current, of which reasoning has now shown the existence. For the volume of water in the Mediterranean, incessantly increased by the Atlantic current and the rivers that flow into it, must raise the level of the sea every year, for its evaporation is insufficient to restore the equilibrium. As this is not the case, we must naturally admit the existence of a lower current that pours through the Straits of Gibraltar, the overplus of the Mediterranean into the Atlantic.

We proved this fact. The *Nautilus* profited by this counter-current. It rushed rapidly through the narrow passage. For an instant I caught a glimpse of the admirable ruins of the temple of Hercules, sunk, according to Pliny and Avienus, with the low island on which it stood, and a few minutes later we were afloat on the waves of the Atlantic.

CHAPTER THIRTY-TWO

VIGO BAY

THE ATLANTIC! That vast extent of water the superficial area of which covers twenty-five millions of square miles nine thousand miles long, with a mean breadth of two thousand seven hundred miles. An important ocean almost unknown to the ancients, except, perhaps, to the inhabitants of Carthage, those Dutchmen of antiquity who, in their commercial peregrinations, followed the western coasts of Europe or Africa! An ocean whose parallel winding shores embrace an immense perimeter, watered by the largest rivers in the world, the Saint Lawrence, the Mississippi, Amazon, La Plata, Orinoco, Niger, Senegal, Elba, Loire, and Rhine, which bring down the waters of the most civilised as well as those of the most savage countries! A magnificent plain, incessantly ploughed by ships of all nations, sheltered under the flags of every nation, and terminated by the two terrible points, dreaded by navigators, Cape Horn and the Cape of Tempests.

The *Nautilus* was culling its waters under her sharp prow after having accomplished nearly ten thousand leagues in three months and a half, a distance greater than one of the great circles of the earth. Where were we going now, and what had the future in store for us?

The *Nautilus* once out of the Straits of Gibraltar came up to the surface again, and our daily walks on the platform were thus restored to us.

I immediately went up there, accompanied by Ned Land and Conseil. At a distance of twelve miles, Cape Vincent, which forms the SW. point of the Spanish peninsula, was dimly to be seen. It was blowing a rather strong gale. The sea was rough. It made the *Nautilus* rock violently. It was almost impossible to keep on the platform, which enormous seas washed at every moment. We therefore went down again after taking in some mouthfuls of fresh air.

I went back to my room, and Conseil returned to his cabin, but the Canadian, with a preoccupied air, followed me. Our rapid passage across the Mediterranean had prevented him putting his projects into execution, and he did not hide his disappointment.

When the door of my cabin was shut, he sat down and looked at me in silence.

"Friend Ned," I said, "I understand you, but you have nothing to reproach yourself with. To have attempted to leave the *Nautilus* while it was going at that rate would have been madness."

Ned Land answered nothing. His compressed lips and frowning brow indicated the violent possession this fixed idea had taken of his mind.

"Well," said I, "we need not despair yet. We are going up the coast of Portugal. France and England are not far off, where we should easily find a refuge. If the *Nautilus*, once out of the Straits of Gibraltar, had gone southward, if it had carried us towards those regions where land is wanting, I should share your uneasiness. But now we know that Captain Nemo does not avoid civilised seas, and in a few days I think we can act with some security."

Ned Land looked at me more fixedly still, and at length he opened his lips.

"It is for to-night," said he.

I started. I must acknowledge I was little prepared for this communication. I wanted to answer the Canadian, but words would not come.

"We agreed to wait for an opportunity," said Ned Land. "I have that opportunity. This night we shall be only a few miles off the Spanish coast. The night will be dark. I have your word, M. Aronnax, and I depend upon you."

As I still was silent, the Canadian rose, and coming nearer to me, said:

"This evening at 9 o'clock. I have told Conseil. At that time Captain Nemo will be shut up in his room, and probably in bed. Neither the engineers nor any of the crew can see us. Conseil and I will go to the central staircase. You, M. Aronnax, must remain in the library not far off, and await our signal. The oars, mast, and sail are in the boat, and I have even succeeded in putting some provisions into it. I procured an English wrench to unscrew the bolts that fasten the boat to the hull of the *Nautilus*. Thus everything is ready for to-night."

"The sea is bad."

"That I allow," answered the Canadian, "but we must risk that. Liberty is worth paying for. Besides, the boat is solid, and a few miles with the wind in our favour are not of any consequence. Who knows if to-morrow we shall not be a hundred leagues out? If circumstances favour us we shall land, living or dead, on some point of solid ground between 10 and 11 o'clock. Then to-night, by the grace of God!"

Thereupon the Canadian withdrew, leaving me almost stunned. I had imagined that when the matter turned up I should have time to reflect and discuss it. My stubborn companion had not allowed me to do that. And, after all, what could I have said to him? Ned Land was quite right.

It was almost an occasion, and he took advantage of it. Could I take back my word, and assume the responsibility of compromising, by personal interest, the future of my companion? To-morrow Captain Nemo might carry us far away from any land.

At that moment a rather strong hissing sound informed me that the reservoirs were being filled, and then the *Nautilus* sank under the waves of the Atlantic.

I remained in my room. I wished to avoid the captain in order to hide from his eyes the emotion I was labouring under. It was a sad day I passed thus between the desire of being free again and the regret of abandoning the marvellous *Nautilus*, leaving my submarine studies unfinished! To leave my ocean, "my Atlantic," as I liked to call it, thus, without having observed its lowest strata, or learnt from it those secrets that the Indian seas and the Pacific had taught me! My romance had fallen from my hand while I was yet at the first volume, my dream was interrupted at its most delightful moment! What wretched hours passed thus, sometimes seeing myself safely on board with my companions, sometimes wishing, in spite of my reason, that some unforeseen circumstance would prevent the realisation of Ned Land's projects!

Twice I went into the saloon. I wished to consult the compass, and to see if the *Nautilus* was approaching or going farther away from the coast. But no. The *Nautilus* kept constantly in the Portuguese waters. It was making for the north along the shores of the ocean.

I was, therefore, obliged to make up my mind to it, and prepare for flight. My baggage was not heavy, and consisted of my notes, nothing more. I asked myself what Captain Nemo would think of our flight, what uneasiness it might cause him, what harm it might do him, and what he would do in case it was discovered or it failed. Certainly I had no fault to find with him—on the contrary. Hospitality was never given more freely than his. In leaving him I could not be accused of ingratitude. No oath bound us to him. He counted upon the force of circumstances alone, and not upon our word to keep us with him for ever. But his intention, openly avowed, of keeping us eternally prisoners on board his vessel justified our attempts.

My dinner was served as usual in my room. I ate little, being too much preoccupied. I left the table at seven o'clock. A hundred and twenty minutes—I counted them—still separated me from the time when I was to join Ned Land. My agitation redoubled. My pulse beat violently. I could not remain immovable. I walked about, hoping to calm the trouble of my mind by movement. The idea of failing in our bold enterprise was the least painful of my thoughts; but at the idea of seeing our project discovered before leaving the *Nautilus*, and of being brought before Captain Nemo, irritated, or, what would have been worse, saddened by my leaving him, my heart palpitated.

I wished to see the saloon for the last time. I went by the waist, and entered that museum where I had passed so many useful and agreeable hours. I looked at all these riches and treasures like a man on the eve of eternal exile, and who is going away never to return. These marvels of Nature, these masterpieces of art, amongst which for so many days my life had been concentrated, I was going to leave them for ever. I should have liked to look through the windows across the waters of the Atlantic; but the panels were hermetically shut, and an iron sheet separated me from that ocean which I did not know as yet.

As I moved thus about the saloon, I reached the door, let into the angle, which opened into the captain's room. To my great astonishment this door was ajar. I drew back involuntarily. If Captain Nemo was in his room he could see me. However, hearing no noise, I drew near it. The room was empty. I pushed open the door and entered. Still the same severe monklike aspect.

At that moment some prints, hung up, that I had not noticed during my first visit, struck me. They were portraits, portraits of great historical men whose existence was but a perpetual devotion to one great humane idea: Kosciusko, the hero who fell to the cry of " Finis Poloniæ!" Botzaris, the Leonidas of modern Greece; O'Connell, the defender of Ireland; Washington, the founder of the American Union; Manin, the Italian patriot; Lincoln, who fell by the hand of a slave-owner; and, lastly, martyr to the freedom of the black race, John Brown, hanging on his gallows as Victor Hugo's pencil has so terribly drawn him.

What tie could exist between these heroic souls and the soul of Captain Nemo? Could I at last, from that assemblage of portraits, find out the mystery of his existence? Was he the champion of oppressed nations, the liberator of slaves? Had he figured in the last social or political commotions of this century? Had he been one of the heroes of the terrible American War?—a war lamentable, but for ever glorious.

Suddenly the clock struck eight. The first stroke awoke me to reality. I trembled as if some invisible eye could see to the bottom of my thoughts, and I rushed out of the room.

There I glanced at the compass. Our course was still north. The log indicated moderate speed, the manometer a depth of about sixty feet. Circumstances, therefore, were favouring the Canadian's project.

I went back to my room and clothed myself warmly in my sea boots, sealskin cap, and vest of byssus lined with sealskin. I was ready. I waited. The vibration of the screw alone disturbed the profound silence that reigned on board. I listened attentively. Would not a shout tell me all at once that Ned Land had been caught in his effort to escape? A mortal dread took possession of me. I tried in vain to regain my *sang-froid*.

At a few minutes to nine o'clock I put my ear against the captain's door. No sound, I left my room and went back to the saloon, which was insufficiently lighted, but empty.

I opened the door communicating with the library. The same insufficient light, the same solitude. I went and placed myself near the door that opened into the cage of the central staircase, and awaited Ned Land's signal.

At the moment the vibration ·from the screw sensibly diminished, then ceased altogether. Why was this change made in the working of the *Nautilus*? Whether this halt would be favourable to or against Ned Land's plans I could not tell.

The silence was only broken by the beatings of my heart.

Suddenly I felt a slight shock. I understood that the *Nautilus* had just stopped on the bottom of the ocean. My anxiety increased. The Canadian's signal did not reach me. I wanted to go to Ned Land and beg him to put off his attempt. I felt that something was changed in our usual navigation.

At that moment the saloon door opened, and Captain Nemo appeared. He perceived me, and said without further preamble, in an amiable tone:

"Ah, Professor, I was looking for you. Do you know your Spanish history?"

Anyone knowing the history of his own country thoroughly under the same conditions of mental worry and anxiety, would not be able to quote a single word of it.

"Well," continued Captain Nemo, "you heard my question. Do you know the history of Spain?"

"Very badly," I replied.

"That is like *savants*," said the captain, "they know nothing. Well, sit down," added he, "and I will relate a curious episode of that history to you."

The captain stretched himself upon a divan, and I mechanically took a place beside him, with my back to the light.

"Professor," he said, "give me all your attention. This history will interest you in some sort, for it will answer a question that doubtless you have not been able to solve."

"I hear, Captain," said I, not knowing what my interlocutor was driving at, and wondering whether it had anything to do with our projects of flight.

"Professor," resumed the captain, "if you have no objection we will go as far back as 1702. As you know, your king, Louis XIV, thinking that the gesture of a potentate was sufficient to make the Pryenees sink into the ground, had imposed his grandson, the Duke of Anjoy, on the Spaniards.

This prince, who reigned more or less badly under the name of Philip V, had a strong party against him from without.

"In fact, the year before, the Royal houses of Holland, Austria and England had concluded a treaty of alliance at The Hague, for the aim of taking the crown of Spain from Philip V and placing it on the head of an archduke, to whom they gave the premature title of Charles III.

"Spain had this coalition to resist. But she was nearly destitute of soldiers and sailors. However, money would not be wanting, provided that their galleons, loaded with gold and silver from America, could enter her ports. Now, towards the end of 1702, she was expecting a rich convoy that France had sent a fleet of twenty-three vessels, commanded by the Admiral Château-Renaud, to escort, for the combined fleets were then scouring the Atlantic.

"This convoy was bound for Cadiz; but the admiral, having learnt that the English fleet was cruising in the neighbourhood, resolved to make for a French port.

"The Spanish commanders of the convoy protested against this decision. They wished to be accompanied to a Spanish port, and if not to Cadiz, to Vigo Bay, situated on the NW. coast of Spain, which was not blockaded.

"The Admiral Château-Renaud was weak enough to obey this injunction, and the galleons entered Vigo Bay.

"Unfortunately, this bay is an open roadstead that cannot be in the least defended. They were, therefore, obliged to hasten the unloading of the galleons before the arrival of the combined fleets, and there would have been plenty of time to do it in, but for a miserable question of rivalry that arose suddenly.

"You are following the links of these facts?" said the captain.

"Perfectly," said I, not knowing why I was receiving this lesson in history.

"Then I continue. This is what happened. The merchants of Cadiz had a privilege by which they were to receive all the merchandise that came from the East Indies, and the landing of the ingots from the galleons at the port of Vigo was a contravention of their rights. They made complaints at Madrid, and obtained from the feeble Philip V the order to make the convoy remain without unloading in the roadstead of Vigo until the enemy's fleets should be out of the road.

"Now whilst this decision was being arrived at, on the 22nd of October, 1702, the English ships arrived in Vigo Bay. The Admiral Château-Renaud, notwithstanding his inferior forces, fought courageously. But when he saw that the riches of the convoy were about to fall into the hands of enemies, he burnt and scuttled the galleons that went to the bottom with their immense treasures."

Captain Nemo stopped. I acknowledged that I did not perceive as yet how this story could interest me.

"Well?" I asked him.

"Well, M. Aronnax," answered Captain Nemo, "we are in Vigo Bay, and it rests with yourself whether you will penetrate its mysteries."

The captain rose and begged me to follow him. I had had time to recover myself. I obeyed. The saloon was dark, but across the transparent panes glittered the sea. I looked.

For a radius of half a mile round the *Nautilus* the waters seemed impregnated with electric light, the sandy bottom clear and distinct. Some of the crew, clothed in their bathing dresses, were at work emptying half-rotten casks, splintered cases, amidst still blackened spars. From these cases and casks escaped ingots of gold and silver, cascades of piastres and jewels. The sand was strewed with them. Then, loaded with their previous booty, these men returned to the *Nautilus*, deposited their load, and went back to continue their inexhaustible gold and silver fishery.

I understood. It was the battlefield of the 22nd of October, 1702. In this very place the galleons laden for the Spanish government had sunk. Here Captain Nemo came, according to his needs, to encase the millions with which he ballasted his *Nautilus*. It was for him, and for him alone, that America had given up her precious metals. He was the direct heir, without anyone to share, of these treasures taken from the Incas and Ferdinand Cortez's conquered people.

"Did you know, Professor," he asked me, smiling, "that the sea contained such riches?"

"I knew," I answered, "that the silver held in suspension in the sea is estimated at two millions of tons."

"Doubtless, but in order to extract the silver the expense would be greater than the profit. Here, on the contrary, I have only to pick up what men have lost, not only in this Vigo Bay, but in a thousand other scenes of shipwreck, all marked on my marine chart. Now do you understand why I am so many times a millionaire?"

"Yes, Captain. But allow me to tell you that in your work in Vigo Bay you have only been beforehand with a rival company."

"What company, pray?"

"A company that has received from the Spanish government the privilege of seeking the shipwrecked galleons. The shareholders are tempted by the bait of an enormous profit, for they estimate the value of these shipwrecked treasures at five hundred millions of francs."

"Five hundred millions!" answered Captain Nemo; "they were that much once, but are so no longer."

"Just so," said I, "and a warning to the shareholders would be an act of charity. Who knows, however, if it would be well received? What speculators regret, above all, generally, is less the loss of money than that of their insane hopes. I pity them, after all, less than the thousands of unfortunates to whom so much wealth, well distributed, would have been profitable, whilst it is for ever lost to them."

I had no sooner expressed this regret than I felt it must have wounded Captain Nemo.

"Lost to them!" he answered, getting animated. "Do you think, then, that this wealth is lost when it is I that gather it? Do you think I give myself the trouble to pick up these treasures for myself? Who says that I do not make a good use of them? Do you believe that I ignore the existence of suffering beings, of races oppressed in this

world, of miserable creatures to solace, of victims to revenge?
Do you not understand——"

Captain Nemo stopped, regretting, perhaps, having said
so much. But I had guessed. Whatever might be the motives
that had forced him to seek independence under the seas,
he was still a man! His heart still beat for the sufferings
of humanity, and his immense charity was given to oppressed
races, as well as to individuals.

And I then understood to whom the millions were sent
by Captain Nemo, while the *Nautilus* was cruising in the
waters of revolted Crete.

CHAPTER THIRTY-THREE

A VANISHED CONTINENT

ON THE morning of the next day, the 19th of February, I
saw the Canadian enter my room. I was expecting his visit.
He looked much disappointed.

"Well, sir," he said to me.

"Well, Ned, luck was against us yesterday."

"Yes, that captain must stop at the very time we were
going to escape from his vessel."

"Yes, Ned, he had business with his banker."

"His banker?"

"Yes, or rather his bank. I mean by that this ocean, where
his wealth is in greater safety than it would be in the coffers
of a state."

I then related to the Canadian the incident of the preceding evening, in the secret hope of making him wish not
to leave the captain; but the only result of my account
was an energetic regret expressed by Ned at not being able
to take a walk on the Vigo battlefield on his own account.

"But all is not over," he said. "It is only one harpoon
throw lost. Another time we shall succeed, and this very
evening, if necessary——"

"What is the direction of the *Nautilus*?" I asked.

"I do not know," answered Ned.

"Well, at noon we shall find our bearings."

The Canadian returned to Conseil. As soon as I was dressed I went into the saloon. The compass was not reassuring. The direction of the *Nautilus* was SSW. We were turning our backs on Europe.

I waited impatiently for our bearings to be taken. About 11.30 a.m. the reservoirs were emptied, and our apparatus went up to the surface of the ocean. I sprang upon the platform. Ned Land preceded me there.

There was no land in sight. Nothing but the immense sea. A few sails on the horizon, doubtless those that go as far as San Roque in search of favourable winds for doubling the Cape of Good Hope. The weather was cloudy. A gale was springing up.

Ned, in a rage, tried to pierce the misty horizon. He still hoped that behind the mist stretched the land so much desired.

At noon the sun appeared for an instant. The first officer took advantage of the gleam to take the altitude. Then, the sea becoming rougher, we went down again, and the panel was closed.

An hour afterwards, when I consulted the map, I saw that the position of the *Nautilus* was indicated upon it by 16° 17' long. and 33° 22' lat., at 150 leagues from the nearest coast. It was no use to dream of escaping now, and I leave Ned Land's anger to be imagined when I informed him of our situation.

On my own account I was not overwhelmed with grief. I felt relieved from a weight that was oppressing me, and I could calmly take up my habitual work again.

That evening, about 11 p.m., I received the very unexpected visit of Captain Nemo. He asked me very graciously if I felt fatigued from sitting up so late the night before. I answered in the negative.

"Then, Mr. Aronnax, I have a curious excursion to propose to you."

"What is it, Captain?"

"You have as yet only been on the sea bottom by daylight. Should you like to see it on a dark night?"

"I should like it much."

"It will be a fatiguing walk, I warn you. You will have to go far, and climb a mountain. The roads are not very well kept in repair."

"What you tell me makes me doubly curious. I am ready to follow you."

"Come, then, Professor. We will go and put on our diving dresses.

When we reached the ward-room I saw that neither my companions nor any of the crew were to follow us in our excursion. Captain Nemo had not even asked me to take Ned or Conseil.

In a few minutes we had put on our apparatus. They placed on our backs the reservoirs full of air, but the electric lamps were not prepared. I said as much to the captain.

"They would be of no use to us," he answered.

I thought I had not heard aright, but I could not repeat my observation, for the captain's head had already disappeared under its metallic covering. I finished harnessing myself, felt that someone placed an iron spiked stick in my hand, and a few minutes later, after the usual manœuvre, we set foot on the bottom of the Atlantic, at a depth of 150 fathoms.

Midnight was approaching. The waters were in profound darkness, but Captain Nemo showed me a reddish point in the distance, a sort of large light shining about two miles from the Nautilus. What this fire was, with what fed, why and how it burnt in the liquid mass, I could not tell. Anyway it lighted us, dimly it is true, but I soon became accustomed to the peculiar darkness, and I understood, under the circumstances, the uselessness of the Ruhmkorff apparatus.

Captain Nemo and I walked side by side directly towards the light. The flat soil ascended gradually. We took long strides, helping ourselves with our sticks, but our progress was slow, for our feet often sank in a sort of mud covered with seaweed and flat stones.

As we went along I heard a sort of pattering above my head. The noise sometimes redoubled, and produced something like a continuous shower. I soon understood the cause. It was rain falling violently and crisping the surface of the waves. Instinctively I was seized with the idea that I should be wet through. By water, in water! I could not help laughing at the odd idea. But the truth is that under a thick diving dress the liquid element is no longer felt, and it only seems like an atmosphere rather denser than the terrestrial atmosphere, that is all.

In the meantime the reddish light that guided us increased and inflamed the horizon. The presence of this fire under the seas excited my curiosity to the highest pitch. Was it some electric effluence? Was I going towards a natural phenomenon still unknown to the *savants* of the earth? Or —for this thought crossed my mind—had the hand of man any part in the conflagration? Had it lighted this fire? Was I going to meet in this deep sea companions and friends of Captain Nemo living the same strange life, and whom he was going to see? All these foolish and inadmissible ideas pursued me, and in that state of mind, ceaselessly excited by the series of marvels that passed before my eyes, I should not have been surprised to see at the bottom of the sea, one of the submarine towns Captain Nemo dreamed of.

Our road grew lighter and lighter. The white light shone from the top of a mountain about eight hundred feet high. But what I perceived was only a reflection made by the crystal of the water. The fire, the source of the inexplicable light, was on the opposite side of the mountain.

It was one o'clock in the morning. We had reached the first slopes of the mountain. But the way up led through the difficult paths of a vast thicket.

Yes, a thicket of dead trees, leafless, sapless, mineralised under the action of the water, overtopped here and there by gigantic pines. It was like a coal-series, still standing holding by its roots to the soil that had given way, and whose branches, like fine black paper-cuttings, stood out against the watery ceiling. My readers may imagine a forest on the side of the Hartz Mountains, but forest and mountain sunk, to the bottom of the sea. The paths were encumbered with seaweed and fucus, amongst which swarmed a world of crustaceans. I went on climbing over the rocks, leaping over the fallen trunks, breaking the sea-creepers that balanced from one tree to another, startling the fish that flew from branch to branch. Pressed onwards I no longer felt any fatigue. I followed my guide, who was never fatigued.

What a spectacle! How can I depict it? How describe the aspect of the woods and rocks in this liquid element, their lower parts sombre and wild, the upper coloured with red tints in the light which the reverberating power of the water doubled? We were climbing rocks which fell in enormous fragments directly afterwards with the noise of an avalanche. Right and left were deep dark galleries where sight was lost. Here opened vast clearings that seemed made by the hand of man, and I asked myself sometimes if some inhabitant of these submarine regions was not about to appear suddenly.

But Captain Nemo still went on climbing. I would not be left behind. My stick lent me useful aid. A false step would have been dangerous in these narrow paths, hollowed out of the sides of precipices; but I walked along with a firm step without suffering from vertigo. Sometimes I jumped over a crevice the depth of which would have made me recoil on the glaciers of the earth; sometimes I ventured on the vacillating trunks of trees thrown from one abyss to another without looking under my feet, having only eyes to admire the savage sites of that region. There, monumental rocks perched on these irregularly-cut bases seemed to defy the laws of equilibrium. Between their stony knees grew trees like a jet of water under strong pressure, sustaining and sustained by the rocks. Then, natural towers, large scarps cut perpendicularly like a fortress curtain, inclining at an angle which the laws of gravitation would not have authorised on the surface of the terrestrial regions.

And did I not myself feel the difference due to the powerful density of the water, when, notwithstanding my heavy garments, my brass headpiece, my metal soles, I climbed slopes impracticably steep, clearing them, so to speak, with the lightness of an isard or a chamois?

I feel that this recital of an excursion under the sea cannot sound probable. I am the historian of things that seem impossible, and that yet are real and incontestable. I did not dream. I saw and felt.

Two hours after having quitted the *Nautilus* we had passed the trees, and a hundred feet above our heads rose the summit of the mountain, the projection of which made a shadow on the brilliant irradiation of the opposite slope. A few petrified bushes were scattered hither and thither in grimacing zigzags. The fish rose in shoals under our footsteps like birds surprised in the tall grass. The rocky mass was hollowed out into impenetrable confractuosities, deep grottoes, bottomless holes, in which I heard formidable noises. My blood froze in my veins when I perceived some enormous antennæ barricading my path, or some frightful claw shutting up with noise in the dark cavities. Thousands of luminous points shone amidst the darkness. They were the eyes of gigantic crustaceans, giant lobsters setting themselves up like halberdiers and moving their claws with the clanking sound of metal; titanic crabs pointed like cannon on their carriages, and frightful poulps, intertwining their tentacles like a living nest of serpents.

What was this exorbitant world that I did not know yet? To what order belonged these articulates to which the rock formed a second carapace? Where had Nature found the secret of their vegetating existence, and for how many centuries had they lived thus in the lowest depths of the ocean?

But I could not stop. Captain Nemo, familiar with these terrible animals, paid no attention to them. We had arrived at the first plateau, where other surprises awaited me. There rose picturesque ruins which betrayed the hand of man, and not that of the Creator. They were vast heaps of stones in the vague outlines of castles and temples, clothed with a world of zoophytes in flower, and, instead of ivy, seaweed and fucus clothed them with a vegetable mantle.

But what, then, was this portion of the globe swallowed up by cataclysms? Who had placed these rocks and stones like dolmens of anti-historical times? Where was I? Where had Captain Nemo's whim brought me to?

I should have liked to question him. As I could not do that, I stopped him. I seized his arm. But he, shaking his head, and pointing to the last summit, seemed to say to me: "Higher! Still higher!"

I followed him with a last effort, and in a few minutes I had climbed the peak that overtopped for about thirty feet all the rocky mass.

I looked at the side we had just climbed. The mountain only rose seven or eight hundred feet above the plain; but on the opposite side it commanded from twice that height the depths of this portion of the Atlantic. My eyes wandered over a large space lighted up by a violent fulguration. In fact, this mountain was a volcano. At fifty feet below the peak, amidst a rain of stones and scoriæ, a wide crater was vomiting forth torrents of lava which fell in a cascade of fire into the bosom of the liquid mass. Thus placed, the volcano, like an immense torch, lighted up the lower plain to the last limits of the horizon.

I have said that the submarine crater threw out lava, but not flames. The oxygen of the air is necessary to make a flame, and it cannot exist in water; but the streams of red-hot lava struggled victoriously against the liquid element, and turned it to vapour by its contact. Rapid currents carried away all this gas in diffusion, and the lava torrent glided to the foot of the mountain like the eruption of Vesuvius on another Torre del Greco.

There, before my eyes, ruined, destroyed, overturned, appeared a town, its roofs crushed in, its temples thrown down, its arches dislocated, its columns lying on theground, with the solid proportions of Tuscan architecture still discernible upon them; further on were the remains of a gigantic aqueduct; here, the encrusted base of an Acropolis, and the outlines of a Parthenon; there, some vestiges of a quay, as if some ancient port had formerly sheltered, on the shores of an extinct ocean, merchant vessels and war triremes; farther on still, long lines of ruined walls, wide deserted streets, a second Pompeii buried under the waters, raised up again for me by Captain Nemo.

Where was I? Where was I? I wished to know at any price. I felt I must speak, and tried to take off the globe of brass that imprisoned my head.

But Captain Nemo came to me and stopped me with a gesture. Then picking up a piece of clayey stone he went up to a black basaltic rock and traced on it the single word:

'ATLANTIS'

What a flash of lightning shot through my mind! Atlantis, the ancient Meropis of Theopompus, the Atlantis of Plato, the continent disbelieved in by Origen, Jamblichus, D'Anville, Malte-Brun, and Humboldt, who placed its disappearance amongst legendary tales; believed in by Possidonius, Pliny, Ammianus, Marcellinus, Tertullian, Engel, Sherer, Tournefort, Buffon, and D'Avezac, was there before my eyes bearing upon it the unexceptionable testimony of its catastrophe! This, then, was the engulfed region that existed beyond Europe, Asia and Lybia, beyond the columns of Hercules, where the powerful Atlantides lived, against whom the first wars of Ancient Greece were waged!

The historian who put into writing the grand doings of the heroic times was Plato himself. His dialogue of Timotheus and Critias was, thus to speak, written under the inspiration of Solon, poet and legislator.

One day Solon was talking with some wise old men of Saïs, a town already eight hundred years old, as the annals engraved on the sacred walls of its temples testified. One of these old men related the history of another town, a thousand years older. This first Athenian city, nine hundred centuries old, had been invaded and in part destroyed by the Atlantides. These Atlantides, said he, occupied an immense continent, larger than Africa and Asia joined together, which covered a surface between the twelfth and fortieth degree of north latitude. Their dominion extended even as far as Egypt. They wished to impose it upon Greece, but were obliged to retire before the indomitable resistance of the Hellenes. Centuries went by. A cataclysm occurred with inundations and earthquakes. One night and one day sufficed for the extinction of this Atlantis, of which the highest summits, the Madeiras, Azores, Canaries, and Cape Verd Islands still emerge.

Such were the historical souvenirs that Captain Nemo's inscription awoke in my mind. Thus, then, led by the strangest fate, I was treading on one of the mountains of this continent! I was touching with my hand these ruins a thousand times secular and contemporaneous with the geological epochs. I was walking where the contemporaries of the first man had walked. I was crushing under my heavy soles the skeletons of animals of fabulous times, which these trees, now mineralised, formerly covered with their shade.

Ah! why did time fail me? I should have liked to descend the abrupt sides of this mountain, and go over the whole of the immense continent that doubtless joined Africa to America, and to visit the great antediluvian cities. There, perhaps, before my gaze, stretched Makhinios the warlike, Eusebius the pious, whose gigantic inhabitants lived entire centuries, and who were strong enough to pile up these blocks which still resisted the action of the water. One day, perhaps, some eruptive phenomenon would bring these engulfed regions back to the surface of the waves. Sounds that announced a profound struggle of the elements have been heard, and volcanic cinders projected out of the water have been found. All this ground, as far as the Equator, is still worked by underground forces. And who knows if in some distant epoch, increased by the volcanic dejections and by successive strata of lava, the summits of ignivome mountains will not appear on the surface of the Atlantic?

Whilst I was thus dreaming, trying to fix every detail of the grand scene in my memory, Captain Nemo, leaning against a moss-covered fragment of ruin, remained motionless as if petrified in mute ecstasy. Was he dreaming about the long-gone generations and asking them the secret of human destiny? Was it here that this strange man came to refresh his historical memories and live again that ancient existence?—he who would have no modern one. What would I not have given to know his thoughts, to share and understand them!

We remained in the same place for a whole hour, contemplating the vast plain in the light of the lava that sometimes was surprisingly intense. The interior bubblings made rapid tremblings pass over the outside of the mountain. Deep noises, clearly transmitted by the liquid medium, were echoed with majestic amplitude.

At that moment the moon appeared for an instant through the mass of waters and threw her pale rays over the engulfed continent. It was only a gleam, but its effect was indescribable. The captain rose, gave a last look at the immense plain, and then, with his hand, signed to me to follow him.

We rapidly descended the mountain. When we had once passed the mineral forest I perceived the lantern of the *Nautilus* shining like a star. The captain walked straight towards it, and we were back on board as the first tints of dawn whitened the surface of the ocean.

CHAPTER THIRTY-FOUR

SUBMARINE COALFIELDS

THE NEXT day, the 20th of February, I awoke very late. The fatigues of the previous night had prolonged my sleep until eleven o'clock. I dressed promptly. I was in a hurry to know the direction of the *Nautilus*. The instruments informed me that it was running southward at a speed of twenty miles an hour and a depth of fifty fathoms.

Conseil entered. I gave him an account of our nocturnal excursion, and the panels being opened, he could still get a glimpse of the submerged continent.

In fact, the *Nautilus* was moving only five fathoms from the soil of the Atlantis plain. It was flying like a balloon before the wind above terrestrial prairies; but it would be more according to fact to say that we were in this saloon like being in a carriage of an express train. In the foreground were fantastically shaped rocks, forests of trees transformed from the vegetable to the mineral kingdom whose immovable outlines appeared under the waves. They were also stony masses, buried under a carpet of axides and anemones, bristling with long vertical hydrophytes; then blocks of lava strangely twisted that attested the fury of the underground expansions.

About 4 p.m. the ground, generally composed of thick mud and mineralised branches, gradually changed; it became more rocky and appeared strewn with conglomerations of basaltic tufa, with pieces of lava and sulphurous obsidians. I thought that a mountainous region would soon succeed the long plains, and in fact, during certain evolutions of the *Nautilus*, I perceived the southern horizon bounded by a high wall that seemed to close all issue. Its summit evidently passed above the level of the ocean. It must be a continent, or at least an island—either one of the Canaries or one of the Cape Verd Islands. Our bearings not having been taken—perhaps purposely—I was ignorant of our whereabouts. In any case such a wall appeared to me to mark the end of that Atlantis of which, after all, we had seen so little.

The night did not put a stop to my observations. Conseil had gone to his cabin. The *Nautilus*, slackening speed, fled over the confused masses on the ground, sometimes almost touching them as to rest on them, sometimes going up whimsically to the surface of the waves. I then caught a glimpse of some bright constellations through the crystal waters, and precisely five or six of these zodiacal stars that hang in the trail of Orion.

I should have remained much longer at my window, admiring the beauties of sea and sky, but the panels were shut. At that moment the *Nautilus* was close to the high wall. What it would do now I could not guess. I went to my room. The *Nautilus* did not move. I went to sleep with the firm intention of waking after a few hours' slumber.

But the next day it was eight o'clock when I returned to the saloon. I looked at the manometer. It showed me that the *Nautilus* was floating on the surface of the ocean. I heard besides, a noise of footsteps on the platform. However, no rolling betrayed to me the undulation of the upper waves.

I went up as far as the panel. It was open. But instead of the broad daylight I expected I was surrounded by profound darkness. Where were we? Had I made a mistake? Was it still night? No—there was not a star shining, and no night is so absolutely dark.

I did not know what to think when a voice said to me:

"Is that you, Professor?"

"Ah, Captain Nemo," I answered; "where are we?"

"Under the ground, Professor."

"Under ground!" I cried, "and the *Nautilus* still floating?"

"Yes; it floats still."

"But I do not understand."

"Wait a few minutes. Our lantern is going to be lighted,

and if you want a light on the subject you will soon be satisfied."

I set foot on the platform and waited. The darkness was so complete that I did not even see Captain Nemo. However, in looking at the zenith exactly above my head, I thought I could perceive a vague light—a sort of twilight—that filled a circular hole. At that moment the lantern was suddenly lighted, and its brilliancy made the vague light vanish.

I looked after having closed my eyes for an instant, dazzled by the electric flame. The *Nautilus* was stationary, near a bank something like a quay. The sea on which it was riding was a lake imprisoned in a circle of walls which measured two miles in diameter or six miles round. Its level—the manometer indicated it—could only be the same as the exterior level, for a communication naturally existed between this lake and the sea. The high walls, inclined at the base, were rounded like a vault, and made a vast tundish upside down, the height of which was about 1,200 feet. At the summit was a circular orifice through which I had seen the vague light evidently made by daylight.

Before examining the interior dispositions of this enormous cavern more attentively, before asking myself if it was the work of man or Nature, I went up to Captain Nemo.

"Where are we?" I said.

"In the very heart of an extinct volcano," he answered, "a volcano the interior of which has been invaded by the sea after some convulsion of the ground. Whilst you were asleep, Professor, the *Nautilus* penetrated into this lagoon by a natural channel opened at a depth of five fathoms below the surface of the ocean. This is its port, a sure, convenient and mysterious port, sheltered from all the winds of heaven. Find me on the coasts of your continents or islands a road-stead that equals this assured refuge against the fury of tempests."

"You certainly are in safety here, Captain Nemo. Who could get at you in the heart of a volcano? But did I not perceive an aperture at its summit?"

"Yes, a crater formerly filled with lava, smoke and flames, which now gives entrance to the life-giving air we are breathing."

"But what volcanic mountain is this then?"

"It belongs to one of the numerous islets with which this sea is strewn. A simple rock for ships, for us an immense cavern. I discovered it by accident, and accident has done me a good service."

"But could not someone descend by the orifice that forms the crater of the volcano?"

"No more than I could go up through it. For about a hundred feet the base of the mountain is practicable, but above the sides overhang and could not be climbed."

"I see, Captain, that Nature serves you everywhere and always. You are in safety on this lake, and no one but you can visit its waters. But what do you want with such a refuge? The *Nautilus* needs no port?"

"No, Professor, but it needs electricity, the elements to produce electricity, sodium to feed these elements, coal to make its sodium, and coalfields to extract the coal. Now here it happens that the sea covers entire forests that were buried in geological epochs; now mineralised and formed into coal they are an inexhaustible mine to me."

"Then your men here, Captain, do miners' work?"

"Precisely. These mines extend under the water like the coalfields of Newcastle. It is here that, clad in their bathing dresses, pickaxe and spade in hand, my men go to extract the coal that I do not even ask for from the mines of earth. When I burn this fuel for the fabrication of sodium, the smoke that escapes through the crater gives it once more the appearance of an active volcano."

"Shall we see your companions at work?"

"Not this time, at least, for I am in a hurry to continue our voyage round the submarine world. So I shall content myself with taking some of the reserves of sodium that I possess. One day will suffice to embark them, and then we shall continue our voyage. If, therefore, you wish to inspect this cavern and make the tour of the lake, take advantage of to-day, M. Aronnax."

I thanked the captain and went to look for my two companions, who had not yet left their cabin. I invited them to follow me without telling them where they were.

They came up on to the platform. Conseil, whom nothing astonished, thought it quite natural to wake up under a mountain after going to sleep under the sea. But Ned Land's only idea was to try and find out whether the cavern had any other issue.

After breakfast, about 10 a.m., we descended on the bank.

"Here we are once more on land," said Conseil.

"I don't call this land," answered the Canadian. "And, besides, we are not upon but underneath."

Between the foot of the mountain slopes and the waters of the lake ran a sandy shore, which in its widest part measured five hundred feet. Upon this it was easy to make the tour of the lake. But the base of the slopes formed an irregular soil, on which lay, in picturesque heaps, volcanic blocks and enormous pieces of pumice-stone. All these disintegrated masses, covered under the action of subterranean fires with polished enamel, shone in the lantern's electric flames. The micaceous dust of the shore that rose under our footsteps flew up like a cloud of sparks.

The ground gradually rose from the water, and we soon reached long and sinuous slopes, veritable ascents that allowed us to climb by degrees, but we were obliged to walk prudently amongst the conglomerates that no cement joined together, and our feet slipped on the glassy trachyte formed of crystal, felspar and quartz.

Our ascension continued. The slopes became steeper and narrower. Sometimes profound excavations lay in the way which we were obliged to cross. Overhanging masses had to be avoided. We crawled on our hands and knees. But by the help of Conseil's skill, and the Canadian's strength, we overcame all obstacles.

However, our ascent was soon stopped at a height of about 250 feet by impassable obstacles. There was quite a vaulted arch overhanging us, and our ascent was exchanged for a circular walk. Here and there chrysanthemums grew timidly at the foot of aloes with long and sickly-looking leaves. But amongst the lava streams I perceived little violets, still slightly scented, and I admit that I smelt them with delight. Perfume is the soul of flowers, and the sea flowers—the splendid hydrophytes—have no soul!

We had arrived at the foot of a thicket of robust dragon-trees which had pushed aside the rocks by the effort of their muscular roots, when Ned Land exclaimed:

"Why, here's a swarm of bees, sir!"

"A swarm?" replied I, with a gesture of perfect incredulity.

"Yes, a swarm," repeated the Canadian; "and the bees are buzzing all about it."

I approached and was forced to surrender to evidence. There, at the orifice of a hole in the trunk of a dragon-tree, were several thousands of the industrious insects so common in all the Canaries, and whose produce is so particularly esteemed.

The Canadian naturally wished to make a provision of honey, and it would have been churlish of me to refuse it. He lighted a quantity of dry leaves, mixed with sulphur, by means of a spark from his flint, and began to smoke out the bees. The buzzing gradually ceased, and the hive eventually yielded several pounds of perfumed honey, with which Ned Land filled his haversack.

"When I have mixed this honey with some artocarpus paste," said he, "I shall be able to offer you a delicious cake."

"It will be as good as gingerbread," said Conseil.

"Gingerbread let it be," said I; "but let us go on with our interesting walk."

At certain turns of the path we were following, the lake appeared in its whole extent. The lantern lighted up the whole of its peaceful surface that knew neither ripple nor wave. The *Nautilus* kept perfectly still. On the platform and the shore the ship's crew were working like black shadows clearly cut against the luminous atmosphere.

We were now obliged to descend towards the shore, the

crest becoming impracticable. Above us the gaping crater looked like the wide mouth of a well. From this place the sky could be clearly seen, and I saw the dishevelled clouds running before the west wind touching the summit of the mountain with their misty fringes—a certain proof that these clouds were low ones, for the volcano did not rise more than 800 feet above the sea-level.

Half an hour after the Canadian's exploit we had reached the inner shore. At that place opened a magnificent grotto. My companions and I were delighted to lie down on its fine sand. The fire had polished its enamelled and sparkling sides all dusted over with mica. Ned Land tapped the walls to try and find out their thickness. I could not help smiling. The conversation then turned upon the eternal projects of flight; and I thought I would, without saying too much, give him the hope that Captain Nemo had only come down south to renew his provision of sodium. I therefore hoped that now he would go near the coasts of Europe and America, which would allow the Canadian to renew with more success his former abortive attempt.

We had been lying for an hour in this charming grotto. The conversation, animated at first, was then languishing. We began to feel sleepy, and as I saw no reason why I should not give way to slumber, I fell fast asleep. I was dreaming (one does not choose one's dreams) that my existence was reduced to the vegetating life of a simple mollusc. It seemed to me that this grotto formed the double valve of my shell. All at once I was awakened by Conseil's voice.

"Look out!—look out!" cried the worthy fellow.

"What is it"? I asked, raising my head.

"The water is coming up to us!"

I rose. The water was rushing like a torrent into our retreat, and as we certainly were not molluscs, we were obliged to fly.

In a few minutes' time we were in safety on the summit of the grotto isself.

"What was it?" asked Conseil. "Some new phenomenon?"

"No, my friends," replied I; "it was the tide, the tide

that almost caught us as it did Walter Scott's hero! The ocean outside rises, and, by a natural law of equilibrium, the level of the lake rises likewise. We have escaped with a bath. Let us go to the *Nautilus* and change our clothes."

Three-quarters of an hour later we had ended our circular walk, and were back on board. The men of the crew were then finishing taking the sodium on board, and the *Nautilus* could have started at once.

But Captain Nemo gave no order. Perhaps he meant to wait for night, and go out secretly by his submarine passage.

However that may be, the next day the *Nautilus*, having left its moorings, was navigating far from all land, and a few yards beneath the waves of the Atlantic.

CHAPTER THIRTY-FIVE

THE SARGASSO SEA

THE DIRECTION of the *Nautilus* had not been changed. All hope of returning to the European seas must for the present be given up. Captain Nemo kept to the south. Where was he taking us to? I dared not imagine.

That day the *Nautilus* crossed a singular part of the Atlantic Ocean. Everyone knows of the existence of that great current of warm water known under the name of the Gulf Stream. After leaving the Gulf of Florida it goes towards Spitzbergen; but some time after quitting the Gulf of Mexico, about the 44th degree of north latitude, this current divides into two arms, the principal one going towards the coasts of Ireland and Norway, whilst the second bends southwards abreast of the Azores; then striking against the African shores and describing a long oval, it comes back towards the Antilles.

Now this second arm (it is rather a collar than an arm) surrounds with its circles of warm water that portion of the cool, quiet, immovable ocean called the Sargasso Sea. A perfect lake in full Atlantic, the waters of the great current takes no less than three years to go round it.

The Sargasso Sea, properly speaking, covers all the submerged part of Atlantis. Certain authors have even stated that the numerous herbs with which it is strewn are torn from the prairies of that ancient continent. It is more probable, however, that these herbs, sea-wrack and fucus, carried away from the shores of Europe and America, are brought to this zone by the Gulf Stream. That was one of the reasons that brought Columbus to suppose the existence of a new world. When the ships of this bold navigator arrived at the Sargasso Sea they sailed with difficulty amidst the herbs that impeded their course to the great terror of their crews, and they lost three long weeks crossing it.

Such was the region the *Nautilus* was now visiting, a veritable prairie, a thick carpet of sea-wrack, fucus, and tropical berries, so thick and compact that the stem of a vessel could hardly tear its way through it. And Captain Nemo, not wishing to entangle his screw in that herby mass, kept at a depth of some yards beneath the surface of the waves.

The name "Sargasso" comes from the Spanish "sargazzo," that signifies varech. This varech, or kelp, or berry-plant, principally forms this immense bank. The reason given by the learned Maury, the author of the *Physical Geography of the Sea*, for the presence of these hydrophytes in the peaceful basin of the Atlantic is the following:

"The explanation that may be given," said he, "seems to me to result from an experiment known by everyone. If some fragments of cork, or other floating bodies, are placed in a vessel of water, and a circular movement is given to the water, the scattered fragments will be seen united in a group in the centre of the liquid surface—that is to say, at the least agitated point. In the phenomenon that occupies us the vessel is the Atlantic, the Gulf Stream is the circular current, and the Sargasso Sea, the central point where the floating bodies unite."

All that day of February 22nd was passed in the Sargasso Sea, where the fish that feed on marine plants and crustaceans find abundant food. The next day the ocean had resumed its accustomed aspect.

From that date, for nineteen days, from the 23rd of February to the 12th of March, the *Nautilus*, keeping in the midst of the Atlantic, carried us along at a constant speed of one hundred leagues in twenty-four hours. Captain Nemo evidently intended to accomplish his submarine programme, and I had no doubt that after doubling Cape Horn he meant to go back into the South Pacific.

During this part of the voyage we went along for whole days on the surface of the waves. The sea was abandoned. A few sailing vessels only were to be seen, bound for the Indies, and making for the Cape of Good Hope. One day we were pursued by the boats of a whaler that had doubtless taken us for some enormous whale of great value. But Captain Nemo did not wish the brave fellows to lose their time and trouble, and he ended the pursuit by plunging under the water. This incident seemed greatly to interest Ned Land. I do not think I am mistaken in saying that the Canadian regretted that our iron-plated cetacean could not be struck dead by the harpoon of the fishers.

Until the 13th of March our navigation went on under the same conditions. That day the *Nautilus* was employed in sounding experiments that greatly interested me.

We had then come nearly 13,000 leagues since our departure from the high seas of the Pacific. Our bearings gave us 45° 37′ south lat. and 37° 53′ west long. It was the spot where Captain Denham of the *Herald*, ran out 7,000 fathoms of line without finding the bottom. There, too, Lieutenant Parker, of the American frigate *Congress*, was not able to reach the submarine depths with a line of 7,200 fathoms.

Captain Nemo resolved to send his *Nautilus* to the very bottom in order to verify these different soundings, I prepared to take notes of the result. The saloon panels were

opened, and the manœuvres necessary to reach such prodigious depths were begun.

It will be readily imagined that the filling of the reservoirs would not suffice. They would probably not have
sufficiently increased the specific weight of the *Nautilus*.
Besides, to go up again it would have been necessary to get
rid of the extra stock of water, and the pumps would not
have been powerful enough to conquer the exterior pressure.

Captain Nemo resolved to seek the oceanic bottom by a
sufficiently elongated diagonal by means of his lateral
planes, which were inclined at an angle of 45° with the water-
lines of the *Nautilus*. Then the screw was worked at its
maximum of speed, and its quadruple branch beat the water
with indescribable violence.

Under this powerful propulsion the hull of the *Nautilus*
vibrated like a sonorous wire and sank regularly under the
water. The captain and I, in the saloon, followed the needle
of the manometer that rapidly moved. We had soon passed
the habitable zone where most of the fish dwell. Some can
only live on the surface of seas or rivers, whilst others, less
numerous, inhabit greater depths. Amongst these latter I
noticed the hexanch, a species of sea-hound, furnished with
six gills; the enormous-eyed telescope; the cuirassed
malarmat, with grey thorax, black pectorals which protected his chest-plate of pale red bony plates; and lastly,
the grenadier, which, living at a depth of six hundred
fathoms, supports a pressure of a hundred and twenty
atmospheres.

I asked Captain Nemo if he had ever seen fish at greater
depths.

"Rarely," he replied.

I looked at the manometer. The instrument indicated a
depth of 3,000 fathoms. Our submersion had lasted an hour.
The *Nautilus*, gliding on its inclined planes, was still sinking.
The solitary water was admirably transparent and of a
diaphaneity that nothing could depict. An hour later we
were at a depth of 6,500 fathoms—about three leagues and
a quarter—and still there was no sign of the bottom.

However, at a depth of 7,000 fathoms I perceived some blackish summits arise amidst the waters. But these summits might belong to mountains as high as the Himalayas or Mont Blanc, higher even, and the depth of these abysses remains unknown.

The *Nautilus* sank still lower, in spite of the powerful pressure it endured. I felt the steel plates tremble under the jointures of their bolts; its bars bent; its partitions groaned; the windows of the saloon seemed to curve under the pressure of the water. And the apparatus would doubtless have been crushed in, if, as the captain said, it had not been as capable of resistance as a solid block.

Whilst skirting the declivity of these rocks, lost under the water, I still saw some shells, serpulæ, and spinorbis, still linvig, and some specimens of asteriads.

But soon these last representatives of animal life disappeared, and below three leagues the *Nautilus* passed the limits of submarine existence, like a balloon that rises above the respirable atmosphere. We had reached a depth of 8,000 fathoms—four leagues—and the sides of the *Nautilus* then supported a pressure of 1,600 atmospheres—that is to say, 3,200 lb. on each square centimetre of its surface.

"What a situation!" I cried. "To traverse these deep regions to which man has never reached! Look, Captain, look at those magnificent rocks, those uninhabited grottoes, those last receptacles of the globe where life is no longer possible! What unknown sites, and why must we be forced to keep nothing of them but the remembrance?"

"Should you like to take away anything better than the remembrance?" asked Captain Nemo.

"What do you mean?"

"I mean that nothing is easier than to take a photographic view of this submarine region!"

I had not time to express the surprise that this fresh proposition caused me before, at an order from Captain Nemo, a camera was brought into the saloon. Through the wide-opened panels the liquid, lighted up by electricity, was distributed with perfect clearness. No shade, not a gradation, was to be seen in our manufactured light. The sun would not have been more favourable to an operation of this nature. The *Nautilus*, under the propulsion of its screw, mastered by the inclination of its planes, remained motionless. The camera was pointed at these sites on the oceanic bottom, and in a few seconds we had obtained an exceedingly pure negative.

However, after Captain Nemo had terminated his operation, he said to me:

"We must go up again now, Professor. It would not do to expose the *Nautilus* too long to such pressure."

"Go up again!" I expostulated.

"Hold tight."

I had not time to understand why the captain gave me this caution before I was thrown upon the carpet.

At a signal from the captain the screw had been shipped, the planes raised vertically, and the *Nautilus*, carried up like a balloon into the air, shot along with stunning rapidity. It cut through the water with a sonorous vibration. No detail was visible. In four minutes it had cleared the four leagues that separated it from the surface of the ocean, and after emerging like a flying-fish it fell again, making the waves rebound to an enormous height.

CHAPTER THIRTY-SIX

CACHALOTS AND WHALES

During the night, from the 13th to the 14th of March, the *Nautilus* resumed her southerly direction. I thought that, once abreast of Cape Horn, the head would be turned westward, so as to make for the seas of the Pacific, and so complete its voyage round the world. Nothing of the kind was done, however, and the vessel kept on its way to the austral regions. Where was it going? To the Pole? That was madness! I began to think that the daring of the captain justified Ned Land's fears.

For some time past the Canadian had not spoken to me about his projects of flight. He had become less communicative, almost silent. I could see how much this prolonged imprisonment was weighing upon him. I felt how his anger was accumulating. When he met the captain his eyes lighted up with sombre fire, and I always feared that his natural violence would lead him into some extreme.

That day, the 14th of March, about 11 a.m., the *Nautilus*, being then on the surface of the ocean, fell in with a troop of whales—an encounter that did not surprise me, for I knew that these animals, hunted to death, had taken refuge in the high latitudes.

We were seated on the platform, with a quiet sea. The month of October in those latitudes gave us some beautiful autumnal days. It was the Canadian—he could not be mistaken—who signalled a whale on the eastern horizon. Looking attentively, we could see its black back rise and fall above the waves at five miles' distance from the *Nautilus*.

"Ah!" cried Ned Land, "if I was on board a whaler now what pleasure that sight would give me! It is one of large size. Look with what strength its blow-holes throw up columns of air and vapour! Confound it all! Why am I chained to this piece of iron?"

"What, Ned!" said I, "you have not yet got over your old fishing ideas?"

Ned Land was not listening. The whale was drawing nearer. He devoured it with his eyes.

"Ah!" cried he, "it is not one whale, but ten, twenty, a whole troop of them! And I can't do anything! I'm bound hand and foot!"

"But, friend Ned," said Conseil, "why not ask the captain's permission to pursue them?"

Conseil had not finished his sentence before Ned Land had lowered himself through the panel, and was running to seek the captain. A short time afterwards both appeared on the platform.

Captain Nemo looked at the troop of cetaceans that were playing on the waters about a mile from the *Nautilus*.

"They are austral whales," said he. "There's the fortune of a fleet of whalers there."

"Well, sir," asked the Canadian, "can't I pursue them just to prevent myself forgetting my old trade of harpooner?"

"What is the use?" answered Captain Nemo. "We have no use for whale-oil on board."

"But, sir," resumed the Canadian, "you allowed us to pursue a dugong in the Red Sea!"

"That was to procure fresh meat for my crew. Here it would only be for the pleasure of killing. I know that it is a privilege reserved to man, but I do not approve of such murderous pastime. By destroying the austral as well as the ordinary whale, both inoffensive creatures, people like you, Ned Land, commit a blamable action. It is thus they have depopulated the whole of Baffin's Bay, and they will annihilate a class of useful animals. Therefore let the unfortunate cetaceans alone. They have quite enough of their natural enemies, the cachalots, sword-fish and saw-fish, without your interfering."

I leave the Canadian's face during this moral lecture to be imagined. It was a waste of words to give such reasons to a sportsman. Ned Land looked at Captain Nemo, and evidently did not understand what he meant. However, the captain was right. The barbarous and inconsiderate greed of the fishermen will one day cause the last whale to disappear from the ocean.

Ned Land whistled "Yankee Doodle" between his teeth, and turned his back upon us.

However, Captain Nemo looked at the troop of cetaceans, and addressing me:

"I was right in saying whales had enough natural enemies, sir. They will have plenty to do before long. Do you see those black moving points, M. Aronnax, about eight miles to leeward?"

"Yes, Captain," I replied.

"They are cachalots—terrible animals that I have some-times met with in troops of two or three hundred. As to those cruel and mischievous creatures, it is right to exterminate them."

The Canadian turned quickly at these last words.

"Well, Captain," I said, "in the interest of the whales there is still time."

"It is useless to expose oneself, Professor. The *Nautilus* will suffice to disperse these cachalots. It is armed with a steel spur that I imagine is quite worth Mr. Land's harpoon."

The Canadian did not repress a shrug of the shoulders. Attack cetaceans with a prow! Who had ever heard of such a thing?

"Wait, M. Aronnax," said Captain Nemo. "We will show you a hunt you have never seen before. I have no pity for such ferocious cetaceans. They are all mouth and teeth."

Mouth and teeth! The macrocephalous cachalot, or spermaceti whale, could not be better described; it is some-times more than seventy-five feet long. Its enormous head takes up one-third of its entire body. Better armed than the whale, whose upper jaw is only furnished with whalebone, it is supplied with twenty-five large tusks, about three inches long, cylindrical, and conical at the top, which weigh two pounds each. It is in the upper part of this enormous head, in great cavities divided by cartilages, that from six to eight hundred pounds of the precious oil called sper-maceti is found. The cachalot is an ugly animal, more of a tadpole than a fish, according to Frédol's description. It is badly formed, the whole of the left side being what we might call a "failure," and seeing little except with the right eye.

In the meantime the formidable troop was drawing nearer. They had perceived the whales, and were preparing to attack them. One could prophesy beforehand that the cachalots would be victorious, not only because they were better built for attack than their inoffensive adversaries, but also because they could remain longer under the waves without rising to the surface.

There was only just time to go to the help of the whales when the *Nautilus* came up to them. The *Nautilus* sank: Conseil, Ned and I took our places at the windows of the saloon. Captain Nemo joined the helmsman in his cage to work his apparatus as an engine of destruction. I soon felt the vibration of the screw increase and our speed become greater.

The combat between the cachalots and whales had already begun when the *Nautilus* reached them. It was worked so as to divide the cachalots, who at first showed no fear at the sight of the new monster joining in the conflict. But they soon had to guard against its blows.

What a struggle! Ned Land himself, soon enthusiastic, ended by clapping his hands. The *Nautilus* was now nothing but a formidable harpoon, brandished by the hand of its captain. It hurled itself against the fleshy mass, cut it through from end to end, leaving behind it two quivering halves of an animal. It did not feel the formidable blows on its sides from the cachalots' tails, nor the shocks it produced itself. One cachalot exterminated, it ran to another, tacked on the spot that it might not miss its prey, going backwards and forwards obedient to its helm, plunging when the cetacean dived into deep water, coming back with it to the surface, striking it in front or sideways, cutting or tearing in all directions and at any pace, piercing it through with its terrible spur.

At last the mass of cachalots was broken up, the waves became quiet again. and I felt that we were rising to the surface of the ocean. The panel was opened, and we rushed on to the platform.

The sea was covered with mutilated bodies. A formidable explosion could not have divided or cut up these fleshy masses more effectually. We were floating amidst gigantic bodies, bluish on the back, whitish underneath, covered with enormous protuberances. Some terrified cachalots were flying away on the horizon. The waves were dyed red for several miles round, and the *Nautilus* was floating in a sea of blood.

Captain Nemo joined us.

"Well, Mr. Land?" said he.

"Well, sir," answered the Canadian, whose enthusiasm had calmed down, "it is a terrible spectacle, certainly. But I am not a butcher; I am a hunter, and this is only butchery."

"It is a massacre of mischievous animals," replied the captain, "and the *Nautilus* is not a butcher's knife."

"I like my harpoon better," answered the Canadian.

"Each to his arm," replied the captain, looking fixedly at Ned Land.

From that day I noticed with uneasiness that Ned Land's ill-will for the captain increased, and I resolved to watch the Canadian's doings and gestures very closely.

CHAPTER THIRTY-SEVEN

THE ICE-BANK

THE *Nautilus* resumed her imperturbable southwardly course, following the fiftieth meridian with considerable speed. Did it mean then, to reach the Pole? I did not think so, for hitherto every attempt to reach that point had failed. The season, besides, was far advanced, for in the Antarctic regions the 13th of March corresponds to the 13th of September of Arctic regions, which begins the equinoctial period.

On the 14th of March I perceived floating ice by 55° of latitude—merely pale debris from twenty to twenty-five feet long, forming reefs over which the sea curled. The *Nautilus* kept on the surface of the ocean. Ned Land who had already fished in the Arctic seas, was familiar with the spectacle of icebergs. Conseil and I were admiring it for the first time.

In the air, towards the southern horizon, stretched a white band of dazzling aspect. English whalers have given it the name of "ice-blink." However thick the clouds may be, they cannot hide it, it announces the presence of an ice-pack or bank.

In fact, larger blocks soon appeared, the brilliancy of which was modified according to the caprices of the mist. Some of these masses showed green veins, as if the long undulating lines had been traced by sulphate of copper. Others, like enormous amethysts, let the light shine through them. Some reflected the rays of the sun upon a thousand crystal facets. Others, shaded with vivid calcareous tints, would have sufficed for the construction of a whole town in marble.

The temperature was rather low. The thermometer, exposed to the exterior air, indicated two or three degrees below zero. But we were warmly dressed in furs that seals or Polar bears had furnished us with. The interior of the *Nautilus* regularly heated by its electrical apparatus, defied the most intense cold. Besides, it had only to sink some yards below the surface to find a supportable temperature. Two months earlier we should have experienced perpetual daylight in these latitudes; but we had already three or four hours' night, and by and by there would be six months of darkness in these circumpolar regions.

On the 15th of March we passed the latitude of the New Shetland and New Orkney Islands. The captain informed me that formerly numerous tribes of seals inhabited them; but the English and American whalers, in their rage for destruction, massacred even mothers with young, and left the silence of death where life and animation formerly existed.

On the 16th of March, about 8 a.m., the *Nautilus*, following the fifty-fifth meridian, crossed the Antarctic Polar Circle. Ice surrounded us on every side and closed the horizon. Still Captain Nemo went through one passage after another, and still more southward.

"Where can he be going to?" I asked.

"He is following his nose," answered Conseil. "After all, when he cannot go any farther he will stop."

"I would not swear to that!" I answered. And, to tell the truth, I must acknowledge that this adventurous excursion did not displease me. I cannot express my astonishment at the beauties of these new regions. The ice took most superb forms. Here the grouping formed an Oriental town, with its innumerable minarets and mosques; there an overturned city, looking as if thrown to the earth by some earthquake—aspects incessantly varied by the oblique rays of the sun or lost in the grey mists amidst snowstorms. Detonations and ice-slips were heard on all sides—great overflows of icebergs that changed the scene like the landscape of a diorama.

When the *Nautilus* was submerged at the moment that these equilibriums were disturbed, the noise was propagated under the water with frightful intensity, and the fall of the masses created fearful eddies as far as the greatest depth of the ocean. The *Nautilus* then pitched and tossed like a ship given up to the fury of the elements.

Often, seeing no issue, I thought we were definitely prisoners; but instinct guided him, and on the slightest indication Captain Nemo discovered new passages. He never made a mistake in observing the slender threads of bluish water that furrowed the ice-fields. I did not doubt that he had already steered his *Nautilus* in the Antarctic seas.

However, on the 16th of March ice-fields absolutely barricaded the road. It was not yet the ice-bank, but vast ice-fields cemented by the cold. This obstacle could not stop Captain Nemo, and he threw himself against the ice-field with frightful violence. The *Nautilus* entered the brittle mass like a wedge, and split it up with a frightful cracking noise. It was the ancient battering-ram hurled by infinite power. Pieces of ice, thrown high in the air, fell in hail around us. By its single power of impulsion our apparatus made a canal for itself. Sometimes by the force of its own impetus it fell on the ice-field and crushed it with its weight, or, deeply engaged in the ice, it divided it by a simple pitching movement that opened up wide fissures in it.

At length, on the 18th of March, after many useless assaults, the *Nautilus* was positively blocked up. It was no longer stopped by either streams, packs, or ice-fields, but an interminable and immovable barrier, formed by icebergs soldered together.

There was no longer the slightest appearance of sea or liquid surface before our eyes. Under the prow of the *Nautilus* stretched a vast plain covered with confused blocks, looking like the surface of a river some time before the breaking up of the ice, but on a gigantic scale. Here and there sharp peaks and slender needles rising to a height of two hundred feet; farther, a line of cliffs with precipitous sides, covered with greyish tints, vast mirrors that reflected a few rays of the sun, half drowned in the mists. Then over this desolate scene a savage silence, scarcely broken by the flapping of petrels' or puffins' wings. All was then frozen, even sound.

In fact, notwithstanding all its efforts, notwithstanding the powerful means employed to break up the ice, the *Nautilus* was reduced to immobility. Generally, if you cannot go any farther, all you have to do is to go back. But here going back was as impossible as going on, for the passages had closed up behind us, and if our apparatus remained stationary long it would soon be blocked up. That is what happened about 2 p.m., and the young ice formed on its sides with astonishing rapidity. I was forced to acknowledge that Captain Nemo's conduct was more than imprudent. I was at that moment on the platform. The captain, who had been observing the situation for some minutes, said to me:

"Well, Professor, what do you think of it?"

"I think we are caught, Captain."

"Ah, Professor!" answered the captain in an ironical tone, "you are always the same! You only see obstacles and difficulties. But I affirm to you that not only will the *Nautilus* be set free, but it will go farther still!"

"Farther south?" I asked, looking at the captain.

"Yes, sir, it will go to the Pole."

"To the Pole!" I cried, unable to restrain a movement of incredulity.

"Yes," replied the captain coldly, "to the Antarctic Pole, to that unknown point where all the meridians of the globe meet. You know whether I do all I please with the *Nautilus*."

It then came into my head to ask Captain Nemo if he had already discovered this Pole, which no human being had set foot upon.

"No, Professor," he answered, "and we will discover it together. There, where so many have failed, I shall not fail. I have never brought my *Nautilus* so far south; but, I repeat, it shall go farther still."

"I wish to believe you, Captain," said I in a slightly ironical tone. "I do believe you! There is no obstacle before us! We will break up that ice-bank, and if it resists, we will give the *Nautilus* wings so that we can pass over it!"

"Over it, Professor?" answered Captain Nemo tranquilly. "No, not over it, but under it."

"Under it!" I cried.

A sudden revelation of the captain's projects illuminated my mind. I understood. The marvellous qualities of the *Nautilus* would again be of service in this superhuman enterprise.

"I see that we begin to understand each other, Professor," said the captain, half smiling. "You already catch a glimpse of the possibility—I say of the success—of this attempt. What is impracticable to an ordinary ship is easy to the *Nautilus*. If a continent emerges at the Pole, it will stop before that continent. But if, on the contrary, the Pole is bathed by the open sea, the *Nautilus* will go to the Pole itself."

"It is certain," said I, carried along by the captain's reasoning, "that though the surface of the sea is solidified by ice, its depths are free on account of the providential reason that has placed the maximum of density of sea-water at a superior degree to its congelation. And if I am not mistaken, the submerged part of this ice-bank is to the emerged part as four to one."

"About that, Professor. For every foot that icebergs have above the sea they have three below. Now as these mountains of ice are 300 feet high, they are not more than 900 deep. Well, what is 900 feet to the *Nautilus*?"

"Nothing, Captain."

"It might even go and seek at a greater depth the uniform temperature of sea-water, and there we could brave with impunity the thirty or forty degrees of cold on the surface."

"True, sir, very true," I answered, getting animated.

"The only difficulty," continued Captain Nemo, "will be to remain submerged for several days without renewing the air."

"Is that all?" I replied. "The *Nautilus* contains vast reservoirs; we will fill them, and they will furnish us with all the oxygen we shall want."

"Well imagined, M. Aronnax," said the captain, smiling. "But I did not wish you to accuse me of foolhardiness, so I submit all objections to you beforehand."

"Have you any more to make?"

"One only. It is possible that if sea exists at the South Pole, that sea may be entirely frozen over, and consequently we cannot go up to the surface."

"Well, sir, do you forget that the *Nautilus* is armed with a powerful prow, and can we not hurl it diagonally against the ice-fields, which will open at the shock?"

"Ah, Professor, you have some good ideas to-day!"

"Besides, Captain," said I, getting more and more enthusiastic, "why should we not find an open sea at the South as well as at the North Pole? The cold poles and the poles of the globe are not the same either in the boreal or austral hemispheres, and until we get proofs to the contrary we may suppose there is either a continent or an ocean free from ice at these two points of the globe."

"I think so too, M. Aronnax," answered Captain Nemo. "I will only observe to you that after uttering so many objections to my scheme, you now crush me with arguments in favour of it."

Captain Nemo spoke truly. I had come to rival him in audacity. It was I who was dragging him to the Pole! I out-distanced him. But no, poor fool! Captain Nemo knew the for and against better than you, and was amusing himself with seeing you carried away by your dreams of the impossible.

In the meantime he had not lost an instant. At a signal the first officer appeared. These two men spoke rapidly in their incomprehensible language, and whether it was that the first officer had been told of it beforehand, or that he found the scheme practicable, he manifested no surprise.

But he did not show more impassiveness than Conseil when I told the worthy fellow of our intention of going as far as the South Pole. An "As monsieur pleases" answered my communication, and with that I was obliged to content myself. As to Ned Land, he shrugged his shoulders up as high as they would go."

"I am sorry for you and your captain, M. Aronnax," said he.

"But we shall go to the Pole, Ned!"

"Possibly, but you won't come back!"

The preparations for this audacious attempt was now begun. The powerful pumps of the *Nautilus* were working air into the reservoirs, and storing it at high pressure. About four o'clock Captain Nemo informed me that the panels of the platform were going to be closed. I threw a last look at the thick ice-bank we were going to pass. The weather was clear, the atmosphere pure, and the cold very piercing, twelve degrees below zero; but the wind had lulled, and this temperature did not seem unbearable.

About ten men got up on the sides of the *Nautilus*, and, armed with pickaxes, broke the ice round the hull, which was soon set free. This was a speedy operation, for the young ice was still thin. We all went back into the interior. The usual reservoirs were filled with the liberated water, and the *Nautilus* soon sank.

At a depth of nine hundred feet, as Captain Nemo had foreseen, we were floating under the undulated surface of the ice-bank. But the *Nautilus* sank lower still. It reached a depth of four hundred fathoms. The temperature of the water which gave 12° on the surface was now only 10°. Two degrees were already gained. Of course, the temperature of the *Nautilus* raised by its heating apparatus, kept up to a much superior degree. All the manœuvres were accomplished with extraordinary precision.

Under the sea, the *Nautilus* had gone the direct road to the Pole straight along the fifty-second meridian. There remained from 67° 30' to 90°, twenty-two and a half degrees —to cross—that is to say, rather more than five hundred leagues. The *Nautilus* went at an average speed of twenty-six miles an hour—that of an express train (a *French* express). If it kept it up for forty hours that time would be enough to reach the Pole.

The next day, March 19th, at 5 a.m., I went back to my station in the saloon. The electric log indicated that the speed of the *Nautilus* had only been moderate. It was then going up towards the surface, but prudently, by slowly emptying its reservoirs.

My heart beat quickly. Were we going to emerge and find the free atmosphere of the Pole?

No. A shock told me that the *Nautilus* had struck against the bottom of the ice-bank, still very thick, to judge by the dullness of the sound. We had struck a depth of 1,000 feet. That gave 2,000 feet, above us, 1,000 feet of which emerged. The ice-bank, therefore, was higher than it was on its border—a not very reassuring fact.

During that day the *Nautilus* several times recommenced the same experiment, and always struck against the wall that hung above it like a ceiling. At certain moments it met at a depth of five hundred fathoms. Sometimes it was double the height it was where the *Nautilus* sank.

I carefully noted these different depths, and thus obtained a submarine profile of this chain.

In the evening no change had occurred in our situation.

Still ice between two and three hundred fathoms deep—an evident diminution, but what thickness there still was between us and the surface of the ocean!

It was then 8 p.m. According to the daily custom on board the air ought to have been renewed four hours before. I did not suffer from it much, although Captain Nemo had not yet drawn upon his reservoirs for a supplement of oxygen.

My sleep was restless that night. Hope and fear besieged me by turns. I rose several times. The gropings of the *Nautilus* were still going on. About 3 a.m. I noticed that the lower surface of the ice-bank was met with at a depth of only twenty-five fathoms. A hundred and fifty feet next separated us from the surface of the water. The ice-bank was gradually becoming an ice-field. The mountain was becoming a plain.

My eyes no longer left the manometer. We were still ascending, diagonally following the brilliant surface that shone under the rays of the electric lamp. The ice-bank was getting lower above and below in long slopes. It got thinner from mile to mile.

At last, at 6 a.m. on this memorable 19th of March, the door of the saloon opened. Captain Nemo appeared.

"The open sea!" he said.

CHAPTER THIRTY-EIGHT

THE SOUTH POLE

I RUSHED upon the platform. Yes! There lay the open sea. A few pieces of ice and moving icebergs were scattered about; in the distance a long stretch of sea; a world of birds in the air and myriads of fish in the waters which, according to their depth, varied from intense blue to olive green. The thermometer marked three degrees above zero. It was like a relative spring enclosed behind this ice-bank, whose distant masses were outlined on the northern horizon.

" Are we at the Pole?" I asked the captain, with a palpitating heart.

"I do not crow yet," he answered. "At noon we will take
our bearings."

"But will the sun show itself through these mists?" said
I, looking at the grey sky.

"However little it shows, it will be enough for me,"
answered the captain.

About ten miles south of the *Nautilus* a solitary island rose
to a height of six hundred feet. We were bearing down
upon it, but prudently, for the sea might be strewn with
reefs.

An hour afterwards we had reached the islet. Two hours
later we had been round it. It measured from four to five
miles in circumference. A narrow channel separated it
from a considerable stretch of land, perhaps a continent,
the limits of which we could not perceive. The existence of
this land seemed to prove Maury's hypothesis. The ingenious
American has, in fact, remarked that between the South
Pole and the 60th parallel the sea is covered with floating
icebergs of enormous dimensions, which are never met
with in the North Atlantic. From this fact he drew the
conclusion that the Antarctic circle encloses a considerable
quantity of land, as icebergs cannot form in the open
sea, but only on coasts. According to his calculations,
the mass of icebergs that surround the austral pole forms a
vast cape, the width of which must reach three hundred
miles.

The *Nautilus*, for fear of being stranded, had stopped at
three cables' length from a beach, over which rose a superb
heap of rocks. The boat was launched. The captain, two of
his men carrying the instruments, Conseil, and I embarked.
It was 10 a.m. I had not seen Ned Land. The Canadian,
doubtless, did not wish to acknowledge himself in the wrong
in the presence of the South Pole.

A few strokes of the oars brought the boat on to the
sand, where it stranded. As Conseil was going to jump out
I stopped him.

"Captain Nemo," said I, "to you belongs the honour of first setting foot on this land."

"Yes, Professor," answered the captain, "and I do not hesitate to do so, because, until now, no human being has left the imprint of his footsteps upon it."

That said he jumped lightly on the sand. Keen emotion made his heart beat faster. He climbed a rock which overhung, forming a small promontory, and there, with his arms crossed, mute and motionless, he seemed to take possession with an eager look of these southern regions. After five minutes passed in this rapt contemplation he turned towards us.

"When you are ready, Professor," he called to me.

I disembarked, followed by Conseil, leaving the two men in the boat.

For some distance the soil was composed of a reddish tufa, as if it had been made of crushed bricks. Scoriæ, lava streams, and pumice-stone covered it. Its volcanic origin could not be mistaken. In certain places some slight curls of smoke attested that the interior fires still kept their expansive force. Still, when I had climbed a high cliff, I saw no volcano within a radius of several miles. It is known that in these Antarctic countries James Ross found the craters of the *Erebus* and *Terror* in full activity on the 167th meridian, and in lat. 77° 32′.

The vegetation of this desolate continent seemed to me very restricted. Some lichens of the species *Unsnea melanoxantha* were spread upon the black rocks, certain microscopic plantlets, rudimentary diatomas, a sort of cells placed between two quartz shells, long purple and crimson fucus, supported on small natatory bladders, and which the tide threw upon the shore, composed the whole meagre flora of the region.

But in the air life was superabundant. There thousands of birds of all kinds fluttered and flew about, deafening us with their cries. Others crowded the rocks, gazing at us, as we passed, without fear, and pressing familiarly under our feet. There were penguins as agile and supple in the water, where they are sometimes taken for rapid bonitoes, as they are heavy and clumsy on land. They uttered harsh sounds, and formed numerous assemblies, sober in gesture, but prodigal of clamour.

About half a mile farther on the soil was riddled with ruffs' nests; it was a sort of laying ground from which many birds issued. Captain Nemo had some hundreds killed, for their blackish flesh is very good. They uttered a cry like the braying of an ass, were about the size of a goose, slate-colour on the body, white underneath, with a yellow cravat round their throats. They let themselves be killed with stones without trying to escape.

When I rejoined Captain Nemo I found him silently leaning against a rock, and looking at the sky. He seemed impatient and vexed. But there was no help for it. This powerful and audacious man could not command the sun like he did the sea.

Twelve o'clock came without the sun having showed itself for a single instant. Even the place it occupied behind the curtain of mist could not be distinguished. The mist soon after dissolved in snow.

"We must wait till to-morrow," said the captain simply, and we went back to the *Nautilus* amidst the snow.

The snowstorm lasted until the next day. It was impossible to keep upon the platform. From the saloon, where I was taking notes of the incidents of this excursion, to the Polar continent, I heard the cries of petrels and albatrosses playing amidst the tempest. The *Nautilus* did not remain motionless, and, coasting the continent, it went about ten miles farther south in the sort of twilight that the sun left as it skirted the horizon.

The next day, the 20th of March, the snow had ceased. It was slightly colder. The thermometer indicated two degrees below zero. The mists rose, and I hoped it would be possible to take an observation that day.

Captain Nemo not having yet appeared, the boat took Conseil and me to the land. The nature of the soil was the same—volcanic. Everywhere traces of lava, scoriæ, basalts, but no trace of the crater from which they issued. Here, as there, myriads of birds animated this part of the Polar continent. But they divided this empire with vast troops of marine mammalia, who looked at us with their soft eyes. They were seals of different sorts, some lying on the ground, some on floating pieces of ice, several coming out of the sea or plunging into it. They did not run away at our approach, never having had to do with man, and I counted enough for the provisioning of some hundreds of ships.

It was 8 a.m. We had four hours to employ before the sun could be usefully observed. I guided our steps towards a vast bay that was hollowed out of the granitic cliff of the shore.

There I may say that as far as the eye could reach, land and ice were covered with marine mammalia, and I looked involuntarily for old Proteus, the mythological shepherd who watched over these immense flocks of Neptune. There were more seals than anything else, forming distinct groups, male and female, the father watching over his family, the mother suckling her little ones, some already strong enough to go a few steps. When they wish to move from place to place they take little jumps, made by the contraction of their bodies, and helped awkwardly by their one imperfect fin, which, as with the lamantin, their congener, forms a perfect forearm. I ought to say that in the water, their element *par excellence*, these animals, with their mobile dorsal spine, with smooth and close skin and webbed feet, swim admirably. When resting on the earth they take the most graceful attitudes. Thus the ancients, observing their soft and expressive looks, which cannot be surpassed by the most beautiful look a woman can give—their clear, voluptuous eyes, and their charming positions, turning them into poetry, metamorphosed the males into tritons and the females into syrens.

I made Conseil notice the large development of the lobes of the brain in these interesting creatures. No mammal, except man, has so much cerebral matter. Seals are capable of receiving a certain amount of education, are easily tamed, and I think, with other naturalists, that if properly trained they might render good service as fishing-dogs.

The greater part of these seals slept on the rocks or sand. Amongst those seals, properly so called, which have no external ears—in which they differ from the otter, whose ears are prominent—I noticed several varieties of stenorhynchi, about nine feet long, with white coats, bulldog heads armed with ten teeth in either jaw, four incisive ones top and bottom, and two large canine teeth in the form of a *fleur-de-lys*. Amongst them glided marine elephants—a sort of seals with short and mobile trumpets (the giants of the species), which on a circumference of twenty feet measured ten metres. They made no movement at our approach.

"Are they dangerous animals?" asked Conseil.

"No," I answered, "unless they are attacked. When a seal is defending its young its fury is terrible, and it is not rare for it to break fishing-boats in pieces."

Two miles farther on we were stopped by a promontory which sheltered the bay against the south winds. It fell straight down into the sea, and was covered with foam from the waves. Beyond we heard formidable bellowings such as a troop of oxen might have uttered.

After we had reached the top of the promontory I perceived a vast white plain covered with walruses. They were playing and howling with joy, and not anger.

Walruses resemble seals in the form of their bodies and the disposition of their limbs. But both canine and incisive teeth are wanting in their lower jaw, and the upper canines are two defences a yard long which measure thirty-two inches to the circumference of their alveolus. These tusks—made of compact ivory, not striated, harder than that of elephants and less subject to go yellow—are much sought after. Accordingly walruses are much hunted, and their destroyers massacring indiscriminately females with young and young ones, destroy more than four thousand every year.

Passing near these curious animals I had full leisure to observe them, for they did not disturb themselves. Their skins were thick and rugged, of a fawn colour inclining to red; their hair was short and scanty; some were twelve feet long. Quieter and less timid than their congeners of the north, they did not confide to picked sentinels the care of watching the approaches to their encampment.

After having examined this city of walruses I thought of retracing my steps. It was eleven o'clock, and if Captain Nemo found he could take an observation I wished to be present at his operation. However, I hardly hoped that the sun would show itself that day; piled-up clouds on the horizon hid him from our sight. It seemed as if the jealous planet would not reveal to human beings the unavoidable point of the globe.

However, I thought of returning to the *Nautilus*. We were following a narrow track that ran up to the summit of the cliff. At half-past eleven we had reached the spot where we landed. The stranded boat had landed the captain. I perceived him standing on a block of basalt. His instruments were by him. His eyes were fixed on the northern horizon, above which the sun was describing his elongated curve.

I stood near him and waited without speaking. Twelve o'clock came, and, like the day before, the sun did not appear.

It was like fatality. We still wanted an observation. If it were not taken to-morrow we must definitely renounce taking our position.

In fact, we were at the 20th of March. The next day, the 21st, was the day of the equinox, and the refraction not counting, the sun would disappear below the horizon for six months, and with its disappearance the long Polar night would begin. Since the September equinox it had been above the northern horizon, rising by elongated spirals until the 21st of December. At that epoch, the summer solstice of these austral countries, it had begun to sink, and the next day it would shoot forth its last rays.

The next day, the 21st of March, at 5 a.m., I went up on to the platform and found Captain Nemo there.

"The weather is clearing up a little," said he; "I have

great hopes of it. After breakfast we will land and choose a post of observation."

This agreed upon, I went to Ned Land and tried to persuade him to come with me. The obstinate Canadian refused, and I saw that his taciturnity, like his bad temper, increased every day. After all I did not much regret his obstinacy in this circumstance. There were really too many seals on land, and such a temptation should not be placed before the unreflecting fisher.

Breakfast over, I landed. The *Nautilus* had gone forty miles farther south still during the night. It was at a good league from the coast, which rose to an abrupt peak of 1,600 feet. The boat carried also, Captain Nemo, two of his crew, and the instruments—that is to say, a chronometer, a telescope and a barometer.

We landed at nine o'clock. The sky was getting clearer; the clouds were flying south. The mists were rising from the cold surface of the water. Captain Nemo walked towards the peak, of which he doubtless meant to make his observatory. It was a difficult ascent over the sharp lava and pumice-stones, in an atmosphere often saturated with a sulphurous smell from the smoking fissures. For a man unaccustomed to tread on land, the captain climbed the steep slopes with an agility that I could not equal and that a chamois-hunter might have envied.

When Captain Nemo reached the top he carefully took its height by means of the barometer, for he would have to take it into consideration in taking his observation.

At a quarter to twelve the sun, then only seen by refraction, looked like a golden disc, shedding its last rays over these lands and seas which man had never before ploughed.

Captain Nemo, provided with a reticulated glass which, by means of a mirror, corrected the refraction, watched the sun as it disappeared gradually below the horizon describing an elongated diagonal. I held the chronometer. My heart beat quickly. If the disappearance of half the disc coincided with the noon of the chronometer, we were at the Pole itself.

"Twelve!" I cried.

"The South Pole!" answered Captain Nemo in a grave tone, giving me the glass which showed the sun cut in exactly equal halves by the horizontal.

So saying, Captain Nemo unfurled a black flag, bearing an N in gold, quartered on its bunting. Then, turning towards the sun, whose last rays were lapping the horizon of the sea, he exclaimed:

"Adieu, sun! Disappear, thou radiant star! Rest beneath this free sea, and let a six months' night spread its darkness over my new domain!"

CHAPTER THIRTY-NINE

ACCIDENT OR INCIDENT?

THE NEXT day, March 22, at 6 a.m., preparations for departure were begun. The last gleams of twilight were melting into night. The cold was intense. The constellations shone with wonderful intensity. In the zenith glittered that wondrous southern cross, the Polar star of Antarctic regions.

In the meantime the reservoirs of water were being filled, and the *Nautilus* was slowly sinking. It stopped at a depth of one thousand feet. It beat the waves with its screw, and advanced northwards at the rate of fifteen miles an hour. Towards evening it was already floating under the immense carapace of the ice-bank.

At 3 a.m. I was awakened by a violent shock. I rose up in bed, and was listening amidst the obscurity, when I was roughly thrown into the middle of the room. The *Nautilus* had evidently made a considerable rebound after having struck.

I groped along the partition through the waist to the saloon, which was lighted up by the luminous ceiling. The furniture was all upset. Happily the window-sashes were firmly set, and had stood fast. The pictures on the starboard side, through the vessel being no longer vertical, were sticking to the tapestry, whilst those on the larboard side were hanging a foot from the wall at their lower edge. The *Nautilus* was lying on its starboard side completely motionless.

In the interior I heard a noise of footsteps and confused voices. But Captain Nemo did not appear. At the moment I was going to leave the saloon Ned Land and Conseil entered.

"What is the matter?" said I immediately.

"I came to ask monsieur," answered Conseil.

"*Mille diables!*" cried the Canadian. "I know very well what it is. The *Nautilus* has struck, and to judge by the way it is lying, it won't come off quite so easily as in Torres Straits."

"But at least," I asked, "is it on the surface of the sea?"

"We do not know," answered Conseil.

"It is easy to find out," said I.

I consulted the manometer. To my great surprise it indicated a depth of one hundred and eighty fathoms.

"What can this mean?" I exclaimed.

"We must ask Captain Nemo," said Conseil.

"But where shall we find him?" asked Ned Land.

"Follow me," I said to my two companions.

We left the saloon. There was no one in the library, or on the central staircase, or in the ward-room. I supposed that Captain Nemo must be in the helmsman's cage. The only thing to do was to wait. We all three returned to the saloon.

We had been thus for twenty minutes listening to the least noise in the interior of the *Nautilus*, when Captain Nemo entered. He did not seem to see us. His countenance, habitually so impassive, revealed a certain anxiety. He looked at the compass and manometer in silence, and put his finger on a point of the planisphere in that part that represented the South Seas.

"May I know, sir," I asked, "the cause of this accident?"

"An enormous block of ice, a whole mountain, has turned

over," he answered. "When icebergs are undermined by warmer water or reiterated shocks, their centre of gravity ascends. Then the whole thing turns over. That is what has happened. One of these blocks as it turned over struck the *Nautilus*, which was floating under the waters. Then gliding under its hull, and raising it with irresistible force, it has raised it to less dense waters, and thrown it on its side."

"But cannot the *Nautilus* be got off by employing the reservoirs so as to restore its equilibrium?"

"That is what they are doing now, sir. You can hear the pump working. Look at the needle of the manometer. It indicates that the *Nautilus* is ascending, but the block of ice is ascending with it, and until some obstacle stops its upward movement our position will not be changed."

The *Nautilus* still kept the same position. It would, doubtless, right itself when the block itself stopped. But at that moment how did we know that we should not strike against the ice-bank and so be frightfully squeezed between the two frozen surfaces?

I reflected on all the consequences of this situation. Captain Nemo did not cease to watch the manometer. The *Nautilus*, since the fall of the iceberg, had ascended about one hundred and fifty feet, but it still made the same angle with the perpendicular.

Suddenly a slight movement was felt in the hull. The *Nautilus* was evidently righting itself a little. The objects hung up in the saloon were insensibly recovering their normal position. The partitions became more vertical. No one spoke. With heightened emotion we watched the vessel right itself. The flooring became horizontal under our feet. Ten minutes went by.

"At last we are straight!" I exclaimed.

"Yes," said Captain Nemo, going to the door of the saloon.

"But shall we get afloat again?" I asked him.

"Certainly," he answered, "since the reservoirs are not yet empty, and that when they are the *Nautilus* will ascend to the surface of the sea."

The captain went out, and I soon saw that, following his orders, they had stopped the ascension of the *Nautilus*. In fact, it would soon have struck against the bottom of the ice-bank and it was better to keep it in the water.

"We have had a narrow escape!" then said Conseil.

"Yes. We might have been crushed between two blocks of ice, or, at least, imprisoned. And then, not being able to renew the air—— Yes, we have had a narrow escape!"

"If that is all!" murmured Ned Land.

I did not wish to begin a useless discussion with the Canadian so did not answer him. Besides, at that moment the panels of the saloon were opened and the electric light. shone through the glass panes.

We were in full water, as I have said; but at a distance of thirty feet on each side of the *Nautilus* rose a dazzling wall of ice. Above and below the same wall. Above, because the bottom of the ice-bank formed an immense ceiling. Below, because the overturned block, gliding down by degrees, had found on the lateral walls two resting-places which kept it in that position. The *Nautilus* was imprisoned in a veritable tunnel of ice, about sixty feet wide, filled with tranquil water. It would, therefore, be easy for it to go out of it by going either backwards or forwards, and finding, at some hundreds of feet lower down, a free passage under the ice-bank.

It was then 5 a.m. At that moment a shock took place in the bows of the *Nautilus*. I knew that its prow had struck against a block of ice. This, I thought, must be a mistaken manœuvre, for the submarine tunnel, obstructed by block, was not easily navigated. I therefore imagined that Captain Nemo, changing his direction, would turn round these obstacles, or follow the sinuosities of the tunnel. In any case our forward journey could not be quite prevented. Still, contrary to my expectation, the *Nautilus* began a decided retrograde movement.

"We are going backwards?" said Conseil.

"Yes," I answered, "the tunnel must be without issue on that side."

"And what will be done then?"

"Then," I said, "the manœuvre is very simple. We shall retrace our steps and get out by the southern orifice, that is all."

I walked backwards and forward for some minutes between the saloon and the library. My companions also were silent. I soon threw myself upon a divan, and took a book which my eyes ran over mechanically.

Some hours passed. I often looked at the instruments hung up on the walls of the saloon. The manometer indicated that the *Nautilus* kept at a constant depth of nine hundred feet, the compass that we were going south, the log that our speed was twenty miles an hour—an excessive speed in that narrow space. But Captain Nemo knew that he could not make too much haste, and that now minutes were worth centuries.

At twenty-five minutes past eight a second shock took place, this time at the back. I turned pale. My companions came up to me. I seized Conseil's hand. We questioned each other with a look more directly than if words had interpreted our thoughts.

At that moment the captain entered the saloon. I went to him.

"The route is barricaded on the south?" I asked.

"Yes, sir. As the iceberg turned over it closed all issue."

"Then we are blocked up?"

"Yes."

CHAPTER FORTY

WANT OF AIR

THUS THERE was around the *Nautilus*, above and below, an impenetrable wall of ice. We were imprisoned in the ice-bank. The Canadian struck a formidable blow on the table with his fist. Conseil said nothing. I looked at the captain. His face had regained its usual impassiveness. He had crossed his arms over his breast and was reflecting. The *Nautilus* was quite still.

The captain then spoke.

"Gentlemen," said he, in a calm voice, "there are two ways of dying under our present circumstances."

This inexplicable personage looked like a professor of mathematics stating a problem to his pupils.

"The first," he continued, "is to be crushed to death; the second is to be suffocated. I need not speak of the possibility of dying of hunger, for the provisions of the *Nautilus* will certainly outlast us."

"We cannot be suffocated, Captain," I answered, "for our reservoirs are full."

"True," said Captain Nemo, "but they will only give us air for two days. Now we have already been six and thirty hours under water, and the heavy atmosphere of the *Nautilus* already wants renewing. In forty-eight hours our reserve will be exhausted."

"Well, Captain, we must get out before forty-eight hours."

"We will try, at all events, by piercing through the wall that surrounds us."

"On which side?" I asked.

"The bore will tell us that. I am going to run the *Nautilus* on to the lower bank, and my men will put on their diving dresses and attack the wall where it is the least thick."

"Can we have the saloon panels opened?"

"Certainly; we are no longer moving."

Captain Nemo went out. A hissing sound told me that the reservoirs were being filled with water. The *Nautilus* gradually sank, and rested on the ice at a depth of 175 fathoms.

"My friends," said I, "the situation is grave, but I count on your courage and energy."

"Sir," answered the Canadian, "it is not the time to worry you with my grumbling. I am ready to do anything for the common safety."

"That is right, Ned," said I, holding out my hand to the Canadian.

"I am as handy with the pickaxe as the harpoon," he added, "and if I can be useful to the captain he may dispose of me."

"He will not refuse your aid. Come, Ned."

I led the Canadian to the room where the men of the *Nautilus* were putting on their diving-dresses. I told the captain of Ned's proposition, which was accepted. The Canadian put on his sea-costume, and was ready as soon as his companions. Each wore a Rouquayrol apparatus on his back, to which the reservoirs had furnished a contingent of pure air—a considerable but necessary diminution to the reserve of the *Nautilus*. The Ruhmkorff lamps were useless in the luminous water saturated with electric rays.

When Ned was dressed I went back to the saloon, where the panels were open, and, taking a place beside Conseil, I examined the ambient beds that supported the *Nautilus*.

Some moments after we saw a dozen men of the crew step out on to the ice with Ned Land amongst them, recognisable from his tall stature. Captain Nemo was with them.

Before beginning to dig through the walls he had them bored to assure a good direction to the work. Long bores were sunk into the lateral walls, but after forty-five feet they were again stopped by a thick wall. It was useless to attack the ice ceiling, for it was the ice-bank itself, which was more than 1,200 feet high. Captain Nemo then had the lower surface bored. There thirty feet of ice separated us from the water, such was the thickness of this icefield. It was, therefore, necessary to cut away a part equal in extent to the water-line of the *Nautilus*. There were, therefore, about 7000 cubic yards to detach in order to dig a hole through which we could sink below the icefield.

The work was immediately begun and carried on with indefatigable energy. Instead of digging round the *Nautilus*, which would have been exceedingly difficult, Captain Nemo had an immense trench made, about eight yards from its port quarter. Then his men began simultaneously to work at it in different points of its circumference, and large blocks were soon detached from the mass. By a curious effect of specific gravity, these blocks, being lighter than water, fled up to the vault of the tunnel, which thus became thicker at the top as it became thinner at the bottom. But it was of no consequence so long as the bottom ice was so much the less thick.

After two hours of energetic work, Ned Land entered exhausted. His companions and he were relieved by fresh workers, whom Conseil and I joined. The first officer of the *Nautilus* directed us.

The water seemed to be singularly cold, but I soon grew warmer with handling the pickaxe. My movements were very free, though made under a pressure of thirty atmospheres.

When I re-entered, after two hours of work, to take food and rest, I found a notable difference between the air the Rouquayrol apparatus furnished me with and the atmosphere of the *Nautilus*, already loaded with carbonic acid gas. The air had not been renewed for forty-eight hours, and its life-giving qualities were considerably weakened. However, in twelve hours we had broken off a slice of ice a yard thick, or about six hundred cubic yards. Admitting that we could go on at the same rate, it would take still five nights and four days to accomplish our task.

"Five nights and four days!" said I to my companions, "and we have only air for two days in the reservoirs."

"Without reckoning," replied Ned, "that, once out of this confounded prison, we shall still be imprisoned under the ice-bank without any possible communication with the atmosphere!"

True enough. Who could then foresee the minimum of time necessary for our deliverance? Should we not all be suffocated before the *Nautilus* could reach the surface of the waves? Was it destined to perish in this tomb of ice with all the people it contained? The situation appeared terrible, but each of us looked it in the face, and we were all decided to do our duty to the end.

As I had foreseen, during the night another slice, a yard thick, was dug off the immense alveolus. But in the morning, when clothed in my bathing-dress, I walked in the liquid mass in a temperature of from 6° to 7° below zero, I remarked that the lateral walls were gradually approaching each other. The water away from the trench, which was not warmed, by the men's work and the play of the tools, showed a tendency to solidity. In presence of this new and imminent danger what chance of safety had we, and how could we prevent the solidification of this liquid medium that would have crushed the sides of the *Nautilus* like glass?

I did not make known this new danger to my companions. Why risk the damping of that energy which they were employing in their painful toil? But when I went back on board I spoke to Captain Nemo about this grave complication.

"I know it," he said in his calm tone, which no terrible conjuncture of circumstances could modify. "It is one danger more, but I see no means of avoiding it. The only chance of safety is to work quicker than the solidification. We must be first, that is all."

"Be there first!" I ought by now to be accustomed to this way of speaking.

That day I handled the pickaxe vigorously for several hours. The work kept me up. Besides, to work was to leave the *Nautilus* and breathe the pure air drawn directly from the reservoirs and furnished by the apparatus, and to leave the impoverished and vitiated atmosphere.

That evening Captain Nemo was obliged to open the taps of his reservoirs, and throw some columns of pure air into the interior of the *Nautilus*. Without that precaution we should never have awakened.

The next day, the 26th of March, I went on with my mining work on the fifth yard. The lateral walls and lower surface of the ice-bank thickened perceptibly. It was evident that they would come together before the *Nautilus* could be extricated. Despair came over me for an instant. My axe nearly dropped from my hands. What was the use of digging if I was to perish suffocated, crushed by the water that was turning to stone?—a death that even the ferocity of savages would not have invented. It seemed to me that I was between the formidable jaws of a monster, which were irresistibly closing.

At that moment Captain Nemo, directing the work and working himself, passed close to me. I touched him, and pointed to the walls of our prison. The port wall had advanced to within four yards of the *Nautilus*.

The captain understood me and signed to me to follow him. We re-entered the vessel. Once my diving-dress off, I accompanied him into the saloon.

"M. Aronnax," said he, "we must try some heroic means or we shall be sealed up in this freezing water as in cement."

"Yes, said I, "but what can we do?"

"Ah!" cried he, "if the *Nautilus* were but strong enough to support the pressure without being crushed!"

"What then?" I asked, not seizing the captain's idea.

"Do you not understand," he continued, "that this congelation of water will help us? Do you not see that by its solidification it will break up the icefields that imprison us, as in freezing it breaks up the hardest stones? Do you not see that it would be an agent of salvation instead of an agent of destruction?"

"Yes, Captain, perhaps. But, however capable the *Nautilus*

may be of resisting pressure, it could not bear that, and would be crushed as flat as a steel plate."

"I know it, sir; therefore we must not count upon Nature for help, but upon ourselves. We must prevent this solidification. Not only are the lateral walls closing up, but there does not remain ten feet of water either fore or aft of the *Nautilus*. It is freezing on all sides of us."

"How much longer," I asked, "shall we have air to breathe on board?"

The captain looked me full in the face.

"The day after to-morrow," he said, "the reservoirs will be empty."

I broke out into a cold perspiration. And yet ought I to have been astonished at this answer? On the 22nd of March the *Nautilus* had sunk below the free waters of the Pole. We were now at the 26th. We had been living for five days on the vessel's reserves, and what remained of breathable air must be kept for the workers. Now, whilst I am writing this, my impression of it is still so acute that an involuntary terror takes possession of my whole being, and air seems wanting to my lungs.

In the meantime Captain Nemo was reflecting, silent and motionless. It was visible that his mind had grasped an idea. But he seemed to be driving it away. He answered himself in the negative. At last these words escaped from his lips:

"Boiling water!" murmured he.

"Boiling water?" I cried.

"Yes, sir. We are enclosed in a relatively restricted space. Would not some jets of boiling water, constantly injected by the pumps of the *Nautilus*, raise the temperature of this medium, and delay its congelation?"

"It must be tried," said I resolutely.

"We will try it, Professor."

The thermometer then indicated seven degrees outside. Captain Nemo took me to the kitchens, where vast distilling apparatus was at work, which furnished drinking-water by evaporation. It was filled with water, and all the electric heat of the piles was put into the serpentines, bathed by the liquid. In a few moments the water had attained 100°. It was sent to the pumps, while fresh water constantly supplied its place. The heat given off by the piles was such that the cold water taken from the sea after going through the apparatus arrived boiling in the pump.

The injection began, and three hours after the thermometer outside indicated six degrees below zero. It was one degree gained. Two hours later the thermometer only indicated four.

During the night the temperature of the water went up to one degree below zero. The apparatus could not send it up any higher. But as sea-water does not freeze at less than two degrees, I was at last reassured against the danger of solidification.

The next day, the 27th of March, eighteen feet of ice had been taken from the trench. There still remained twelve. Another forty-eight hours' work. The air could not be renewed in the interior of the *Nautilus*. That day things went from bad to worse.

An intolerable heaviness weighed upon me. About 3 p.m. this feeling of agony became exceedingly violent. I dislocated my jaws with gaping. My lungs panted as they sought the burning fluid, indispensable for respiration, and which became more and more rarefied. A moral torpor took possession of me. I lay down without strength to move, almost without consciousness.

If our situation was intolerable in the interior, with what haste and pleasure we donned our bathing-dresses to work in our turn! The pickaxes rang on the frozen surface. Our arms were tired, our hands skinned, but what mattered fatigues and wounds? Our lungs had vital air. We breathed! We breathed!

And yet no one thought of prolonging his work under water beyond his allotted time. His task accomplished, each gave to his panting companion the reservoir that was to pour life into him. Captain Nemo set the example, and was the first to submit to this severe discipline. When the time came he gave up his apparatus to another, and re-entered the vitiated atmosphere on board, always calm, unflinching, and uncomplaining.

That day the usual work was accomplished with still more vigour. But six feet of ice remained. Six feet alone separated us from the open sea. But the reservoirs of air were almost empty. The little that remained must be kept for the workers. Not an atom for the *Nautilus*.

When I re-entered the vessel I was half suffocated. What a night! Such suffering could not be expressed. The next day my breathing was oppressed. Along with pains in my head came dozy vertigo that made a drunken man of me. My companions felt the same symptoms. Some of the crew had rattling in their throats.

On that day, the sixth of our imprisonment, Captain Nemo, finding the pickaxes' work too slow, resolved to crush in the bed of ice that still separated us from the water. This man kept all coolness and energy. He subdued physical pain by moral force. He thought, planned, and acted.

He ordered the vessel to be lightened—that is to say, raised from the ice by a change of specific gravity. When it floated it was towed above the immense trench dug according to its water-line. Then its reservoirs of water were filled; it sank into the hole.

At that moment all the crew came on board, and the double door of communication was shut. The *Nautilus* was then resting on a sheet of ice not three feet thick, which the the bores had pierced in a thousand places.

The taps of the reservoirs were then turned full on, and a hundred cubic yards of water rushed in, increasing by 200,000 lb. the *Nautilus's* weight.

We waited and listened, forgetting our sufferings, hoping still. We had made our last effort.

Notwithstanding the buzzing in my head, I soon felt the vibrations in the hull of the *Nautilus*. A lower level was reached. The ice cracked with a singular noise like paper being torn, and the *Nautilus sank*.

"We have gone through!" murmured Conseil in my ear.

I could not answer him. I seized his hand and pressed it convulsively.

All at once, dragged down by its fearful overweight, the *Nautilus* sank like a cannon-ball—that is to say, as though it was falling in a vacuum!

Then all the electric force was put into the pumps, which immediately began to drive the water out of the reservoirs. After a few minutes our fall was stopped. Soon even the manometer indicated an ascensional movement. The screw, with all speed on, made the iron hull tremble to its very bolts, and dragged us northwards.

But how long would this navigation under the ice-bank last before we reached the open sea? Another day? I should be dead first.

Half lying on a divan in the library, I was suffocating. My face was violet, my lips blue, my faculties suspended. I saw nothing, heard nothing. All idea of time had disappeared from my mind. I could not contract my muscles.

I do not know how long this lasted. But I knew that my death-agony had begun. I saw that I was dying. Suddenly I came to myself. A few whiffs of air penetrated into my lungs. Had we, then, reached the surface of the water? Had we cleared the ice-bank?

No! Ned and Conseil, my two brave friends, were sacrificing themselves to save me. Some atoms of air had remained at the bottom of the apparatus. Instead of breathing it, they had kept it for me; and while they were suffocating, they poured me out life drop by drop! I wished to push the apparatus away. They held my hands, and for some minutes I breathed voluptuously.

My eyes fell on the clock. It was 11 a.m. It must be the 28th of March. The *Nautilus* was going at a frightful speed of forty miles an hour.

Where was Captain Nemo? Had he succumbed? Had his companions died with him?

At that moment the manometer indicated that we were only some twenty feet from the surface. A simple field of ice separated us from the atmosphere. Could we not break it?

Perhaps. Anyway, the *Nautilus* was going to attempt it. I felt that it was taking an oblique position, lowering its stern, and raising its prowl An introduction of water had been sufficient to disturb its equilibrium. Then, propelled by its powerful screw, it attacked the icefield from below like a powerful battering-ram. It broke it in slightly then drew back, drove at full speed against the field, which broke up, and at last, by a supreme effort, it sprang upon the frozen surface, which it crushed under its weight.

The panel was opened, I might say torn up, and the pure air rushed in to all parts of the *Nautilus*.

CHAPTER FORTY-ONE

FROM CAPE HORN TO THE AMAZON

I HAVE no idea how I got to the platform. Perhaps the Canadian carried me there. But I was breathing, inhaling the vivifying air of the sea. My two companions were beside me, intoxicating themselves with the fresh particles. Unfortunate men, too long deprived of food, cannot throw themselves inconsiderately on the first aliments that are given to them. We, on the contrary, had no reason to restrain ourselves; we could fill our lungs with the atoms of this atmosphere, and it was the sea-breeze itself that was pouring out life to us.

Our strength promptly returned to us, and when I looked around me I saw that we were alone upon the platform. Not a man of the crew was there, not even Captain Nemo. The strange sailors of the *Nautilus* contented themselves with the air that circulated in the interior. Not one came to take delight in the open air.

The first words I uttered were words of thanks and gratitude to my two companions. Ned and Conseil had prolonged my existence during the last hours of this agony. All my gratitude was not too much for such self-sacrifice.

"My friends," I said, much moved, "we are bound to one another for ever, and I am under an obligation."

"Which I shall take advantage of," replied the Canadian.

"What?" said Conseil.

"Yes," continued Ned Land, "by taking you with me when I leave this infernal *Nautilus*."

"That reminds me," said Conseil—"are we going the right way?"

"Yes," I answered, "for we are going towards the sun, and here the sun is north."

"Doubtless," said Ned Land; but it remains to be seen if we are making for the Pacific or the Atlantic—that is to say, the frequented or solitary seas."

That I could not answer, and I feared that Captain Nemo would take us to that vast ocean that bathes the coasts both of Asia and America. He would thus complete his journey round the submarine world, and would return to those seas where the *Nautilus* found the most entire independence. But if we returned to the Pacific, far from all inhabited land, what would become of Ned Land's projects?"

We were soon to be apprised of this important fact. The *Nautilus* was going at great speed. The Polar circle was soon passed, and the vessel's head directed towards Cape Horn. We were abreast of the American point on the 31st of March, at 7 p.m.

The next day, the 1st of April, when the *Nautilus* ascended to the surface of the sea, some minutes before noon, we sighted the west coast. It was Terra del Fuego, to which the first navigators gave this name on seeing the quantity of smoke that was rising from the native huts.

Towards evening the *Nautilus* approached the archipelago of the Falkland Islands, of which the next day I could recognise the steep summits. The depth of the sea was slight; I therefore thought—not without reason—that these two islands, surrounded by many islets, formerly formed part of the Magellan lands. The Falkland Islands were probably discovered by the celebrated John Davis, who gave them the name of South Davis Islands. Later on Richard Hawkins called them Maiden Islands. They were afterwards named the Malouines, at the beginning of the eighteenth century, by some Saint Malo fishermen; and, lastly, Falkland Islands by the English, to whom they now belong.

When the last heights of the Falkland group had disappeared under the horizon, the *Nautilus* sank to a depth of from ten to fifteen fathoms, and coasted the American shore. Captain Nemo did not show himself.

Until the 3rd of April we stayed in these regions of Patagonia, sometimes under the ocean, sometimes on its surface. The *Nautilus* passed the wide estuary formed by the mouth of the La Plata, and on the 4th of April was abreast of Uruguay, but at fifty miles' distance. Its direction kept northwards, and it followed the long sinuosities of South America. We had then come 6,000 leagues since we had embarked in the seas of Japan.

The Equator was crossed. Twenty miles to the west lay the Guianas, a French territory, on which we might have found an easy refuge. But the wind was blowing a great gale, and the furious waves would not have allowed a simple boat to accost them. Ned Land doubtless understood that, for he did not speak to me of anything. For my part I made no allusions to his schemes for flight, for I did not wish to urge him to make any attempt that must inevitably fail.

I easily consoled myself for this delay by interesting studies. During the days of the 11th and 12th of April, the *Nautilus* did not leave the surface of the sea, and its nets brought in a miraculous haul of zoophytes, fish, and reptiles.

The next day, the 12th of April, during the day the *Nautilus* approached the Dutch coast near the mouth of the Maroni. There several groups of sea-cows herded together. They were manatees, that, like the dugong and stellera, belong to the sirenian order. These fine animals, peaceable and inoffensive, from eighteen to twenty-one feet long, weigh at least 800 lb. I told Ned Land and Conseil that foreseeing Nature had assigned an important part to these mammalia. Like seals they are destined to graze on the submarine meadows and thus destroy the agglomerations of herbs that choke up the mouth of tropical rivers.

"And do you know," I added, "what has resulted from the almost entire destruction of these useful creatures? The putrified herbs have poisoned the air, and the poisoned air is the cause of the yellow fever that desolates these beautiful countries. Venomous vegetation has been multiplied under the tropical seas, and the sickness has been irresistibly developed from the mouth of the Rio de la Plata to Florida!"

And if Toussenel is to be believed, this plague is nothing to the one that will fall upon our descendants when the seas will be depopulated of whales and seals. Then, infested with poulps, medusæ, and cuttle-fish, they will become vast hotbeds of infection, since their waters will no longer possess "those vast stomachs that God had charged to skim the surface of the sea."

However, without disdaining these theories, the crew of the *Nautilus* seized a half-dozen manatees, in order to provision the larders with excellent meat, superior to beef or veal. Their capture was not interesting. The manatees allowed themselves to be struck without defending themselves. Several thousand pounds of meat, destined to be dried, were stored on board.

That day's fishing brought our stay on the shores of the Amazon to a close, and by nightfall the *Nautilus* was far out at sea.

CHAPTER FORTY-TWO

POULPS

FOR SEVERAL days the *Nautilus* kept constantly away from the American coast. The captain evidently did not wish to frequent the waters of the Gulf of Mexico, or the seas of the Antilles. However, there would have been plenty of water, for the average depth of these seas is nine hundred fathoms; but probably these regions, strewn with islands and ploughed by steamers, did not suit Captain Nemo.

On the 16th of April, we sighted Martinique and Guadaloupe, at a distance of about thirty miles. I caught a glimpse of their high peaks.

On the 20th of April, we rose to an average depth of 700 fathoms. The nearest land was then the archipelago of the Bahamas, scattered like a heap of stones on the surface of the sea. There rose high submarine cliffs, straight walls of corroded blocks, amongst which were black holes that our electric rays did not light up to their depths.

It was about eleven o'clock when Ned Land attracted my attention to the window.

"The frightful animal!" he cried. I looked in my turn, and could not restrain a movement of repulsion. Before my eyes was a monster worthy to figure in tetralogical legends.

It was a calamary of colossal dimensions, at least thirty-two feet long. It was swimming backwards with extreme velocity in the direction of the *Nautilus*. It was staring with its enormous green eyes; its eight arms, or rather eight feet, starting from its head, which has given the name of "cephalopod" to this animal, were twice as long as its body, and twined about like the hair of the Furies. We could distinctly see the 250 blowholes on the inner side of the tentacles under the form of semi-spherical capsules. Sometimes these blowholes fastened themselves on to the pane and made a vacuum. The mouth of the monster—a horned beak made like that of a parrot—opened and shut vertically. Its tongue, a horny substance armed with several rows of sharp teeth, came quivering out of this veritable pair of shears. What a freak of Nature!—a bird's beak on a mollusc! Its body, fusiform and larger in the middle, made a fleshy mass that must have weighed from 40,000 to 50,000 lb. Its inconstant, colour, changing with extreme rapidity according to the irritation of the animal, passed successively from livid grey to reddish brown.

What had irritated this mollusc? It was doubtless the presence of this *Nautilus*, more formidable than itself, upon which its suckers or mandibles had no hold. And yet what monsters these poulps are!—what vitality the Creator has endowed them with!—what vigour their three hearts impart to their movements!

Chance had brought us into the presence of this calamary, and I would not lose the occasion of carefully studying this specimen of cephalopods. I overcame the horror with which its aspect inspired me, and taking a pencil, began to draw it.

In fact, other poulps had appeared at the port window. I counted seven. They formed a procession after the *Nautilus* and I heard their beaks grating on the iron hull. We had plenty to choose from.

I went on with my work. These monsters kept in our vicinity with such precision that they seemed motionless, and I could have drawn their outline on the window. Besides, we were going at a moderate speed.

All at once the *Nautilus* stopped. A shock made it tremble in every joint.

"Can we be stranded?" I asked.

"Anyway," answered the Canadian, "we must be off again, for we are floating."

The Nautilus was certainly floating, but it was not moving onwards. The branches of its screw were not beating the waves. A minute passed. Captain Nemo, followed by his first officer, came into the saloon.

I had not seen him for some time; he looked to me very gloomy. Without speaking to us, or, perhaps, even seeing us, he went to the panel, looked at the poulps, and said a few words to his officer.

The latter went out. Soon the panels were closed. The ceiling was lighted up again.

I went towards the captain.

"A curious collection of poulps," I said in as indifferent

a tone as an amateur might take before the crystal of an aquarium.

"Yes, Professor," he replied, "and we are going to fight them face to face."

I looked at the captain, thinking I had not rightly heard.

"Face to face?" I echoed.

"Yes, sir. The screw is stopped. I think that the horny mandibles of one of them are caught in its branches. That prevents us moving on."

"And what are you going to do?"

"Go up to the surface and massacre all that vermin."

"A difficult enterprise."

"As you say. The electric bullets are powerless against their soft flesh, and where they do not find enough resistance to make them go off. But we will attack them with axes."

"And with harpoons, sir," said the Canadian, "if you do not refuse my aid."

"I accept it, Mr. Land."

"We will accompany you," said I, and, following Captain Nemo, we went to the central staircase.

There about ten men armed with boarding hatchets were standing ready for the attack. Conseil and I took two hatchets. Ned Land seized a harpoon.

The *Nautilus* was then on the surface of the sea. One of the sailors, placed on the lowest steps, was unscrewing the bolts of the panel. But he had hardly finished before the panel was raised with extreme violence, evidently drawn up by a blowhole in the arm of a poulp.

Immediately one of these long arms glided like a serpent through the opening, and twenty others were brandished above it. With a blow of the hatchet Captain Nemo cut off this formidable tentacle, which glided twisting down the steps.

At the moment we were crowding together to get up to the platform, two other arms stretched down to a sailor placed in front of Captain Nemo, and drew him up with irresistible violence.

Captain Nemo uttered a cry and rushed out. We followed

What a scene! The unhappy man, seized by the tentacle and fastened to its blowholes, was balanced in the air according to the caprice of this enormous trunk. He was choking, and cried out, "*A moi! à moi!*" ("Help! help!"). These French words caused me a profound stupor. Then I had a countryman on board, perhaps several! I shall hear that heartrending cry all my life!

The unfortunate man was lost. Who would rescue him from that powerful grasp? Captain Nemo threw himself on the poulp, and with his hatchet cut off another arm. His first officer was fighting with rage against other monsters that were climbing the sides of the *Nautilus*. The crew were fighting with hatchets.

The Canadian, Conseil and I dug our arms into the fleshy masses. A violent smell of musk pervaded the atmosphere. It was horrible.

For an instant I believed that the unfortunate man, encircled by the poulp, would be drawn away by its powerful suction. Seven of its eight arms had been cut off, one only brandishing its victim like a feather twisted about in the air. But at the very moment that Captain Nemo and his officer were rushing upon it, the animal hurled out a column of black liquid, secreted in a bag in its stomach. We were blinded by it. When this cloud was dissipated the calamary had disappeared, and with it my unfortunate countryman!

With what rage we then set upon these monsters! Ten or twelve poulps had invaded the platform and sides of the *Nautilus*. We rolled pell-mell amongst the serpents' trunks that wriggled about the platform in pools of blood and black ink. It seemed as if thè viscous tentacles kept springing out again like hydra heads. Ned Land's harpoon at each stroke plunged into the green eyes of the calamary and put them out. But my brave companion was suddenly thrown over by one of the tentacles of a monster which he had not been able to avoid.

Ah, how my heart beat with emotion and horror! The calamary's formidable beak opened over Ned Land. The unfortunate man was about to be cut in two. I rushed to his aid. But Captain Nemo was before me. His hatchet disappeared in the two enormous mandibles, and, miraculously preserved, the Canadian rose and plunged the whole of his harpoon into the poulp's triple heart.

"We are quits," said Captain Nemo to the Canadian.

Ned bowed without answering.

This combat had lasted a quarter of an hour. The monsters, vanquished, mutilated, and death-stricken, left the place clear at last, and disappeared under the waves.

Captain Nemo, covered with blood, stood motionless near the lantern, and looked at the sea that had swallowed one of his companions, whilst tears rolled from his eyes.

CHAPTER FORTY-THREE

THE GULF STREAM

WE NONE of us can forget that terrible scene of April 20. I wrote it under the impression of violent emotion. Since then I have revised it and read it to Conseil and the Canadian. They find it exact as to facts, but insufficient as to effect. To depict such a scene it would take the pen of the most illustrious of our poets, Victor Hugo.

Captain Nemo went back to his room, and I saw him no more for some time. But how sad, despairing, and irresolute he was, I judged by the vessel of which he was the soul, and which received all his impressions! The *Nautilus* no longer kept any determined direction. It went and came, floating like a lifeless thing on the waves. Its screw was free again, but was little used. It went about at random. But it could not tear itself away from the theatre of its last struggle—from that sea which had devoured one of its children.

Ten days passed thus. It was not till the 1st of May that the *Nautilus* frankly took a northerly direction after sighting the Bahamas at the opening of the Bahama Channel. We were then following the current of that largest sea river, which has its own banks, fish, and temperature, I have named the Gulf Stream.

It is, in fact, a river that flows freely in the midst of the Atlantic, and its waters do not mix with those of the ocean. It is a salt river—salter than the surrounding sea. Its average depth is three thousand feet, its average breadth sixty miles. In certain places its current goes along at a speed of more than a league an hour. The invariable volume of its water is more considerable than that of all the rivers of the globe.

I may add that during the night the phosphorescent waters of the Gulf Stream rivalled the electric brilliancy of our lantern; above all, in the stormy weather which threatened us frequently.

On the 8th of May we were still abreast of Cape Hatteras, at the height of the North Carolinas. The Gulf Stream is seventy-five miles wide there, and one hundred and five fathoms deep. The *Nautilus* continued to move about at random. All supervision seemed banished from the vessel. I acknowledge that under those circumstances an escape might succeed. In fact, the inhabited shores offered easy refuges on all sides. The sea was incessantly ploughed by numerous steamers that run between New York or Boston and the Gulf of Mexico, and night and day by little schooners that do the coasting trade on the different points of the American coast. We might hope to be picked up. It was, therefore, a favourable opportunity, notwithstanding the thirty miles that separated the *Nautilus* from the coasts of the Union.

But one vexatious circumstance thwarted the Canadian's schemes. The weather was very bad. We were approaching the regions where tempests are frequent, that country of gales and cyclones engendered by the current of the Gulf Stream. To tempt such a sea in a fragile boat was to court destruction. Ned Land agreed to that himself, and fretted his life away with nostalgia that nothing but flight could cure.

"Sir," said he to me that day, "there must be an end to this. I want to know how things stand. Your Nemo is going away from land, up north. But I declare to you that I have had enough of the South Pole, and I won't follow him to the North Pole."

"But what is to be done, Ned, as flight is impracticable now?"

"I return to my first idea. The captain must be spoken to. I will not stay here! I am stifled!"

The Canadian had evidently lost all patience. His vigorous nature could not get accustomed to this prolonged imprisonment. His countenance grew daily worse, his temper more sullen. I felt what he must suffer, for nostalgia had seized me too. Nearly seven months had gone by since we had heard any news of earth. What is more, Captain Nemo's isolation, his altered humour, especially since the fight with the poulps, his taciturnity, all made me see things in a different light. I no longer felt the enthusiasm of the first days. One must be a Dutchman like Conseil to accept the situation in this medium reserved for cetaceans and other inhabitants of the sea. Really if the brave fellow had gills instead of lungs I think he would make a distinguished fish.

"Well, sir?" said Ned, seeing that I did not answer.

"Well, Ned, you want me to ask Captain Nemo what his intentions are concerning us?"

"Yes, sir."

I remained alone. Once decided to ask, I resolved to have done with it immediately. I like things better done than about to be done.

I entered my room. There I heard someone walking about in Captain Nemo's. I could not let this occasion of meeting him slip. I knocked at the door. I obtained no answer. I knocked again, and then turned the handle. The door opened.

I entered. The captain was there. Bent over his work-table, he had heard nothing. Resolved not to go out without questioning him, I approached him. He raised his head suddenly, frowned, and said rather rudely:

"You here? What do you want?"

"To speak to you, Captain."

"But I am occupied, sir. I am at work. The liberty I allow you to shut yourself up, may I not enjoy it also?"

My reception was not very encouraging, but I was decided to hear everything in order to answer everything.

"Captain," said I coolly, "I have to speak to you on business that I cannot put off."

"What can that be, sir?" he replied ironically. "Have you made some discovery that has escaped me? Has the sea given up to you any fresh secret?"

We were far from the subject. Before I could answer, the captain pointed to a manuscript on the table, and said in a grave tone:

"Here is a manuscript written in several languages, M. Aronnax. It contains the account of my studies on the sea, and, if God so please, it shall not perish with me. This manuscript, signed by my own name, completed by the history of my life, will be enclosed in an insubmersible case. The last survivor of us all on board the *Nautilus* will throw this case into the sea, and it will go where the waves will carry it."

The name of this man! His history written by himself! Then the mystery that surrounds him will be one day revealed? But at that moment I only saw in this communication an opening for me.

"Captain," I answered, "I can but approve the idea that influences you. The fruit of your studies must not be lost. But the means you employ seem to me very primitive. Who knows where the winds will carry that case, in what hands it will fall? Could you not find some better means? Could not you or one of yours——"

"Never, sir," said the captain, interrupting me.

"But I and my companions will preserve your manuscript if you will give us liberty——"

"Liberty, sir?" said Captain Nemo, rising.

"Yes, Captain, and that is the subject I wished to ask you about. We have now been seven months on your vessel, and I now ask you, in the name of my companions and myself, if you mean to keep us here always?"

"M. Aronnax," said Captain Nemo, "I have only the same answer to give you that I gave you seven months ago. Whosoever enters my vessel never leaves it again."

"But that is slavery!"

"Call it by what name you please."

"But everywhere a slave keeps the right of recovering his liberty! Whatever means offer he has the right to consider them legitimate."

"Who has denied you that right?" answered Captain Nemo. "Have I ever asked you to bind yourself by an oath?"

The captain looked at me and folded his arms.

"Sir," I said to him, "we shall neither of us care to return to this subject. But as we have begun it I must go on. To me study is a help, a powerful diversion, a passion that can make me forget anything. Like you, I could live ignored, obscure, in the hope of bequeathing to the future the result of my work, by means of a case confided to the mercies of waves and winds. In a word I can admire you, follow you with pleasure in a rôle that I understand, up to a certain point; but there are other aspects of your life surrounded with complications and mysteries in which my companions and I alone have no part. And even when our hearts could beat for you, moved by your griefs, or stirred to the bottom by your acts of genius or courage, we are obliged to repress the least manifestation of sympathy that the sight of what is beautiful and right arouses, whether it comes from friend or enemy. It is this feeling of being strangers to everything that concerns you that makes our position unbearable, even to me, but much more for Ned Land. Every man, because he is a man, is worth attention. Have you ever asked yourself what the love of liberty and the hatred of slavery might arouse in a nature like that of the Canadian, what he might think or attempt?"

I was silent. Captain Nemo rose.

"It does not matter to me what Ned Land thinks or attempts. I did not take him; I do not keep him on board my vessel for my own pleasure. As to you, M. Aronnax you are one of the few people who can understand anything, even silence. I have nothing more to answer you. This first time that you come to speak on this subject must also be the last, for I cannot even listen to you again."

I withdrew. From that day our position was clear. I related our conversation to my two companions.

"We now know," said Ned Land, "that there is nothing to expect from that man. The *Nautilus* is approaching Long Island. We will escape, no matter what the weather is."

But the sky became more and more threatening. Symptoms of a hurricane became manifest. The atmosphere became white and misty. Fine streaks of cirrus clouds were succeeded on the horizon by masses of cumulous clouds. Other low clouds swept swiftly by. The sea rose in huge billows. The birds disappeared, with the exception of petrels, those friends of the storm. The barometer fell visibly, and indicated an extreme tension of the vapours in the air. The mixture in the storm glass was decomposed under the influence of the electricity which saturated the atmosphere. The struggle of the elements was approaching.

The tempest broke out on the 18th of May, just as the *Nautilus* was floating abreast of Long Island, at some miles from the port of New York. I can describe this struggle of the elements, for instead of avoiding it in the depths of the sea, Captain Nemo, by an inexplicable caprice, wished to dare it on the surface.

The wind was blowing from the SW. at a speed of 45 feet a second, which became 75 before 3 p.m. That is the figure of tempests.

Captain Nemo, unshaken by the gale, had taken his place on the platform. He had fastened himself by a rope round his waist to resist the monstrous waves that swept over him. I had gone up and fastened myself too, dividing my admiration between this tempest and the incomparable man who defied it.

The sea was swept by ragged clouds that dipped into the billows. I no longer saw any of the intermediary waves that form in the large hollows—nothing but long fuliginous undulations, the crest of which did not break into foam, so compact were they. Their height increased. The *Nautilus*, sometimes lying on its side, sometimes as straight up as a mast, pitched and tossed frightfully.

About 5 p.m. rain fell in torrents, which neither beat down wind nor sea. The hurricane blew at the rate of 40 miles an hour. It is in these conditions that it blows down houses, blows in tiles and doors, breaks iron gates and displaces twenty-four pound cannon. And yet the *Nautilus*, amidst the torment, justified this saying of a learned engineer—"There is no well-built hull that cannot defy the sea!" It was not a resisting rock which the waves would have demolished; it was a steel spindle, obedient and mobile, without rigging or masts, which could defy their fury with impunity.

The intensity of the tempest increased during the night. the barometer fell like it did in 1860 at La Réunion, during a cyclone. At nightfall I saw a large ship pass on the horizon, struggling painfully. It must have been one of the steamers of the lines beteeen New York and Liverpool or Havre. It soon disappeared in the darkness.

At 10 p.m. the sky was all on fire. The atmosphere was streaked with violent lightning. I could not support its brilliancy, whilst Captain Nemo, looking straight at it, seemed the soul of the tempest. A terrible noise filled the air, made by the waves, wind, and thunder. The wind veered to all parts of the horizon, and the cyclone, starting from the east, returned to it, passing north, west and south in the opposite directions to the circular tempests of the austral hemisphere.

To the shower of rain succeeded a shower of fire. The drops of water changed to fulminating sparks. One would have thought that Captain Nemo, seeking a death worthy of him, tried to get struck by lightning. With a frightful pitch the *Nautilus* threw up its steel prow into the air like a lightning conductor, and I saw it give out sparks. Completely worn out, I crawled on all fours towards the panel. I opened it and went down to the saloon. The tempest had then attained its maximum of intensity. It was impossible to keep on one's feet in the interior of the *Nautilus*.

Captain Nemo came in about midnight. I heard the reservoirs gradually filling, and the *Nautilus* slowly sank under the water.

Through the windows of the saloon I saw large frightened fish pass like phantoms in the fiery waters. Some were struck by lightning before my eyes.

The *Nautilus* still sank. I thought it would find calm water at a depth of eight fathoms; but no, the surface was too violently agitated. We were obliged to sink to twenty-five fathoms to find rest.

But there, what tranquillity! what silence! what a peaceful medium! Who would have said that a terrible tempest was going on upon the surface of that same ocean.

CHAPTER FORTY-FOUR

IN LATITUDE 47° 24′ AND LONGITUDE 17° 18′

THE STORM had thrown us eastward once more. All hope of escaping on the shores of New York or the St. Lawrence had vanished. Poor Ned, in despair, shut himself up like Captain Nemo. Conseil and I left each other no more.

I ought rather to have given NE. as the direction of the *Nautilus*, to be more exact. For some days it drifted about, sometimes on the surface, sometimes beneath it, amid those fogs so dreaded by sailors. What accidents are due to fogs! What shocks upon the reefs when the noise of the wind is louder than the breaking of the waves! What collisions between vessels, notwithstanding the fog-signals and alarm-bells!

On the 15th of May we were at the southern extremity of Newfoundland Bank. This bank is formed of alluvia, or large heaps of organic matter, brought either from the Equator by the Gulf Stream or from the North Pole by the counter-current of cold water that skirts the American coast. There also are piled those erratic blocks of stone carried down by the breaking up of the ice. And it is also a vast charnel-house of molluscs and zoophytes, which perish there by millions.

The depth of the sea is not great on Newfoundland Bank— a few hundred fathoms at most. But towards the south is a depression of 1,500 fathoms. There the Gulf Stream widens. It loses speed and heat and becomes a sea.

It was upon this inexhaustible Newfoundland Bank that I surprised cod in its favourite waters.

It may be said that cod are mountain-fish, for Newfoundland is only a submarine mountain. As the *Nautilus* moved through the thick shoals of them, Conseil said:

"Those cod! I thought cod were as flat as soles."

"They are only flat at the grocer's," said I, "where they are open and dried. But in water they are fusiform fish, like mullet, and shaped for speed."

"What a lot of them there is!" said Conseil.

"There would be more but for their enemies—sharks and men! Do you know how many eggs there are in a single female?"

"I'll guess well," answered Conseil; "five hundred thousand!"

"Eleven millions, my friend."

"I have confidence in monsieur," said Conseil; "I will not count them."

"Count what?"

"The eleven millions of eggs. But I must make one remark."

"What?"

"Why, if all the eggs bore, four cods would be enough to feed England, America and Norway."

Whilst we were on Newfoundland Bank, I saw the long lines, armed with two hundred hooks, which each boat hangs out by dozens. Each line had a little grapline at one end, and was fastened to the surface by a buoy-rope, the buoy being made of cork. The *Nautilus* had to be skilfully steered amidst this submarine network.

However, it did not stay long in these frequented regions. It went northwards to the 42nd degree of latitude. It was abreast of St. John's, in Newfoundland, and Heart's Content, where one extremity of the transatlantic cable touches.

The *Nautilus*, instead of keeping to its course northward, took an easterly direction as if to follow the telegraphic plateau on which the cable lies, and of which the multiplied soundings have given the exact plan.

It was on the 17th of May, at about 500 miles from Heart's Content, and at a depth of 1,400 fathoms, that I saw the cable lying on the ground. Conseil, whom I had not told about it, took it for a gigantic serpent, and prepared to classify it according to his usual method. But I consoled the worthy fellow, and by way of consolation told him various particulars about the laying down of the cable.

The first cable was laid during the years of 1857 and 1858; but, after having transmitted about four hundred telegrams, it ceased to act. In 1863 the engineers manufactured a new cable, measuring 2000 miles in length, and weighing 4,500 tons, which was embarked on board the *Great Eastern*. This attempt also failed.

Now on the 25th of May the *Nautilus*, at a depth of 190 fathoms, was in the exact place where the rupture occurred that ruined the enterprise. It was at 638 miles from the Irish coast. It was perceived at 2 p.m. that communication with Europe was interrupted. The electricians on board resolved to cut the cable in order to haul it up again, and at 11 p.m. they had brought in the damaged part. They made a joint, and spliced it, and it was once more submerged.

But a few days later it broke, and could not be found again in the depths of the ocean.

The Americans were not discouraged. The daring Cyrus Field, the promoter of the enterprise, who had risked all his fortune in it, raised a fresh subscription. It was immediately taken up. Another cable was laid under better conditions. The conducting-wires were enveloped in gutta-percha and protected by a wadding of hemp contained in metal armour. The *Great Eastern* set out with it again on the 13th of July, 1866.

The operation went on well. However, one hitch occurred. Several times, whilst unrolling the cable, the electricians observed that nails had recently been driven into it in order to spoil the wire. Captain Anderson, his officers and engineers, met, deliberated, and caused it to be advertised that, if the culprit were caught on board, he should be thrown into the sea without further judgment. After that the criminal attempt was not repeated.

On the 23rd of July the *Great Eastern* was not more than five hundred miles from Newfoundland when the news of the armistice between Prussia and Austria, after Sadowa, was telegraphed to it. On the 27th it sighted, through the fog, the port of Heart's Content. The enterprise was happily terminated, and in the first despatch young America telegraphed to old Europe these wise words, so rarely understood: "Glory to God in the highest, and on earth peace, goodwill towards men."

I did not expect to find the electric cable in its original state as it came from the manufactories. The long serpent, covered with debris of shells, bristling with foraminiferæ, was encrusted in a stony coating that protected it against performing molluscs. It was resting tranquilly, sheltered from the movements of the sea, and under a pressure favourable to the transmission of the electric spark, which passes from America to Europe in ·32 of a second. The duration of this cable will, doubtless, be infinite, for it has been remarked that its gutta-percha envelope is improved by the sea-water.

Besides, on this plateau, so happily chosen, the cable is never submerged at such depths as to cause it to break. The *Nautilus* followed it to its greatest depth, in about 2,200 fathoms, and there it lay without any effort of traction. Then we approached the place where the accident took place in 1863.

The bottom of the sea there formed a wide valley on which Mont Blanc might rest without its summit emerging above the waves. This valley is closed on the east by a precipitous wall 6,000 feet high. We reached it on the 28th of May, when the *Nautilus* was not more than 120 miles from Ireland.

Was Captain Nemo going north to coast the British Isles? No. To my great surprise he went southward again and returned to European seas. Whilst rounding the Emerald Isle I caught a glimpse of Cape Clear and Fastnet Beacon, which lights the thousands of vessels from Glasgow to Liverpool.

The *Nautilus* still went southward. On the 30th of May we sighted Land's End, between the extreme point of England and the Scilly Isles, which were left to starboard.

If the vessel was going to enter the Channel it must go direct east. It did not do so.

During the whole of the 31st of May the *Nautilus* described a series of circles on the water that greatly interested me. It seemed to be seeking a spot there was some difficulty in finding. At noon Captain Nemo came to take the bearings himself. He did not speak to me, and seemed gloomier than ever. What could sadden him thus? Was it his proximity to European shores? Was it some memory of the country he had abandoned? What was it he felt, remorse or regret? For a long time this thought haunted my mind, and I felt a kind of presentiment that before long chance would reveal the captain's secrets.

The next day, the 1st of June, the *Nautilus* continued the same manœuvres. It was evidently trying to find a precise point in the ocean. Captain Nemo came to take the sun's altitude like he did the day before. The sea was calm, the sky pure. Eight miles to the east a large steamship appeared on the horizon. No flag fluttered from its mast, and I could not find out its nationality.

Some minutes before the sun passed the meridian, Captain Nemo took his sextant and made his observation with extreme precision. The absolute calm of the waters facilitated the operation. The motionless *Nautilus* neither pitched nor rolled.

At that moment I was upon the platform. When the captain had taken his observation he pronounced these words:

"It is here!"

He went down through the panel. Had he seen the ship that had tacked about, and seemed to be bearing down upon us? I cannot tell.

I returned to the saloon. The panel was shut, and I heard the water hissing into the reservoirs. The *Nautilus* began to sink vertically, its screw was stopped, and communicated no movement to it.

A few minutes later it stopped at a depth of 418 fathoms, and rested on the ground.

The luminous ceiling of the saloon was then extinguished, the panels were opened, and through the windows I saw the sea lighted up within a radius of half a mile by our electric lantern.

On the starboard appeared a large protuberance which attracted my attention. It looked like a ruin buried under a crust of whitish shells like a mantle of snow. Whilst attentively examining this mass I thought I recognised the swollen outlines of a ship, cleared of her masts, that must have gone down prow foremost. The disaster must have taken place at a distant epoch. This wreck, encrusted with lime, had been lying many years at the bottom of the ocean.

I did not know what to think, when, near me, I heard Captain Nemo say in a slow voice:

"Once that ship was called the *Marseillais*. It carried seventy-four guns, and was launched in 1762. In 1778, on the 13th of August, commanded by La Polype-Vertrieux, it fought daringly against the *Preston*. In 1779, on the 4th of July, it assisted the squadron of the Admiral d'Estaing to take Granada. In 1781, on the 5th of September, it took part in the naval battle of Chesapeake Bay. In 1794 the French Republic changed its name. On the 16th of April of the same year it joined at Brest the squadron of Villaret-Joyeuse as escort to a cargo of wheat coming from America under the command of Admiral Van Stabel. On the 11th and 12th prairial, year II, this squadron encountered the English vessels. Sir, to-day is the 13th prairial, the 1st of June, 1868. It is seventy-four years ago to-day, that in this same place, by 47° 4′ latitude and 17° 28′ longitude, this ship, after an heroic fight, dismasted, the water in her hold, the third of her crew disabled, preferred to sink with her 356 sailors than to surrender, and, nailing her colours to her stern, disappeared under the waves to the cry of 'Vive la République!'" (Carlyle says: "This enormous inspiring feat turns out to be an enormous inspiring nonentity, extant nowhere save as falsehood in the brain of Barrère!")

"The *Vengeur*!" I exclaimed.

"Yes, sir. The *Vengeur*! A glorious name!" murmured the captain, as he folded his arms.

CHAPTER FORTY-FIVE

A HECATOMB

IN THE meantime the *Nautilus* was slowly ascending to the surface of the sea, and I saw the confused outlines of the *Vengeur* gradually disappear. Soon a slight pitching told me we were floating in the open air.

At that moment a dull detonation was heard. I looked at the captain, but he did not stir.

"Captain?" I said.

He did not answer.

I left him and went up on to the platform. Conseil and the Canadian had preceded me there.

"What was that noise?" I asked.

"A gunshot," answered Ned Land.

I looked in the direction of the ship I had perceived before. She had neared the *Nautilus*, and was putting on more steam. Six miles separated us from her.

"What vessel is that, Ned?"

"By her rigging and the height of her low masts," answered the Canadian, "I bet she's a warship. I hope she'll come and sink us, if necessary, along with this confounded *Nautilus*."

"Can you tell me her nationality, friend Ned?" I asked.

The Canadian frowned, screwed up his eyes, and fixed the whole power of his eyes on to the ship.

"No, sir," he answered. "I cannot find out to what nation she belongs. Her colours are not hoisted. But I can affirm that she is a ship of war, for a long pendant is floating from her mainmast."

For a quarter of an hour we went on looking at the ship that was bearing down upon us. Still I did not think she had sighted the *Nautilus* at that distance, still less did she know what it was.

The Canadian soon announced that this vessel was a large warship, a two-decker, and an iron-clad with a ram.

Thick black smoke was issuing from her two funnels. Her reefed sails could not be distinguished from her yards. She bore no colours. Distance prevented us making out the colour of her pendant, which streamed like a narrow ribbon.

She was rapidly approaching. If Captain Nemo allowed her to come near it would offer us a chance of escape.

"Sir," said Ned Land to me, "if that ship passes within a mile of us I shall throw myself into the sea, and I advise you to do the same."

I was going to answer when some white smoke issued from the prow of the vessel. Then, a few seconds afterwards, the water aft of the *Nautilus* was thrown up by the fall of some heavy body. In a short time we heard the report.

"Why, they are firing at us!" I exclaimed.

"Good people!" muttered the Canadian. "Then they do not take us for shipwrecked men on a raft!"

"If monsieur will allow me to say so, that's right," said Conseil, shaking off the water that another shot had sprinkled him with. "If monsieur will allow me to say so, they have sighted the narwhal, and are firing at the narwhal."

"But they must see that they have men to deal with!" I exclaimed.

"Perhaps that is the reason," answered Ned Land, looking at me.

Quite a revelation was made in my mind. They doubtless knew now what to think about the existence of the pretended monster. Doubtless Captain Farragut had found out that the *Nautilus* was a submarine boat, and more dangerous than a supernatural cetacean when it struck against the *Abraham Lincoln*.

In the meantime, cannon-balls were multiplying round us. Some, meeting the liquid surface, ricocheted to considerable distances. But none reached the *Nautilus*.

The iron-clad was then not more than three miles off. Notwithstanding the violent cannonade, Captain Nemo did not make his appearance on the platform. And yet if one of these conical shots had struck the hull of the *Nautilus* in a normal line it would have been fatal to it.

The Canadian then said to me:

"Sir, we ought to attempt anything to get out of this. Let us make signals! *Mille diables!* They will perhaps understand that we are honest men!"

Ned Land took out his handkerchief to wave it in the air. But he had hardly spread it out than, floored by a grasp of iron, notwithstanding his prodigious strength, he fell on the platform.

"Wretch!" cried the captain. "Do you want me to nail you to the ram of the *Nautilus* before it rushes against that ship?"

Captain Nemo, terrible to hear, was still more terrible to

behold. His face had grown pale under the spasms of his heart, which must for an instant have ceased to beat. The pupils of his eyes were fearfully contracted. His voice no longer spoke, it roared. With body bent forward, he shook the Canadian by the shoulders.

Then leaving him, and turning to the iron-clad, whose shots rained round him, he said:

"Ah! you know who I am, ship of a cursed nation!" cried he in a powerful voice. "I do not need to see your colours to recognise you! Look, I will show you mine!"

And Captain Nemo spread out a black flag in the front of the platform like the one he had planted at the South Pole.

At that moment a projectile struck the hull of the *Nautilus* obliquely, and, ricochetting near the captain, fell into the sea.

Captain Nemo shrugged his shoulders. Then, speaking to me:

"Go down," he said in a curt tone—"go down, you and your companions."

"Sir," I cried, "are you going to attack that ship?"

"Sir, I am going to sink it!"

"You will not do that."

"I shall do it!" replied Captain Nemo. "Do not take upon yourself to judge me, sir. Fate has shown you what you were not to see. The attack has been made. The repulse will be terrible. Go down below."

"What is that ship?"

"You do not know? Well, so much the better! Its nationality, at least, will remain a secret to you. Go below."

The Canadian, Conseil and I were obliged to obey. About fifteen of the *Nautilus* crew had surrounded the captain, and were looking with an implacable feeling of hatred at the ship that was advancing towards them. We felt that the same feeling of vengeance animated them all.

I went down as another projectile struck the *Nautilus*, and I heard its captain exclaim:

"Strike, mad vessel! Shower your useless shot! You will

not escape the ram of the *Nautilus*! But this is not the place you are to perish in! Your ruins shall not mix with those of the *Vengeur*!"

I went to my room. The captain and his officer remained on the platform. The screw was put in movement. The *Nautilus* speedily put itself out of range of the ship. But the pursuit went on, and Captain Nemo contented himself with keeping his distance.

Night came. Profound silence reigned on board. The compass indicated that the *Nautilus* had not changed its direction. I heard its screw beating the waves with rapid regularity. It kept on the surface of the water, and a slight rolling sent it from side to side.

My companions and I had resolved to fly when the vessel was near enough to hear or see us, for the moon, that would be full three days later, shone brightly. Once on board the vessel, if we could not prevent the blow that threatened her, we could at least do all that circumstances would allow us to attempt. I thought several times that the *Nautilus* was preparing for the attack. But it contented itself with allowing its adversary to approach, and a short time afterwards fled away again.

A part of the night passed without incident. We were awaiting an occasion to act. We spoke little, being too much excited. Ned Land wanted to throw himself into the sea. I made him wait. I thought the *Nautilus* would attack the two-decker on the surface of the sea, and then it would not only be possible but easy to escape.

At 3 a.m., being uneasy, I went up on to the platform. Captain Nemo had not left it. He was standing near his flag, which a slight breeze was waving over his head. He did not lose sight of the vessel. His look, of extraordinary intensity, seemed to attract her, fascinate her, and draw her onwards more surely than if he had been towing her.

The moon was then passing the meridian. Jupiter was rising in the east. Sky and ocean were equally tranquil, and the sea offered to the Queen of Night the clearest mirror that had ever reflected her image.

And when I compared the profound calm of the elements with the anger that was smouldering in the *Nautilus*, I felt myself shudder all over.

The ship kept at two miles' distance from us. She kept approaching the phosphorescent light that indicated the presence of the *Nautilus*. I could see her green and red lights and white lantern hung from her mainstay. An indistinct reflection lighted up her rigging and showed that the fires were heated to the uttermost. Sparks and flames were escaping from her funnels and starring the atmosphere.

I remained thus till 6 a.m., without Captain Nemo appearing to perceive me. The vessel was a mile and a half off, and with the break of day her cannonade began again. The moment could not be distant when, the *Nautilus* attacking its adversary, my companions and I would for ever leave this man whom I dared not judge.

I was about to go down to tell them about it when the officer came up on the platform. Several sailors accompanied him. Captain Nemo either did not or would not see them. Certain precautions were taken, which might be called the clearing up for the fight. They were very simple. The iron balustrade was lowered. The lantern and pilot-cages were sunk into the hull until they were on a level with the deck. The surface of the long steel-plated cigar no longer offered a single salient point that could hinder its manœuvres.

I returned to the saloon. The *Nautilus* was still above the water. Some morning beams were filtering through their liquid bed. Under certain undulations of the waves the windows were lighted up with the red beams of the rising sun. The dreadful 2nd of June had dawned.

At 5 a.m. the log showed me that the speed of the *Nautilus* was slackening. I understood that it was letting the ship approach. Besides, the firing was more distinctly heard, and the projectiles, ploughing up the surrounding water, were extinguished with a strange hissing noise.

"My friends," said I, " the time is come. One grasp of the hand, and may God help us!"

Ned Land was resolute, Conseil calm, I nervous, scarcely able to contain myself.

We all passed into the library. As I was opening the door that gave on to the cage of the central staircase I heard the upper panel shut with a bang.

The Canadian sprang up the steps, but I stopped him. A well-known hissing sound told me that they were letting water into the reservoirs. In a few minutes' time the *Nautilus* sank a few yards below the surface of the sea.

I now understood its manœuvre. It was too late to do anything. The *Nautilus* did not think of striking the two-decker in her impenetrable armour, but below her water-line, where her metal covering no longer protected her.

We were again imprisoned, unwilling witnesses to the fatal drama that was preparing. We had hardly time to reflect. Taking refuge in my room, we looked at each other without speaking a word. A profound stupor took possession of my mind. My thoughts seemed to stand still. I was in that painful state of expectation that precedes a dreadful crash. I waited and listened. I was all ear.

In the meantime the speed of the *Nautilus* visibly increased. It was taking a spring. All its hull vibrated.

Suddenly I uttered a cry. A shock had taken place, but a relatively slight one. I felt the penetrating force of the steel ram. I heard a grating, scraping sound. But the *Nautilus*, carried along by its force of propulsion, passed through the mass of the ship like a needle through sailcloth.

I could stand it no longer. I rushed like a madman into the saloon.

Captain Nemo was there. Mute, sombre, implacable, he was looking through the port panel.

An enormous mass was sinking through the water, and, in order to lose nothing of its agony, the *Nautilus* was sinking with it. At thirty feet from me I saw the broken hull, into which the water was rushing with a noise like thunder, then the double line of guns and bulwarks. The deck was covered with black moving shades.

The enormous ship sank slowly. The *Nautilus*, following

her, watched all her movements. All at once an explosion took place. The compressed air blew up the decks of the ship as though her magazines had been set fire to. The water was so much disturbed that the *Nautilus* swerved.

Then the unfortunate ship sank more rapidly. Her tops, loaded with victims, appeared; then her spars, bending under the weight of men; then the summit of her mainmast. Then the dark mass disappeared, and with it the dead crew, drawn down by a formidable eddy.

I turned to Captain Nemo. That terrible avenger, a perfect archangel of hatred, was still looking. When all was over he went to the door of his room, opened it, and went in. I followed him with my eyes.

On the end panel, below his heroes, I saw the portrait of a woman still young, and two little children. Captain Nemo looked at them for a few moments, held out his arms to them, and kneeling down, burst into sobs.

CHAPTER FORTY-SIX

CAPTAIN NEMO'S LAST WORDS

THE PANELS were closed on this frightful vision, but light had not been restored to the saloon. In the interior of the *Nautilus* reigned darkness and silence. It was leaving this place of desolation, a hundred feet under the water, at a prodigious speed. Where was it going—north or south? Where was the man flying to after this horrible retaliation?

At eleven o'clock the electric light reappeared. I went into the saloon and consulted the different instruments. The *Nautilus* was flying north at a speed of twenty-five miles an hour, sometimes on the surface of the sea, sometimes thirty feet below it.

By taking our bearings on the chart I saw that we were passing the entrance to the English Channel, and that we were going to the North seas at a frightful speed.

In the evening we had traversed two hundred leagues of the Atlantic. Night came, and the sea was dark till the moon rose.

I went to my room, but could not sleep. I was assailed by nightmare. The horrible scene of destruction was repeated in my mind.

From that day who could tell where the *Nautilus* took us in this North Atlantic basin? Always with inappreciable speed. Always amidst the hyperborean mists. Did it touch at Spitzbergen or the shores of Nova Zembla? Did we explore the unknown White Sea, Kara Sea, Gulf of Obi, Archipelago of Liarrov, and the unknown coast of Asia? I cannot tell. I do not even know how the time went. The clocks on board had stopped. It seemed as if night and day, as in polar countries, no longer followed their regular course. I felt myself carried into that region of the strange where the over-ridden imagination of Edgar Poe roamed at will. At each instant I expected to see, like the fabulous Gordon Pym, "that veiled human face, of much larger proportions than that of any inhabitant of the earth, thrown across the cataract that defends the approach to the Pole!"

I estimate—but perhaps I am mistaken—that this adventurous course of the *Nautilus* lasted fifteen or twenty days, and I do not know how long it would have lasted but for the catastrophe that ended this voyage. Captain Nemo never appeared, nor his officer. Not a man of the crew was visible for an instant. The *Nautilus* kept below the water almost incessantly. When it went up to the surface to renew the air, the panels opened and shut mechanically. The bearings were no longer reported on the chart. I did not know where we were.

One morning—I do not know its date—I had fallen into an uneasy slumber at early dawn. When I awoke I saw Ned Land bending over me, and heard him whisper:

"We are going to fly!"

I sat up.

"When?" I asked.

"To-night. All supervision seems to have disappeared

from the *Nautilus*. Stupor seems to reign on board. Shall you be ready, sir?"

"Yes. Where are we?"

"In sight of land that I have just sighted through the mist, twenty miles to the east."

"What land is it?"

"I do not know, but whatever it is we will seek refuge on it."

"Yes! Ned—yes, we will go to-night, even should the sea swallow us up!"

"The sea is rough, the wind violent, but twenty miles in that light boat of the *Nautilus* do not frighten me. I have put some provisions and a few bottles of water in it without the knowledge of the crew."

"I will follow you."

I had made up my mind to anything. The Canadian left me. I went up on the platform, where I could scarcely stand against the waves. The sky was threatening, but as land lay there in those thick mists, we must fly. We must not lose a day nor an hour.

What a long day was the last I had to pass on board the *Nautilus*! I remained alone. Ned Land and Conseil avoided me, so as not to betray us by talking.

At 6 p.m. I dined, but without appetite. I forced myself to eat notwithstanding my repugnance, wishing to keep up my strength.

At half-past six Ned Land entered my room. He said to me:

"We shall not see each other again before our departure. At ten o'clock the moon will not yet be up. We shall take advantage of the darkness. Come to the boat. Conseil and I will be waiting for you there."

Then the Canadian went out, without giving me time to answer.

I wished to verify the direction of the *Nautilus*. I went to the saloon. We were going NNE. with frightful speed, at a depth of twenty-five fathoms.

I looked for the last time at all the natural marvels and

riches of art collected in this museum, in this unrivalled collection destined one day to perish in the depths of the sea with the man who had made it. I wished to take a supreme impression of it in my mind. I remained thus for an hour, bathed in the light of the luminous ceiling, and passing in review the shining treasures in their glass cases. Then I went back to my room.

There I put on my solid sea garments. I collected my notes together and placed them carefully about me. My heart beat loudly. I could not check its pulsations. Certainly my agitation would have betrayed me to Captain Nemo.

What was he doing at that moment? I listened at the door of his room. I heard a noise of footsteps: Captain Nemo was there. He had not gone to bed. At every movement that he made I thought he was going to appear and ask me why I wanted to escape! I was constantly on the alert. My imagination magnified everything. This impression became so poignant that I asked myself if I had not better enter the captain's room, see him face to face, dare him with look and gesture!

At that moment I heard the vague chords of the organ, a sad harmony under an indefinable melody, veritable wails of a soul that wished to break all terrestrial ties. I listened with all my senses, hardly breathing, plunged like Captain Nemo in one of those musical ecstasies which took him beyond the limits of this world.

Then a sudden thought terrified me. Captain Nemo had left his room. He was in the saloon that I was obliged to cross in my flight. There I should meet him for the last time. He would see me, perhaps speak to me. A gesture from him could annihilate me, a single word could chain me to his vessel.

Ten o'clock was on the point of striking. The moment had come to leave my room and rejoin my companions.

I could not hesitate should Captain Nemo stand before me. I opened my door with precaution, and yet it seemed to make a fearful noise. Perhaps that noise only existed in my imagination.

I felt my way along the dark waist of the *Nautilus*, stopping at every step to suppress the beatings of my heart.

I reached the corner door of the saloon and opened it softly. The saloon was quite dark. The tones of the organ were feebly sounding. Captain Nemo was there. He did not see me. I think that in a full light he would not have perceived me, he was so absorbed.

I dragged myself over the carpet, avoiding the least contact, lest the noise should betray my presence. It took me five minutes to reach the door into the library.

I was going to open it when a sigh from Captain Nemo nailed me to the place. I understood that he had got up. I even saw him, for some rays from the lighted library reached the saloon. He came towards me with folded arms, silent, gliding rather than walking, like a ghost. His oppressed chest heaved with sobs, and I heard him murmur these words—the last I heard:

"Almighty God! Enough! Enough!"

Was it remorse that was escaping thus from the conscience of that man?

Desperate, I rushed into the library, went up to the central staircase, and following the upper waist, reached the boat through the opening that had already given passage to my two companions.

"Let us go! Let us go!" I cried.

"At once," answered the Canadian.

The orifice in the plates of the *Nautilus* was first shut and bolted by means of a wrench that Ned Land had provided himself with. The opening in the boat was also closed, and the Canadian began to take out the screws that still fastened us to the submarine vessel.

Suddenly a noise was heard in the interior. Voices answered one another quickly. What was the matter? Had they discovered our flight? I felt Ned Land glide a dagger into my hand.

"Yes," I murmured, "we shall know how to die!"

The Canadian had stopped in his work. But one word, twenty times repeated, a terrible word, revealed to me the cause of the agitation on board the *Nautilus*. It was not we the crew were anxious about.

"The Maëlstrom! the Maëlstrom!" they were crying.

The Maëlstrom! Could a more frightful word in a more frightful situation have sounded in our ears? Were we then on the most dangerous part of the Norwegian shore? Was the *Nautilus* being dragged into a gulf at the very moment our boat was preparing to leave its side?

It is well known that at the tide the pent-up waters between the Faroë and Loffoden Islands rush out with irresistible violence. They form a whirlpool from which no ship could ever escape. From every point of the horizon rush monstrous waves. They form the gulf justly called "Navel of the Ocean," of which the power of attraction extends for a distance of ten miles. There not only vessels but whales and bears from the boreal region are sucked up.

It was there that the *Nautilus* had been voluntarily or involuntarily run by its captain. It was describing a spiral, the circumference of which was lessening by degrees. Like it, the boat fastened to it was whirled round with giddy speed. I felt it. I felt the sick sensation that succeeds a long-continued movement of gyration. We were horror-stricken with suspended circulation, annihilated nervous influence, covered with cold sweat like that of death! What noise surrounded our fragile boat! What roaring, which echo repeated at a distance of several miles! What an uproar was that of the water breaking on the sharp rocks at the bottom, where the hardest bodies are broken, where the trunks of trees are worn away and are "made into fur" according to a Norwegian saying!

What a situation! We were frightfully tossed about. The *Nautilus* defended itself like a human being. Its steel muscles cracked. Sometimes it stood upright, and we with it!

"We must hold on and screw down the bolts again," said Ned Land. "We may still be saved by keeping to the *Nautilus*——"

He had not finished speaking when a crash took place. The screws were torn out, and the boat, torn from its groove, sprang like a stone from a sling into the midst of the whirlpool.

My head struck on its iron framework, and with the violent shock I lost all consciousness.

CHAPTER FORTY-SEVEN

CONCLUSION

SO ENDED this voyage under the sea. What happened during that night, how the boat escaped the formidable eddies of the Maëlstrom, how Ned Land, Conseil and I got out of the gulf, I have no idea. But when I came to myself I was lying in the hut of a fisherman of the Loffoden Isles. My two companions, safe and sound, were by my side pressing my hands. We shook hands heartily.

At this moment we cannot think of going back to France. Means of communication between the north of Norway and the south are rare. I am, therefore, obliged to wait for the steamer that runs twice a month to Cape North.

It is here, therefore, amidst the honest folk who have taken us in, that I revise the account of these adventures. It is exact. Not a fact has been omitted, not a detail exaggerated. It is a faithful narrative of an incredible expedition in an element inaccessible to man, and to which progress will one day open up a road.

Shall I be believed? I do not know. After all, it matters little. All I can now affirm is my right to speak of the seas under which, in less than ten months, I journeyed twenty thousand leagues during that submarine tour of the world that has revealed so many marvels of the Pacific, the Indian Ocean, Red Sea, Mediterranean, Atlantic, and the austral and boreal seas!

But what has become of the *Nautilus*? Has it resisted the pressure of the Maëlstrom? Is Captain Nemo still alive? Is he still pursuing his frightful retaliations under the ocean, or did he stop before that last hecatomb? Will the waves one day bring the manuscript that contains the whole history of his life Shall I know at last the name of the man? Will the ship that has disappeared tell us by its nationality the nationality of Captain Nemo?

I hope so. I also hope that his powerful machine has conquered the sea in its most terrible gulf, and that the *Nautilus* has survived where so many other ships have perished! If it is so, if Captain Nemo still inhabits the ocean, his adopted country, may hatred be appeased in his savage heart! May the contemplation of so many marvels extinguish in him the desire of vengeance! May the judge disappear, and the *savant* continue his peaceful exploration of the sea! If his destiny is strange, it is sublime also. Have I not experienced it myself? Have I not lived ten months of this unnatural life? Two men only have a right to answer the question asked in Ecclesiastes 6,000 years ago, "That which is far off and exceeding deep, who can find it out?" These two men are Captain Nemo and I.

THE END